NO

REMORSE

A Chance and Choices Adventure

Book Three

Lisa Gay

Chance and Choices

This book is a work of fiction. The names, characters, places, and incidents either are the product of the author's imagination or used factitiously. Any resemblance to an actual person, living or dead, business establishment, or event is entirely coincidental.

ISBN-13: 978-1-945858-06-2
ISBN -10: 1-945858-06-0

Those Involved in these incidents:

Place of Origin – Harmony

Chris Williams – father of Ann, Stephanie, and Sally

Emma Williams – mother of Ann, Stephanie, and Sally

Ann Williams – oldest sister – Noah's wife

Stephanie Yates – middle sister – Eli's wife

Sally Williams – youngest sister

Eli Yates – Stephanie's husband

Tom Yates - Eli's father

Hattie Yates – Eli's mother

Smithfield Wyman – sheriff of Harmony

Earl – previous owner of Eyanosa

Eyanosa – Noah's horse

Dusty – Williams' dead horse

Place of Origin – Indian Territory

Noah Swift Hawk – Ann's husband

Arabella – Noah's dead horse

Place of Origin – Kuhn Bayou

Harry – gatekeeper of the bridge across Kuhn Bayou/ previous owner of clothes Minnie gave to Stephanie

Place of Origin – Pine Bluff

Roscoe Bacon – owner Bacon's Trading Post

James Bacon – Eli's alias as Roscoe's nephew

Nancy Bacon – Sally's alias as Roscoe's niece

Roscoe's donkeys:

Little Jenny – miniature donkey

Little Jack – miniature donkey

Big Jenny

Shaggy

Spot
Blanco
Chocolate
Smiley
Honey
QuickSilver

Roscoe's mules:
King
Ace
Rose
Hector
Molly
Jumper
Blue
Chief
Diamond
Stubborn - (Redeemed)

Roscoe's goats:
Snowflake
Bella
Fancy
Billy

Place of Origin – Unknown
Butterfield Gang – Gus, Ben, Roy, and others
Russell French – Traveling Resupply Business co-owner
Arnold Buzmann - Traveling Resupply Business co-owner
William – Resupply Business worker (Will)
George - Resupply Business worker

Russell's mule team:

Mule 1, 6, 10, 19 - Arnold's share of the mules - left at Pine Bluff

Mule 2, 5, 16, 18 – injured mules kept by Arnold

Mule 3, 9, 12, 13, 14, 15 – injured mules traded by Arnold

Mule 17 – severely injured mule given to Nancy (Beauty)

Mule 4 – mule with injured eye purchased by Nancy

Mule 7 & 8 –injured mules purchased by Nancy

Mule 11 & 20 – injured mules earned by Dr. Luke Smith

Place of Origin – Little Rock

Daniel Hall – Judge of State of Arkansas

Mrs. Daniel Hall – Judge Hall's wife

Ansel- Judge Hall's son

William – Clerk of Court

Harold LeBarron – Associate Clerk of Court Mr.

Beamis– white man guilty of interracial relations

Sheriff Taylor – Sheriff of Little Rock

Luke Smith –Noah's alias / doctor

Isabelle Smith –Ann's alias / Luke's wife

Marie - Stephanie's alias

Thaddeus Pratt - preacher / Jeremiah's uncle

Martin Harrow – livery owner

Dollie Harrow – Martin's wife

John Peabody - Peabody Inn owner

Bradford Logan – miller / Amelia's father

Amelia Logan - Henry's girl / Melvin Hatcher's cousin

Edwin – stablehand at Martin Harrow's

S.R. – Edwin's father

Robert – Edwin's friend

Bertha – girl Robert wants to marry

Bertha's Father

Clark – owner of the general store

U.S. Army - Little Rock Arsenal

Miles Cornish – Captain

Jeremiah Pratt – Specialist

Melvin Hatcher – Private

Henry Fenn – Private

Peppermint – army milk cow

ONE

The man with all the power had the law on his side, and he knew it. He sat behind his high desk and demanded answers. "Ann Williams, did you marry Noah Swift Hawk?"

Ann sat in the witness chair in the courtroom, crowded with hostile feelings. She stated her opinion of the law that forbade interracial marriage. "Yes, and not you or anybody else can convince me that's wrong."

Judge Daniel Hall's stomach turned over. Of her own free will, the woman had joined herself to an Indian, and she felt no remorse. "Go to your seat."

Hoping for justice, Ann had walked a hundred miles. She did not go to her seat. "But we came here to press charges against the Butterfield Gang. They tried to burn me up with my sisters and our farmhands. Won't you even listen?"

"This case has nothing to do with that. Do as I told you." Ann walked to the defendant's seats and sat with her back to Noah.

Noah knew he was hurting her. He wanted to hold her and make everything all right, but he knew that he absolutely could not.

The last thin shreds of Ann's hope shattered as Judge Daniel Hall rammed his beliefs down her throat. "Ann Williams and Noah Swift Hawk, I find you guilty of interracial marriage. The penalty is fifty-nine lashes for Noah Swift Hawk and twenty-nine for Ann Williams. The marriage is annulled. Sheriff Taylor, take the prisoners and carry out the sentence."

Noah couldn't let anybody hurt Ann. He begged, "I'm the guilty one. I wanted to have relations with her. I manipulated her. She's the victim of my intentions. Give me all the lashes."

Ann stood beside the man she loved. "Give me my lashes because I AM going to live with Noah, I AM going to have all kinds of relations with him and fill the world with our babies, and I'll be right before God, and you'll still be wrong."

In his heart, Noah smiled. Ann was magnificent as she stood for her right to love him.

The judge demanded respect, "Silence!"

Ann was not silent. "You can't legislate who I love or who loves me."

Judge Hall stood up and thrust his red face toward Ann. "Silence or I'll charge you with contempt of court and add ten more lashes!"

"Then, do it."

"Sheriff Taylor, gag her."

Smithfield Wyman, the sheriff from Ann's hometown of Harmony, Arkansas, interrupted, "One moment, let me read the law you wanted me to study." Sherrif Wyman read the passage then stated his request. "Ann is not pregnant. They have not been living in a house as man and wife, and there is no evidence that immoral sexual relations have occurred. Even though Ann says she is married, there are no papers. Therefore, they are not. In conclusion, I ask that the sentence be hard labor rebuilding the Cadron Ferry. That will spare Arkansas the expense, as well as punish Ann Williams and Noah Swift Hawk."

Judge Hall contemplated. He wanted the woman whipped, maybe even to do it himself, but saving the state a large expense could be beneficial to his career. "I agree, but a military unit is to be dispatched with them to ensure that the work is done satisfactorily. No other person is to participate or help in any way. Keep Ann and Noah separated and chained until they have completely rebuilt the crossing and the ferry.

"Ann Williams and Noah Swift Hawk, if I find you together, I will order maximum flogging and a year of hard labor. As for you, Ann Williams, you are insolent and abrasive. I don't know why any man would want to be with you for even one night. You're lucky I don't whip you for contempt of court. Sheriff Taylor, arrange for the military escort. You have until morning to prepare. Court is adjourned."

As the sheriff took them back to jail, Ann tried to speak with Noah, "I won't deny that I love you."

Noah knew it would have been better if Ann had denied their marriage, but he felt the proof that nothing would change Ann's love for him was amazing, and he loved her even more. Still, due to his fear of the consequences to Ann, he didn't say a word.

Noah and Ann served their hard labor sentence

at the military road crossing of Cadron Creek in the fall of 1839. For three months, under the supervision of Specialist Jeremiah Pratt, Noah and Ann felt tortured by their proximity but forced separation. Days packed with pain and exhaustion, not only of their bodies but also of their hearts, did not stop Noah from sabotaging the work to make it last as long as possible.

Nevertheless, much to their unhappiness, the day arrived when the ferry and dock had been rebuilt. Noah thought his days in that Hell had been much too few, but he knew that he could not say goodbye face-to-face, so he slipped out of the tent during the night, gathered his few belongings, and walked to the pasture to get his horse, Eyanosa.

A few of the soldiers overseeing the construction believed that Noah and Ann should be allowed to love each other, but Private Henry Fenn took action. Noah found him waiting beside Eyanosa. "Noah, it will be weeks of winter travel, but I think you can make it to Pine Bluff."

"You're a good man, Henry. I'll think about going there." Without any hope of ever being happy again, Noah mounted up and left behind the woman he loved. He thought he would never again see Ann, her sisters, or Eli, who had all stayed at the creek. As Noah rode his horse south in misery, he felt it was more than cruel that God had deserted them and had allowed this to happen. He felt desperate for answers.

Before his unit left the following day, Henry passed on his secret message to Ann and her family.

"I want you to know that I told Noah to go to the trading post south of Little Rock. In the spring, you might find the west more tolerant."

Ann and her family refused to allow Noah to desert them. They didn't definitively know where Noah had gone, but they took the chance that the clue given to them would lead them to him. Determined to find Noah, they loaded their supplies into the handcarts made by Eli, Stephanie, and Sally while Ann and Noah had built the ferry.

Ann, her sisters, and Eli went the opposite direction from the place where they hoped to find Noah. At Point Remove Creek, they ferried across the Arkansas River to the south then trudged a hundred miles east.

On the first day of the year of 1840, they arrived at the top of the cliff overlooking the box canyon at Pine Bluff. Almost out of supplies, they prayed that Noah was there and started down the very steep and treacherous trail.

In the field below, they saw the large trading post built of logs, and also a corral, barn, and smokehouse to its left. High cliffs almost entirely encircled the compound. Straight across from the trail they descended, the talc that had piled in a gap rose only a fifth of the height of the cliffs.

Eli and the girls stepped into the trading post through the door facing the gap. The cold air rushed into the room filled with tables, chairs, a bar, and a fireplace. To their right, the store held all kinds of items for sale. Straight ahead, they saw a large stone oven in the kitchen. To their left, one opening had a closed door. The other had no door at all. Through the open doorway, they saw what appeared to be a cross and a man lying prostrate on the floor. Ann spoke to the thin man who walked into the room from the kitchen. "Hello, sir. We're looking for somebody."

The voice brought the man on the floor immediately to his feet. He hurried to the front room. "Ann?"

Ann's beautiful green eyes, framed by her long, wavy raven-colored hair, turned toward him. She dashed across the room and threw herself into the man's embrace. "I've needed your arms around me so much."

Stephanie, Sally, and Eli joined them. Noah had told the owner of the trading post about his anguish over losing his family. The man looked at Noah, with the arms of his family around him, and thought it was the most beautiful sight he had ever seen.

Noah held Ann. "I've needed your arms around me just as much."

Eli stepped back, but Noah pulled him up to his side again. When Stephanie began to move away, Noah didn't let her go either. Ann and Sally didn't let go at all. They held each other and tried to squeeze four months of missed hugs into that one embrace.

Noah finally let them loose. "Let me introduce you. This fine man is Roscoe Bacon," Noah swept his hand from one side to the other, "and this is his trading post. Roscoe, this beautiful woman is Ann Williams, my wife," Noah briefly kissed Ann's lips, "and this is her sister, Sally." Noah mentioned them first because they still had their arms wrapped around his waist. "Those two are my sister-in-law and brother-in-law, Stephanie and Eli Yates." Noah looked at them affectionately.

It was only the second time Stephanie had heard herself referred to as Stephanie Yates. She loved it. She held Eli's hand and smiled at him before she turned back to Roscoe.

Roscoe greeted them, "I'm glad you're here."

Since he was a man that paid attention to practical issues and they needed a place to stay, Eli immediately asked, "It looks like you're set up to serve meals. Do you also offer lodging?"

"People usually camp in the field. I serve vittles and antifogmatics in here, but this is the first winter anybody has been here. Take off your coats. I'll fix us hot coffee to warm you up while we figure out what we can do."

Sally had been fantasizing about hot coffee for days on end while they had traveled outside in the cold. "Coffee would be wonderful."

Noah led his family to the coat rack. He helped Ann out of her coat more as a hug than as a coat removal. He hung the coat on the peg then actually did get her back into his arms. "I've missed you so much."

"I've missed you too." Ann raised her lips to his. Since they were in the company of the whole family, their lips touched only for a second.

Faster than greased lightning, Roscoe slipped back into the room with a big pot filled with hot water and ground coffee, along with six cups. "We'll give the coffee some time, but come on over, and sit a spell."

Roscoe, Stephanie, and Eli sat together on one side of the table. Noah leaned over Stephanie, moved her long, blonde hair out of the way, and hugged her around the shoulders. He pressed his cheek to hers. "I'm so happy that you're here."

Noah looked down at Eli's short, dark-brown hair. He put his hand on Eli's shoulder. "And you too." Eli turned. Noah looked him squarely in his dark brown eyes. "I'm sorry for causing you to hike across the state instead of enjoying each other in your new marriage."

Noah then walked around the table and sat between Sally and Ann. He knew Sally would have been especially hurt because of the way he had left. Family meant everything to Sally. She felt that Noah was her brother, and he had deserted her. He put his arms around Sally and pressed his cheek against her long, curly chestnut hair. He leaned back and looked into her hazel eyes. "I'm very glad that you're here, and I'm so sorry that I left without saying goodbye. Will you forgive me?"

Sally scolded him, "This whole thing is very upsetting and confusing. I forgive you, and I love you, but don't ever leave us again."

"Thank you for forgiving me. You can be sure I won't leave you again."

Noah turned to Ann, took her calloused hands in his, and looked into the green eyes that mesmerized him. "I especially have to ask for your forgiveness. I want to talk with you more about it later. Right now, I want everybody to know how sorry I am. I should have done what you asked me to do, instead of running away."

Ann wrapped her arms around Noah and held him. "You're forgiven and loved. We can talk about all that's happened later."

With no condemnation and his wife's arms around him, Noah felt so much relief and comfort that tears came to his eyes. To not be completely overcome by the feelings that swept over him, he asked, "Is that coffee ready?"

Roscoe poured coffee, whether it was ready or not.

Eli shifted to a different topic, "We have all our supplies at the top of the ridge. Is there any way we can get everything down here?"

Roscoe filled Eli's cup. "How is it packed?"

"We have it in carts."

"If you want to bring carts down, you'll have to bring them around the top of the ridge, down the side, and then in through the gap."

"How long would that take?" Eli thought that sounded like much too long of a process.

"It takes most of a day to walk around the ridge. Pulling carts will make it even slower. Before that, you'll have to get back to them, either by climbing the cliff or going around the same way you would bring them down."

"I hate to leave everything up there, but I guess

we won't be getting it today." Eli held the coffee cup to warm his hands.

Noah knew what was in the store. "We should be able to get most of it here today if we bring it down in packs. We can get the rest later."

Eli informed them, "We can get the food, our clothes, and the blankets into packs, but not the tent or the tarp."

Roscoe offered, "Let's see what's in my store."

Ann carried her coffee. "I don't see a pack big enough to get the tent inside. Maybe we could tie it onto one and wear the pack like a harness."

"Wouldn't you be too back heavy?" asked Roscoe.

"What if I wore it on the front?" Noah sipped his coffee.

Stephanie strolled past the other items in the store. "We also have to get the poles down here."

Roscoe picked up some ropes. "If you're going today, you need to get started."

Noah and Ann walked with their arms around each other. All the way, every few seconds, one turned and gave the other a quick kiss. Even though she was very glad to have her family together, Sally rolled her eyes as she walked behind them with Roscoe.

Ann pulled her handkerchief from her pocket. "I have a Christmas present for you."

Noah had no idea what Ann could have. "You do?" Ann opened the handkerchief containing the remaining peppermint that Eli had given her as a Christmas present.

"Thank you." Noah put a piece in his mouth. "You eat some."

Ann folded up the handkerchief and handed it to Noah. "It's yours."

Noah insisted, "If I want to give some to the woman I love, I should be able to do it."

"That's very sweet. You know I love peppermint." Ann took a small piece out of the handkerchief that Noah held open. Noah took another piece because he had already crunched up and swallowed the first one.

Eli started up the steep path with Stephanie right behind him. Ten feet up, he turned to say, "This way." He lost his footing, slid a few feet, and then rammed into Stephanie. She landed on top of him. So that she wouldn't go down with them, Sally quickly sidestepped. Ann held onto a rock and tried to grab them, but Eli's hand touched hers for only a second.

At the bottom, Eli slid to a stop. "Maybe going up today isn't a good plan."

Noah tried not to laugh as he looked at Eli lying on his back with Stephanie on top of him. "Maybe not, but I bet that ride was exciting."

As Noah helped Stephanie to her feet, she confirmed, "It was."

"It didn't feel nice to my back." Eli got up and bent from side to side.

Sally remained at her perch. "Maybe we shouldn't all go up."

"Put your things into the packs and lower them down." Roscoe held out the ropes.

"How about Eli and I go up. The rest of you release the packs after we lower them. We'll pull the rope back to send down more."

Ann wanted to let Noah and Eli decide the plan. The words, "Sally, let's carefully go back down," barely got out of her mouth. "Ahhh!" Gravity sent her traveling in the same mode as Eli and Stephanie. She arrived at the feet of Noah, where the previous two had stopped.

"Welcome back to the bottom. Are you all right?" Noah helped her up.

"I feel like climbing up and doing it again."

Sally wasn't going against her will and decided to make the most likely path to the bottom, her own choice. She sat in the track left by the others. "I've got a hankering for some fun. I'm coming down by gum." She pushed off and slid down then jumped up. "I'm going again!"

"Let us go first." Noah kissed Sally on her forehead.

"Then get going." Sally shooed the men toward the cliff.

Ann, on the other hand, worried. "Be careful. Don't follow too close."

Sally let the men get above the mudslide before sliding down again. "Roscoe, it's fun! Take a turn."

"I probably shouldn't, but it does look fun."

Ann sat at the top of the track. "It is. You don't have to come up this far."

"Maybe once." Roscoe climbed a short way then slid down laughing. "I haven't had so much fun in decades!" The path was smooth and well established, so he decided to go again. As he swished to the bottom, his hair flapped in the wind and mud pushed up into his pants leg. "That's cold!" He shook his leg to dislodge the dirt. Like the girls, he went up again and took another turn.

Stephanie's bum slipped to the edge of the track. She tipped to the side and put her hand down to stop her rotation. She rode the last half of the trip on her side. It was still fun.

During Sally's most memorable ride, mud flew into her nostril. She missed her next turn as she blew mud and snot out of her nose. After she had cleared out the dirt, she took another turn.

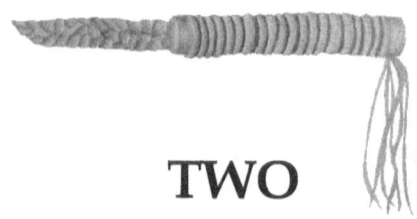

TWO

High above the girls, a rock rolled out from under Eli's foot. He took a quick step back to stop his fall. His foot sank into the mud. He tried to raise his foot, but stones pressed against his ankle. It didn't budge. "Doesn't that beat all?" Eli unlaced his boot.

Noah took hold of Eli's hand. "I hope this is the worst thing that happens." He pulled Eli out of his boot. Eli then yanked it out before he slipped his foot back into it with the muck.

Once at the top, Eli led them to the place where they had hidden their supplies. They randomly crammed a few items into the packs before Eli stopped. "In case we don't have time to get everything, we should decide what things to send down first."

Noah held some of Harry's clothes that had been given to the family when the girls had sold their farm. "Clothes, you think?"

"I'll pack our clothes. You tie up the tent, tarp, and poles." As Eli packed their clothes, he tucked in the spice bottles to prevent them from breaking.

Noah left Eli on the bag filling detail while he wrapped the poles in the blankets and laid the bundle on the tarp. Afterward, Noah secured all the tools, the eating, and the cooking items in a different blanket and placed it on top of the bundle of poles. He then

14

folded the tarp around the two bundles and tied it up securely.

After the clothes and spices, Eli packed the smidgen of food they had left. "I can't fit the pillows. We'll have to bring the packs back up for them."

Noah tied the five packs together through the shoulder straps. He wrapped the other end several times around the tree closest to the edge of the cliff then tied it off with only a little slack.

Eli looked over the edge of the cliff. It was a long, sheer drop to the sharp rocks piled at the bottom. The bundle of packs was heavy and could easily pull him over. He got the packs then crawled to the edge dragging them behind. He lay on his belly and dropped them over. "Stand clear. We're sending down the first batch."

Ann hollered back, "We're ready. Send it down." She took her last ride in the mud.

Noah untied the rope at the fulcrum tree. He slowly lowered the bundle until he reached the end of the rope. Eli walked to the cliff's edge. "We're out of rope. How much farther?"

Stephanie yelled back, "Ten feet. You could let them fall."

Eli rejected the plan. "We need to get the packs back. We still need to send down the pillows, and we can't drop the poles from all the way up here either."

Noah continued to hold the packs suspended in the air. "Bring the loose end of the other rope and tie it to this one." Eli secured the ropes together. They worked the knot around and around the tree and unwound the rope until they had lowered the packs to the ground.

As Ann struggled to work the knot loose, she thought back to when she had untied the bundle with the few things that Noah had lowered from the bedroom window when their home was burning down. She freed the current bags. "We got them off." Ann, Sally, and Stephanie each put on a pack. They carried the other two between them and headed to the trading post.

With only a tiny bit of slack, the two men gently rolled the pole bundle over the edge. When it was still, they lowered it. Roscoe untied the bundle and then hollered, "You can take the rope."

Eli, Stephanie, and Sally had put a lot of effort into building the carts, and they had pulled them a hundred miles across the state. Eli wanted to keep them. As they lowered the tent, he asked, "What about the carts?"

"With all these clouds, it's going to be dark soon. We already might not get down before nightfall. I think we need to come back for them later." The tension on the rope ceased.

By the time Roscoe had freed the tent, the girls were back with the empty packs. Sally called out, "The packs are on the line."

Noah pulled the rope up while Eli unwound the other end of the rope from the tree. They left the bags tied to the rope and shoved in the pillows. Noah walked to the edge. "Here comes the packs and rope." When he heard those below call out that they were ready, Noah threw all of it over the edge.

Roscoe and the girls took the pole bundle and tent to the trading post. Ann asked, "Roscoe, will you cook supper for us? I'll pay you when Eli gets here with our money. Also, how much do we owe for Noah?"

Roscoe walked toward the kitchen. "I'll fix supper. Noah has been helping me. He doesn't owe anything."

The girls left Roscoe to cook and went back for the pillows and ropes.

As he and Noah walked back to the trail, Eli brought up the subject that had been haunting him for months. "I'm sure you're mad at me. You probably think I'm making it so you can't be with Ann because I don't want to leave my father. I swear, I really do want us all to be together, but I'm all my father has."

"If you won't leave Harmony, it won't be possible for us to stay together. For a while, I wanted to knock you into a cocked hat, but not anymore. This is hurting all of us, not just me. I'm sure you don't want to decide between horrible choices. You're probably mad at me for marrying Ann."

"I hate the whole mess, but I've never been mad at you. I'm the one who told you to marry Ann."

"Reverend Pratt told me–"

Eli interrupted, "You talked with Thaddeus?"

"When I was coming here, I stopped because I wanted answers. He went all the way to Cadron Creek to marry you and Stephanie, so I thought he would be willing to help me, but he didn't give me answers. Instead, he gave me more questions. He asked me what I had promised God I would do when I married Ann. Did I promise God I would keep Ann from hard labor or whippings, or did I promise God I would be with her until death, whether things were good or bad? He asked me if I loved Ann more than God loves her, and if I should or should not do what I promised God I would do. The only thing he actually told me to do was to trust God.

"He also said, no matter what the state of Arkansas says that I'm married to Ann in the eyes of God. Even then, I couldn't convince myself to chance getting Ann hurt, so I came here. I can hardly believe that God brought you here, but He did. I want you to know it means so much to me that you didn't go home, but came to find me instead."

"Trying to find you was the only right thing to do. I don't want you to leave the family, but I am fit to be tied. I don't know what we'll do if Pop won't go west with us."

"I have no idea how we're going to solve this, but I told God that I'm going to trust Him no matter how it works out, and I completely mean it. I want you to trust Him as well. For now, we need to love and protect our wives as well as we can, and believe that God is working everything out."

Noah stopped at the top of the trail down. "Sit. Then set your foot against an unmovable rock, rise on your hands, and then scoot forward." They started down, glad that they had cleared the tension between them. In the falling darkness, neither could see the trail. They descended at a snail's pace.

"They should be here already. Now it's too dark to come down. The trail is barely visible." Ann wrung her hands. *I can't lose Noah, especially not after I just found him.*

Stephanie and Sally worried with her. They stood at the bottom of the trail. Stephanie yelled, "Are you there?!"

Eli moved another few inches. "We're coming down! We can't see! We're being very careful!"

Before he raised his bottom, Noah put his foot on what felt like firm support. When all of his weight pushed against the rock, the trail below his foot went to pieces. The girls heard loud crashing and dashed away. Noah felt for another place to support his foot.

Ann ran back to the cliff. "Are you all right?"

"We're safe. It was the rocks below us. Any of you down there get hurt?"

Sally answered, "Nobody got squished. The rocks came down on the side. You're too far to the right. You can't make it all the way down over there."

It didn't appear that he was going the wrong way, but Noah could barely see a foot ahead. "Your right or our right?"

Ann answered, "Our right. You're too far to your left. Come right about fifteen feet."

"We'll move to our right."

Noah finally got to the mudslide. "Whoo hoo!" He slid past the girls.

Sally hurried to where he stopped. "I told you it was fun!"

As Ann offered her hand to Noah, they heard,

"Get out of the way!" She pulled Noah up just before Eli slid into the same spot.

Eli looked up at Stephanie, who was also standing beside the landing zone. "I enjoyed the first ride more."

They walked across the field, muddy but happy. Their few possessions sat safely in Roscoe Bacon's Trading Post, but the most important things they had walked with them: their God and each other.

Noah held Ann's hand and slowed down. Sally shivered. "Come on, you two."

"We'll be there in a minute." Noah hung back.

"Don't stay out here long. It's too cold." Sally ran to join Stephanie and Eli.

Noah needed to put things right between him and Ann. "I want you to know, I absolutely do not have a wife in Indian Territory or anywhere else. The only wife I have or want is you, and you are my wife, no matter what Judge Hall says."

"And you, Noah, my love, are the only husband I'll ever want, and I never believed that you have another wife."

"It's also not true that I don't love you or that I never did. The truth is that I was waiting to love you when I lay on that saloon floor dying. When you came to visit me at Dr. Gridley's house, and I saw you for the very first time, I loved you, and I've loved you every minute since."

Remembering the heartache she'd felt when Noah had continually insisted that he did not care about her, Ann replied with tears, "I know you love me. You convinced me when you wanted to take my lashes on top of the fifty-nine you were already going to receive. I know you were trying to protect me by telling Judge Hall that you don't love me, but it did hurt when you kept on saying it, even after you didn't need to."

Noah gently wiped frozen tears from Ann's face. "When you told Judge Hall to give you your lashes because you were going to love me no matter what, and that you were going to fill the world with my babies, my heart was completely and forever sealed to you. But I tried to convince myself that I'd forget you. I thought you could go on with your life and marry somebody else and that you'd be safe."

Ann stopped. "Understand completely. I'm not going through this life without you, even if it brings whippings or prison." She kissed Noah.

Even after he drank in the love of that kiss, Noah still wanted to make more apologies. "Also, I'm very sorry for the way I left. I shouldn't have run away in the night like a coward."

"Don't apologize for that; there is only so much a person can stand. Even though there was no way we could have gone together, I would have begged you not to go, and Sally would have too. It would have ripped out all our hearts. What you did was a kindness and a blessing."

"Thank you for understanding. You always say the right thing. I thought I would never see you again or the rest of the family. I've been mad, confused, and so very sad. Now, you are all with me again. I can hardly believe it, and I am so happy. I wish I could explain to you how much you mean to me, and how much I love and want you."

"I feel the same way."

Noah drew Ann close and repeated, "I thought I was never going to see you again."

"And I was afraid we wouldn't find you, but now it's as it should be. I'm sorry if I made it harder on you by always putting my love right in front of you."

"At the time, it drove me crazy because I wanted you so much, and I thought that I couldn't have you. Now that I look back on it, knowing that you wouldn't stop loving me was a blessing. I'm glad you always let me know that you love me." Noah sought Ann's lips again. She felt his deep love in that tender kiss.

They drew apart. "I love you, Noah, but we better go in before we freeze." They hurried but stopped at the door to share one more kiss before entering the building.

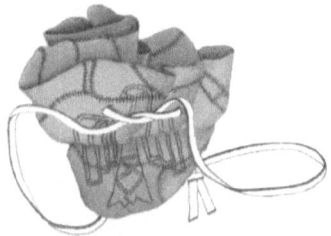

THREE

"You're just in time." Stephanie carried two full bowls out of the kitchen.

Sally put hers on the table. "I'll get yours. Take off your muddy clothes. Let's eat this delicious smelling food."

Ann and Noah put their coats in the pile of dirty clothes before Noah sat at the table. "What were you doing three nights ago?"

"That was when we were trying to sneak through Little Rock." Sally inhaled strongly to draw in the aroma of the food.

Ann sat close beside Noah. "Several times, I was sure we were going to be caught."

"But Eli got us safely across town and to a shed where we were able to sleep. He's very brave." Stephanie looked at Eli with adoring eyes.

Eli confessed, "I don't know how brave I was. I was scared to death that we were going to get caught, especially when Judge Hall was coming toward us."

Very concerned, Noah asked, "You saw Judge Hall out in the night?"

Sally remembered the name they had heard. "It wasn't only him. There were all kinds of people out looking for somebody. We heard Judge Hall say he wasn't going to let Beamis or his family get away."

Roscoe exclaimed, "Oh no! I hope they got away!"

"You know what that's about?" Ann was very curious about what had created such a big stir in Little Rock. She also felt angry that Judge Hall was hunting people like animals. "I couldn't believe how many people were out trying to find this Beamis person. Anyway, we thought we were safe, but then we heard men talking about coming into the shed to get shovels. If they found those people, they planned to kill and bury them. I don't understand why this is so important to them."

"I don't either. I hope they got away. I know them. He's a white man who bought a female person of color then had eight children with her. He owns all of them, but he loves them."

Even though she didn't know the people, Sally concurred with the sentiment because of the injustice of the situation. "I also hope they got away."

Noah stabbed a chunk of meat with his fork. "You want to know how I knew something happened that night?"

Sally wanted to hear a story while she enjoyed Roscoe's stew. "I do."

"I was asleep that day but suddenly woke with a thought screaming in my mind, 'Pray for your family's safety right now!' I felt extremely afraid for you. I went straight to the chapel. I prayed for hours before I stopped feeling that you were in danger."

"Was it right after sunset?" Ann asked.

"Yes. I had been awake for two days, so I had gone to bed early."

Sally felt awed. "God sent an angel to tell you to pray for us. You're so blessed. You had an angel talk directly to you!"

"I didn't hear an angel." Still, as he put another serving of stew in Ann's bowl, Noah wondered if he had.

Ann took the food. "But what else could it have been?"

Stephanie picked up the basket of bread. "Whatever it was, we're all blessed that God specifically kept us safe."

"I thought God wasn't there. Now I know He was working everything out all along." Noah buttered his slice of bread.

Roscoe did not believe that anything happens by the hand of God. However, this family presented things that were beyond what he thought was normal or even possible. He didn't know what ulterior motive they would have, but he decided to watch for clues that they were deceiving him.

With his last crust of bread, Eli sopped up the thick stew that clung to the bottom of his bowl. He remembered that Roscoe had said that people camped in the field. He thought they should get prepared. "I guess we better set up the tent."

"You don't have to do that. If you're only staying the night, you might as well sleep in here. I don't think anybody else will be arriving, and I don't mind if you're inside."

Stephanie had been worried. "We would appreciate that. The temperature really dropped today. It's going to be very cold tonight."

The women had asked Eli to be responsible for their financial affairs. He felt honored that they trusted him, and he wanted to spend their money wisely. He asked, "How much will you charge?"

"Two dollars for the whole lot of you."

Ann put down her spoon. "Eli, I agreed to one dollar and two bits for the coffee we had earlier and this supper."

Eli handed Roscoe three dollars and fifty cents. "Where do you want us to sleep?"

"I only have one bedroom. The rest of you will have to sleep on the floor, but there are feather mattresses you can use."

Sally told them, "I like the stained-glass window," then pulled a mattress into the chapel.

Eli looked at Noah and Ann. "You have the bedroom. We want to be warm." He and Stephanie put two mattresses together in the store next to the kitchen wall. Then, so they wouldn't slip apart, they stacked two more on top of them going the opposite direction.

"Baths are complimentary tonight." Roscoe explained, "To protect my mattresses."

Sally thought her sisters should have the most time, so they could enjoy privacy with their husbands. "I'm also going to take a second mattress if that will be acceptable. Then I'll help you clean up while the others bathe."

Roscoe had set up one of the storerooms as a bathhouse. He filled the big, cast-iron, claw-foot tub with warm water from the cistern in the kitchen. After Ann and Noah's baths, mud had soiled the water beyond further use. Roscoe drained the tub and then filled it again. "That was the last of the warm water."

Sally worked the pump in the kitchen that filled the holding tank by the stove. "Stephanie and Eli, you two go next. I'll wait for the new water to warm up."

FOUR

Very early the next morning, Ann woke and felt Noah beside her. She thanked God again, kissed her husband's cheek, and pressed closer to his side. Noah opened his eyes. "Good morning, wife." He believed God had affirmed to him that Ann truly was his when He brought her to him. With her body, Ann again passionately conveyed her agreement that she and Noah were married. To her, what Judge Daniel Hall thought did not matter one iota.

Much later, when Ann finally left the bedroom, she went to the chapel to talk with Sally about one of the things she and Noah had spoken about the night before. "What do you think about staying here this winter? That is if Roscoe will let us and if we can come to an agreement on the cost."

"We're close to Little Rock, but we don't have any place else to go, and it's too cold to be outside all the time."

Stephanie was already in the main room when Sally and Ann arrived, so they asked her the same question. She didn't think long. "That's a good idea. It's too cold and too late in the winter to try to go anywhere else."

When Noah entered the main room, he saw that

all the girls were there. He went into the store to discuss with Eli the same thing that Ann had talked about with her sisters.

Eli pulled on his shirt. "It's too late in the winter to go anywhere else."

Noah brought up something else that was on his mind. "On a different topic, you may feel that it's none of my business, but I was thinking we should not get Ann or Stephanie pregnant until we're all somewhere safe, or at least until we know what we're going to do. I know it's your decision, you and Stephanie I mean, but if we do have to travel, it would be harder for everybody if either of them was pregnant."

"I already talked with Stephanie about that when we were at Kuhn Bayou selling their land."

"Good. I told Ann I thought it would be best if we didn't make a baby until we're safe. She agreed, but she wanted me to promise we'd have twenty children."

"That's a lot of children! Did you promise?"

Noah smiled. "I promised I'd do my best to make that happen. I also want many children to surround us. I can't think of anything I'd like more, except adding you, Stephanie, Sally, and her future husband with all of your children."

"It's good that you both have the same feelings about having that many children. I hope we do get to stay together and that we have many grandchildren as well. Let's go see what Roscoe is cooking and try to work out something to stay here."

"It would be best if you talk to him. He told me I could just stay here. We didn't talk about how long, but I don't want him to think I'm trying to get him to let all of us stay here for nothing, and I don't think we should anyway. Also, Ann says you're an excellent negotiator and always fair."

Noah stopped in the room where the girls sat beside the fire. Eli continued into the kitchen. "Good morning, Roscoe."

"Good morning, Eli."

"We'd like to stay here this winter. I don't know what Noah has told you, but we have a problem with having a safe place to go. We want to pay you for room and board if you can stand having five people here with you all winter. We have a hundred dollars that we can give you, we would also do all the work like chopping wood, feeding the animals, or whatever needs to be done, and we'll give you all the food and spices we have left."

Not only could Roscoe stand to have them there, he was glad that he wouldn't have to live through another lonely winter. "Bring the food and spices in here with the hundred dollars. You and the others do all the work until you leave, except I'll cook."

They shook hands on the deal. Eli gave Roscoe the money he had brought with him then walked back into the main room. "We're staying here. Help me carry the food into the kitchen."

The family carefully dumped out the packs. Noah praised his brother-in-law. "Good negotiating. You were definitely the right person."

They separated the food and spices from everything else in the pile. Sally added, "We would've eaten the food anyway, and none of us mind doing work, so I agree; you're a great negotiator."

"That's my wonderful husband for you." Stephanie hugged Eli as he reloaded spice bottles to carry to the kitchen.

"Put it over on that counter then go to the table. Breakfast is ready." Roscoe then went into a coughing fit.

"Can I get you some water?" Sally picked up a glass. Roscoe waved for her to bring the water. He drank a few swallows as Ann and Stephanie carried the food to one of the front room tables. They ate omelets made of fresh eggs with dried then rehydrated bell peppers and onions, cheese, and ham accompanied with freshly baked bread, jam, and honey, all washed down with hot coffee.

Sally wanted to remain with Roscoe in the trading post. The rest of her family decided to get the carts from the clifftop. Roscoe packed dried beef jerky and apricots. Ann and Stephanie got india rubber canteens from the store and filled them with water.

Even though Eli didn't want to fire it unless necessary, he got his rifle. None of them felt it would be a good idea to draw attention by shooting a gun in the forest above Pine Bluff. In case they saw an animal he could shoot, or he needed to protect his family, Noah hung the bow and quiver of arrows on his back.

Noah, Ann, Eli, and Stephanie climbed the

slippery path. As they moved away from the trail to take the carts around the clifftop along the route laid out by Roscoe, they heard a horse approaching. They hid and waited.

Noah peeked out. At a distance, the rider looked like the soldier who had seen him hug Ann at Cadron Creek but had never told his commander. "It's Henry Fenn," he whispered. "Don't show yourselves, no matter what." He walked to the trail alone. "Henry, how are you? What are you doing here?"

"I came to tell you that Judge Hall gave Captain Cornish orders to discover your whereabouts. The judge was furious when he wasn't able to find some other people he was hunting. He said he wasn't going to let you and Ann get away with it if you had gotten back together. He questioned all of us who supervised you while you rebuilt the ferry. We all told Judge Hall and Captain Cornish that we knew nothing.

"That was not entirely accurate. I know what I did. Keeping you and Ann apart was wrong, so I tried to bring you back together. First, I told you to come here. Then, I told Ann to come here. When I found out that Judge Hall is looking for you, I wanted to warn you, but I needed help. I know that Melvin made a strong friendship with Sally. I think he fell in love with her. I'm confident that I can trust him. I privately told him you are probably all here at Pine Bluff. We came up with a plan."

"Does anybody else know you came here?"

"Only Melvin. I'm going back immediately. I

don't want anybody else to realize that I've been gone, or if they do realize I left town, they won't know how far I went."

"I appreciate your concern. Ann is not down there in Bacon's Trading Post, but she probably didn't go to Harmony. Gus burned down her farm. I hope she's somewhere safe."

Henry noticed that the bow and arrows Noah had left behind at Cadron Creek hung across his back. "I didn't know that had happened to Ann. I wish you both the best." Henry turned and started back to Little Rock.

In case it was a trap, Noah silently moved his family deeper into the woods. Stephanie feared they now had to leave Pine Bluff. "What do you think we should do?"

They all looked at Noah. "For now, we wait. We need to think about this before we decide anything. Henry may be bait to lure you into the open. They could be watching to see if we run."

Henry had a special place in Ann's heart. "Henry didn't turn us in at Cadron Creek. He won't turn us in now. I hope he gets back to Little Rock safely. Let's pray for him."

Deep in the woods, Noah, Ann, Stephanie, and Eli called out to God to protect Henry then waited an hour before they went close enough to the trail to get the carts. It took most of the rest of the day for them to navigate around the ridge. During the descent from the clifftop, they walked on a soft bed of pine needles. The smell of the trees that covered the gentle slope filled the air. As they approached the base of the bluff, they heard a gaggle of Canada Geese settle onto the river.

Stephanie thought back. "It would be plum wonderful to eat a goose like we did when Eli first came to our farm."

Ann also reminisced, "Those were hard days, but they were easier than this."

Eli said, "Seems like that was a different life and not just last spring."

"It was a different life," Ann sighed.

"Wait here. I'll get us some geese." Noah stealthily made his way to the edge of the river. He whispered to the goose spirit. "I acknowledge the right of these geese to thrive and fill this river, but I ask for two geese for food." Without disturbing any other goose, he silently shot an arrow through the one he saw in the reeds close to the shore. Noah looked for a second goose next to the edge of the water. When he saw another in easy reach, he shot it then felt the wind created by hundreds of wings as the whole gaggle rose into the air as one fluid mass.

Before Noah rejoined his family hiding in the pines, he retrieved the dead geese, gutted them, and left the entrails in the water to feed the fish. He plopped the geese into his cart.

"Well done, my husband. I can't wait to eat roasted goose."

Noah gave Ann a quick peck on her lips. "Anything for you, my love."

They followed the road by the river but kept

close to the base of the bluff then rounded the prominence and went into the cove. Eli commented, "There sure are a lot of mallards. We can probably eat them all winter."

"Look!" Ann pointed at ducks disappearing into the cliff.

Eli stopped. "Let's find out where they're going." When they got to the place that was magically swallowing ducks, they leaned down, looked under the ledge, and discovered a hole.

Stephanie peeked in. "There must be a big space behind this hole. A lot of ducks went in, and I haven't seen any come out."

Noah examined the fissure. "It's not pitch black in there. There must be another opening." He stuck his hand into the hole. "I feel air moving. You want to see if we can get inside?"

Ann loved to explore, but the day was ending. "We shouldn't spend much time in there."

Eli was the first one into the short passage that was just big enough for him to pull himself through and into the duck nest. "If you're coming in, be prepared to stand in duck poop." That didn't keep any of the others out. So she wouldn't have to put her hands into the filth, Eli pulled Ann in when she got to the inner end of the tunnel. He did the same for Stephanie and then Noah. "The ducks went that way when I came in." Eli pointed to an area of dim light.

"It smells horrible in here." Stephanie held her nose closed.

Ann pondered, "Makes you wonder if ducks can smell."

Noah looked around. "Ducks can smell. You have to be upwind when you're hunting. They just don't mind the smell of their droppings." They walked across the cave that was about half the width of the main room of the trading post, but every bit as long. On the left side, about three feet high, a ledge ran almost the entire twenty-foot length of the cave. It made a shelf that took up six feet of the width of the cave and left about four feet of floor. The floor rose toward the rear of the cave where there was a five-foot-high and three-foot-across opening. A dense mat of vines dangled and blocked out most of the light. The ducks detached the bottom edge of the foliage each time they made their way out of the cave. Noah walked up the small bank of dirt to the opening, raised the curtain of plants, and stepped out onto the same slope they had come down only a short time before.

Eli followed Noah out. "I bet coming this way saves fifteen minutes or more over walking around."

Ann asked, "Should we go down this slope and figure out where we are or go back through the cave?"

Noah offered his advice, "I think we have enough time to get into the canyon if we go down the slope again. It might be important to know the layout if somebody comes looking for us. This cave would be a good hiding place and escape route."

Eli looked around the hillside. "I think Noah's right. We should go back around."

36

Ann turned toward her sister, "Is that all right with you, Stephanie?"

Stephanie nodded, "Do you think Roscoe knows about this cave?"

"We should keep it to ourselves." Noah started down the slope.

Their hands were free, so Eli held Stephanie's hand as they navigated down the hill for the second time. "If we have to hide, it would be better if he doesn't know where we are."

Noah saw what Eli had done. "Even if he does know about the cave he wouldn't know that we know." He slipped his hand into Ann's.

Ann gently squeezed the hand that she was very happy to hold. "Then we'll only tell him about everything else."

Noah passed on what his father had taught him. "Pay attention to the look of the trees and anything easily recognizable. We want to be able to find our way back to this opening from the hillside. Keep looking back, so you know what the trail looks like coming up." Even though they frequently stopped to look back, they made their way down and back around to the entrance of the duck's cave in only twenty minutes. They recovered the carts at the cave's opening and then continued on to the trading post.

As the sun went down, Ann and Noah stood on the top of the mound that was the talc hill and looked back toward the river. A pair of perfectly matched hunters, at the same instant, reached into the water with their feet. They carried the fish in their talons to their nest in the large dead tree that stood as a sentinel of death guarding the entrance into the box canyon. Noah's face held an expression of reverence. "How graceful!"

FIVE

Eli entered the trading post. "We have the carts in the barn."

Noah held up the dead birds. "Maybe we can eat these geese tomorrow."

"Very nice. I haven't gone goose hunting for quite some time." *That's another reason why it will be nice to have Noah and his family here.* Roscoe coughed all the way to the washbasin in the kitchen where he hung the geese.

Ann took off her coat. "Henry came to warn us. He said that the Beamis family got away, so now Judge Hall is hunting Noah and me. He sent somebody to Harmony to see if we're there."

"Are they coming? Do we have to run?" Sally nervously shifted from foot to foot.

Noah put his arm around Sally's shoulder. "Henry didn't see anybody but me. I told him Ann wasn't here, but she probably didn't go to Harmony either because Gus burned down your farm."

"Did you have your bow on your back when you spoke with him?"

"Oh no! I did, and I had left it there for you!"

Ann still didn't feel afraid. "Henry might have

noticed, but I feel sure he won't tell on us. He had months of time when he could have told Jeremiah that Noah and I hugged, but he didn't. I think he actually did come to warn us, not to turn us in."

Noah agreed. "I think Ann is right, but I'm still sorry I had the bow on my back. It feels so natural that I didn't think about it being there."

Of all the Little Rock soldiers, Sally only completely trusted Melvin. "We shouldn't take a chance, but where would we go? Let's pray for direction, read the Bible, and listen for an answer."

After his last wait, Noah wasn't sure how quickly God would answer if he asked for guidance. *I hope somebody else asks God to direct us.*

Eli slipped into the store to get the Bible they had read almost every night since they had left Harmony. While Eli was gone, Ann spoke her prayer, "God, if Noah and I did something wrong by getting married, let us suffer and not the rest of the family. Let an arrow shoot through my heart from the cliffs and solve this problem."

Noah immediately spoke up, "No! God, prove to Ann that there is nothing wrong with our marriage by letting us rest here all winter."

Sally felt danger equal to the level presented by the outlaw, Gus, when he and others of the Butterfield Gang had tried to burn them alive inside their house. She spoke her prayer as soon as Eli sat at the table, "God, don't let this year be like last year. We can't run, not right now. We don't have any place we can go. Let us stay here this winter. Save us from the intentions of this judge who thinks he is protecting society by persecuting us. God, we believe that Ann and Noah have done nothing wrong. Just as Noah asked, let us know that You approve of their marriage. Keep the world away from us this winter. If we do need to run away, I will, because I want Noah to be my brother."

Eli flipped the Bible open. "Proverbs 4:10-27. 'Listen, my son, accept what I say, and the years of your life will be many. I instruct you in the way of wisdom and lead you along straight paths. When you walk, your steps will not be hampered; when you run, you will not stumble. Hold on to instruction; do not let it go. Guard it well, for it is your life. Do not set foot on the path of the wicked or walk in the way of evildoers. Avoid it, do not travel on it; turn from it, and go your way. For they cannot rest until they do evil; they are robbed of sleep till they make someone stumble. They eat the bread of wickedness and drink the wine of violence. The path of the righteous is like the morning sun shining ever brighter till the full light of day. But the way of the wicked is like deep darkness; they do not know what makes them stumble. My son, pay attention to what I say; turn your ears to my words. Do not let them out of your sight, keep them within your heart; for they are life to those who find them and health to one's whole body. Above all else, guard your heart, for everything you do flows from it. Keep your mouth free of perversity; keep corrupt talk far from your lips. Let your eyes look straight ahead; fix your gaze directly before you.

Give careful thought to the paths of your feet and be steadfast in your ways. Do not turn to the right or the left; keep your foot from evil'." Eli's eyes noticed something on the opposite page. "Look at Proverbs 5:15-19. 'May your fountains be blessed, and may you rejoice in the wife of your youth. A loving doe, a graceful deer – may her breasts satisfy you always, may you ever be intoxicated with her love'."

Noah looked at Ann. "You see? God says right there that I am always to rejoice in you, the wife of my youth. You intoxicate me now with your love. God says I should always be intoxicated by your love. We have not done anything wrong."

"If God lets us stay here all winter, we'll know for sure that He blesses our marriage. And I think when Proverbs 4 says we should keep our paths straight and stay off the path of evil, that He means for us to stick to the plan we have. We should not step onto the path that an evil person has tried to make us take, as in running out into the winter with no place to go."

Stephanie hoped they would all agree. "So, do we remain here?"

Sally wanted Ann and Noah to know that their marriage was acceptable to God, she wanted to keep Noah as her brother, and she was worried about Roscoe's cough. "I say we stay."

"I do too." Eli shut the Bible.

That made Roscoe happy. "Good. Now, tell me about your journey to get the carts. Did you have any problems following my directions?"

Noah described the hike around the ridge and down the slope through the pines. They told of all the ducks, geese, and fish they could hunt, and the eagles that they had seen catching fish. They did not mention the duck cave. After the recounting of the trip, they slept in the place where they hoped God would let them remain for the winter.

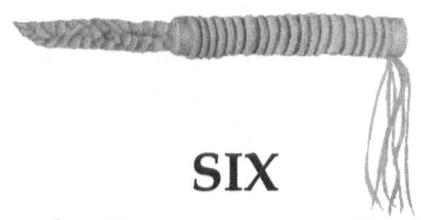

SIX

That night, Henry came upon his pursuers. The soldiers had assumed that the man they thought was riding to Pine Bluff to warn Noah and Ann had stopped each night to rest. They had done the same. Henry rode out into the forest to sneak around the men. He was glad that he had only stopped for the few minutes he had spoken with Noah. Shortly after leaving Noah, Henry had developed a strong feeling that he should rapidly return to Little Rock, and he was attempting to do so. Now, he knew that it was a good thing that he had created an alibi with Melvin.

As he sneaked around the sleeping men, Henry believed he had completed the first part of his mission; warn Noah and Ann. Now, he had to complete the second half; get back to Little Rock without anybody realizing that he had gone to Pine Bluff. Not long after Henry had evaded the men tracking him, snow started to fall. It completely covered his tracks. Even though his horse was exhausted, he persisted and returned to Little Rock after only two days and two nights away. He went straight to Melvin's cousin, Amelia. Later that morning, fellow soldiers found Henry with Amelia and escorted him to Captain Cornish.

"You've been AWOL. Where did you go?"

"I spent some time with my girl. You can ask the men who brought me here where they found me."

Captain Cornish issued orders to the other soldier in the room, "Send in the soldiers who found Private Fenn." He questioned the men who came in. "Where did you find Private Fenn?"

"With Amelia Logan."

"Did you ask how long Private Fenn had been there?"

"She said her father was away, so Henry had stayed there all weekend to protect her."

"What kind of girl is she? Is she likely to be lying?"

"Her father, Bradford Logan, is the miller. I don't think she would do anything that would give her father a bad reputation."

Captain Cornish, nor the two soldiers who had apprehended Henry, realized that Henry knew that Noah and his whole family were together at Pine Bluff. They also did not know that Henry, Melvin, and Amelia had tried to help them. In either case, Henry had broken military law and been AWOL. Captain Cornish wasn't letting Henry go unpunished. "Confine Private Fenn for a week." He instructed Henry, "The next time you plan to go outside the garrison, request leave." Once the soldiers escorted Henry out of the building, the captain stepped out of his office and gave orders to the soldier still outside his door. "As soon as they return, send the men who followed Henry to see me."

Henry walked into the stockade. *That worked perfectly.*

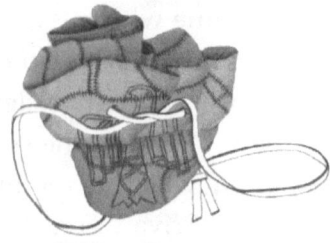

SEVEN

The snow that fell during the night had not only covered the tracks of Henry; it had also covered those that Noah, Ann, Stephanie, and Eli had made. It was an answer to the prayers spoken in the forest the previous day and those voiced in the trading post the night before.

After a delicious breakfast, Noah picked up two spyglasses. "Before anybody, other than Roscoe or myself, goes out of this building, we need to check the ridges."

"Remember how the light glinted off Ben's rifle and gave him away?" Eli didn't wait for an answer. "We need to make lookouts where we can't be seen, and the sunlight won't reflect off the spyglass."

Sally looked into the storeroom. "We could put up curtains."

Roscoe had never hung a curtain in his trading post. "If something that feminine changed here, an observer would guess that you're here. Besides, you don't need to. Thinking somebody might want to rob me, I built this place with that in mind. A person on the ridge can see inside only if they walk all the way around to the side, but still can't see beyond what is right at the window. From the cliff trail or the talc hill, you can't see inside at all. Once in the canyon, you can see only into the store, bedroom, chapel, and storerooms.

"Nobody can see into or shoot into this room or the kitchen because I offset the windows from the doors. As you can see, I built thick storm and attack shutters on all the windows. I also made very thick doors, and water comes directly into the kitchen from under the bedrock. With everything shut, we could hole up in here for a very long time.

"I'll show you where you can walk and not be seen by anybody. You have to come this way," Roscoe led his guests into the store, "then stand right here." He placed a spyglass into a shielded groove that he had designed to block any glint as he looked up at the cliff. He put his eye to the other end and meticulously searched the ridge. "I haven't bothered to look for many years. I don't see anybody up there." He walked the hiding path to the front of the room then examined the talc blockade between the trading post and the river at the south viewing position. "All clear. I'll show you my other spy holes."

The scouts, who had followed Henry, arrived at Pine Bluff and stood at the top of the trail made invisible and unnavigable by the snow. Roscoe searched the clifftop from the rear viewing position. "By the horn spoons! I swan we're in a fix now! Somebody's up there looking down with a spyglass."

Each of those inside the trading post looked at the observers. Eli stepped down from the spying perch. "Dad-blame it!"

Noah felt horrible. "This is my fault. I had that bow on my back when I spoke with Henry. I'm so sorry."

Sally hugged Noah. "Don't blame yourself. I don't think that's it. If it was, whoever's up there would already know we're here or at least that you are. They would sneak in and not stand up there, trying to see what's going on down here."

"Maybe I should go outside. If they don't see anybody but me, they might assume we're not together, because they'll know I'm here. Maybe that would stop them from looking for us."

Ann didn't like the plan. "I don't want you to go outside. What if they decide to remove the question by shooting you?"

"Then, like you said yesterday, we'll know we shouldn't have gotten married. This will be a test to see what God thinks about our marriage."

Stephanie thought it best not to test God. "God doesn't stop every bad thing from happening just because we're doing right. I don't think that's a wise test."

Eli looked at the men on the ridge again. "I doubt they would shoot Noah straight out. If Judge Hall wanted to kill him, why wait until now? If you work outside frequently, they might be convinced that you're the only one here. They would probably think we would share the work and not make you do it all."

"Good thinking. I'll be the only person to go outside. I'll feed and water the animals and bring in the eggs then we can have breakfast. After that, I'll go out and move hay into the loft in the barn before I come back in. I'll stay in for a while as if I'm tired. Later, I'll split wood in front of the barn then bring it in here and rest for a while. Close to the end of the day, I'll go out, cut more wood, and put it in the barn."

Roscoe thought that was too much for Noah to do on his own. "I'll help. Everybody knows I'm here."

"You need to stay in the house and drink hot tea to help your cough." Noah put on his coat and went to the barn alone.

Ann asked, "May we borrow washtubs and washboards and buy soap?"

Roscoe got a pile of items. "There's no charge if you'll wash a few things for me." The girls gladly agreed.

To Eli, the store seemed randomly organized, and it bothered him. He couldn't stop thinking about it. Finally, he asked, "Roscoe, may I reorganize your store?"

"I know where everything is. I'd rather you didn't."

The snow fell as Noah worked outside. The girls strung rope everywhere inside the trading post and then washed. Eli looked into the store repeatedly. "It would be even easier to know where everything is if you'd let me reorganize."

Roscoe could tell that Eli was not going to relax when the store was not set up to his liking. "You have to stay away from the windows, and if I don't like it, you have to put everything back as it is now."

"You'll like it. I'm sure."

Roscoe drank hot tea, prepared the meals, watched the men on the ridge, and fretted about what Eli was doing. At the end of the day, Eli had reorganized the store. The girls had washed everything and had hanged it all to dry. Noah, however, had not cut any wood. Instead, he had moved all the hay into the barn to protect it from the snow. He had also fed and watered the animals and gathered the few eggs that the chickens had laid. He opened the door to the trading post.

Ann met Noah at the door. "The wind has really picked up. Roscoe would like you to close the storm shutters." As Noah handed Ann the basket of eggs, she whispered in his ear, "I promise, I'll warm you up later." Roscoe had roasted the geese he had stuffed with his rice, vegetable, and spice mixture. Sealed away from the inclement weather outside, they ate the delicious meal.

That day, the soldiers on the clifftops had separated and looked into the canyon from many positions but had only discovered that the Indian they were looking for was at Pine Bluff. They met back at the steep trail down. One of the soldiers looked over the edge. "There's supposed to be a trail here."

Another of the men tried to persuade the leader to his way of thinking. "Ain't no way we can get down right here. It'd be days 'for we'd get 'round on the road, and the weather's already bad. We shouldn't try getting in there."

The one making the decisions gave his orders,

"We need ta set up camp an get outta this weather. We don't wanna let them people down there know we're here, so no fire. We'll go back ta Little Rock in the mornin' if we don't see nobody else."

When the sun went down, two feet of snow covered the ground. Throughout the night, a strong wind blew the falling snow through the pines and into the canyon.

Ann took one of the spyglasses from Sally. "You take the west side." She went into the kitchen.

With the shutters closed, Sally didn't bother to navigate the path that hid her from observers. She looked closely at the ridge before she returned to the main room. Ann returned after scrutinizing the north and west ridges. Sally prodded her, "Well?!"

"They're still there like all possessed."

Eli sat at the table. "Doesn't that cap the climax! The way the wind raged last night, I thought they would've vamoosed out of here for sure."

Noah's happiness from his recent lovemaking with Ann evaporated. In a state of high pucker, he put on his coat and opened the front door. A small avalanche of snow slid in the door.

Eli jumped up. "What in tarnation?!"

Noah looked at the wall of white then stepped out of the snow around his legs. He took the spyglass off the table, walked to the back, and looked carefully. He saw men lying at the edge of the cliff looking into the canyon. He wanted to pitch a conniption fit. *Now, I have to do all the work myself again. It was hard enough moving all the hay into the barn yesterday, and it took me the whole day to do it. It's going to take forever to dig a path through six-foot-deep snow to feed the animals.*

Ann went to get a bucket and shovel to scoop up the snow in the building.

Stephanie raised the window sash and tried to push the storm shutters open. "Won't budge."

Roscoe exclaimed, "Now I've seen the elephant! I've lived at Pine Bluff for decades, but I've never been buried alive before!" which was the exact wrong thing to say.

Suddenly, Sally felt that she was suffocating. "We're running out of air!"

Ann put her arm around her sister. "We are not." Ann walked her sister to the door and pointed to the slit of gray at the top. "The door is not blocked."

It wasn't pitch black like when Sally had knocked over her lantern in the cave, but she had the same feeling of being closed in. She yanked the shovel from Ann's hand and dug furiously at the snow in the doorway. "We need to get out!"

"We'll be all right. I'll dig us out." Eli calmly commandeered the shovel and went to work. Noah walked back into the front room. A set of snowshoes sat on one of the tables. Eli rested the shovel blade against the floor. "Noah, I'm going to shovel the snow away from the front of the house. Since the snow is above our heads, those men on the ridge won't be able to see who is in the tunnel. They'll think I'm Roscoe, so I'll keep shoveling after I help you get up onto the roof. You can step out onto the snow and walk to the barn wearing the snowshoes then dig into the barn."

Above the cliffs, less than a foot of snow remained. The soldiers were shocked when they saw the trading post snowed under. They wondered if the people inside the trading post would be able to get out.

Ann handed the snowshoes up to Noah as he sat on the roof. "First, walk around right here. If you sink in, we can get you out."

Noah stood on the trading post roof with the snowshoes attached to his feet. The men on the ridge watched. Everybody above and below held their breath as Noah stepped off the roof. The snowshoes pressed down into the fluff, but only a few inches. Noah took another step. He remained on the correct side of the snow, so he walked across the front of the trading post not far from the small space Eli had dug out. He had no problem staying in the cold open air. He moved farther from the opening by the door.

After many test steps close to help, Noah went to the barn, opened the loft door, and walked into the barn. Inside, he took off the snowshoes and climbed down the ladder. The fire was out, so he started it again. While he gave out hay and grain, he melted snow to water the animals. As Noah packed the hen boxes with extra hay, so they would stay warmer, he felt for eggs. Due to the cold, the hens had laid only two eggs.

At the trading post, Roscoe watched the men on the ridge. Eli shoveled a path toward the barn. Stephanie, Ann, and Sally took down and folded the dry clothes, linens, and blankets. They also continued to put the snow Eli dug into ten-gallon tubs, melted it by the fire, and then poured it down the drain in the kitchen.

Noah left the barn from the loft. When he sat on the trading post roof and took off the snowshoes, Roscoe saw the soldiers get to their feet and walk away from the ridge. Roscoe hurried to the front room. "They're leaving. I think this proves you're supposed to stay here. With this much snow, you can't go anywhere even if you want to. And if those men couldn't come down the cliff trail, nobody else is going to be able to either. You'll be safe here."

The rest of the day, Roscoe's five guests shoveled then melted the snow. Just before sundown, they got to the barn. They fed the animals and stacked the fire in the barn with enough wood to keep it burning all night.

EIGHT

As they sat by the fire, Roscoe divulged some distressing news. "We're not going to have enough food for the whole winter. You'll have to hunt."

Noah said, "The only hunting possibilities are on the other side of the talc hill. We'll have to clear a passageway to the river."

"It's a long way. Noah can't do it alone. We'll all have to help dig the path." Ann looked at each of them.

Sally tapped her finger on the side of her face. "That would expose anybody digging to an observer on the ridge. Anybody other than Noah going outside is risky, but maybe we can if one of us keeps an eye on the ridge."

"I didn't know there would be so much snow when I said you would have to do all the work, so I'll be your lookout."

Sally helped Roscoe prepare breakfast. "I learned a lot about cooking from a man named Melvin. He told me he could make a sad person happy with food. I think enjoyable healthy meals are important. I can see that you do too and that you're very knowledgeable. I'd love to learn if you'll share what you know."

Roscoe struggled to speak, "I've seen men eat plenty of food and still get sick. That's why I make good tasting meals that satisfy your appetite and give your body what it needs."

"Noah shared the story you told him about people who don't eat oranges. He thinks you made it up, especially about their hair getting curly and their eyes bulging out."

"I've seen it happen. I'll show you what I put in my food packs, and you can tell me about Melvin." Roscoe encouraged Sally to talk because he sensed that the man was important to her and because he could barely talk.

"Melvin was the cook for the military detachment assigned to assure that Noah and Ann built the ferry at Cadron Creek and that they stayed apart."

"And he taught you about cooking?" Roscoe pulled up a stool so he could sit down and catch his breath while he listened.

"It all started when it was my turn to cook for us civilians. I went to camp with Melvin. We cooked dinner with my recipe, and we talked. That evening, we made supper using one of Melvin's recipes. Everybody liked both meals and asked us to be permanent cooks. We agreed."

"Was he a nice young man?"

"Yes. I liked him very much, but it couldn't have worked out between us. I'm only fourteen. He's nineteen. I had to go with my family, and he had to go with his unit back to Little Rock. I'm silly to think about him, but I do. I told him when I find a husband that I hoped he would be like him."

"What did he say?"

"He said whoever he was, that he would be a lucky man."

"Sounds like he also liked you."

Sally replied with sadness, "But he let me go."

"As you said, he had to go with his unit. He probably didn't want it to be that way."

"Maybe not, but I won't ever forget him. Now, tell me about you."

"I'm just an old man without a family."

"Why don't you have a family?"

"I guess I did what Melvin did," Roscoe coughed. "Except for one," he coughed. "I let the women I loved walk away, or I walked away myself. Not very smart, was I?" Roscoe coughed then coughed and coughed some more.

Sally got a glass of water. "Maybe you didn't have a choice either."

Roscoe drank a few swallows and then tried to breathe. "Thanks for thinking that, but I had a choice. I made the wrong one." Roscoe and Sally placed the food on the table.

After eating, Roscoe got a spyglass and followed the others out the door. He inhaled the cold air then coughed uncontrollably. Noah felt Roscoe burning up with fever. He scooped him up. "We need to get Roscoe and his cot into the bathroom."

With lips and fingernails blue from lack of oxygen, Roscoe gasped, "I'm fine. I just have to catch my breath."

"You are not fine. You have pneumonia." Noah

carried Roscoe into the house. "Eli, move Roscoe's cot. Roscoe, cover up with blankets."

Noah and Eli searched Roscoe's storerooms. They hadn't looked into them before because they felt they would have been invading Roscoe's privacy. Now, they had to find something to help. Noah perused Roscoe's treasure trove of plants, herbs, and spices. "I should have known Roscoe would have a lot of native plants and herbs. Studying the effects of what you eat requires knowledge of plants and their uses. It also creates knowledge." Noah handed Eli an armload of plants.

"I'm too hot!" Roscoe threw the blankets off. It wasn't long before he wanted the covers back. "I'm freezing!" The girls obliged and covered him again. A few minutes later, he was too hot again. One or the other of the girls removed or returned the blankets as Roscoe requested.

In a big cooking pot, Noah mixed dried mullein leaves, crushed dried yellow coneflower, rosemary, thyme, oregano, and dried goldenseal root. He boiled water and then poured it over the plant mixture. In another pot, Noah poured boiling water over dried butterfly weed roots. He came into Roscoe's sick room with a cup of butterfly weed tea sweetened with honey. "Sally, please make some garlic paste. I also need something to burn sage. I couldn't find anything." Noah handed the cup of tea to Roscoe. "Drink this."

Roscoe coughed out the words, "Last room on the left, under the flaxseeds." Ann, Eli, and Stephanie went to look where directed.

Roscoe finished the drink. Noah took the cup. "Breathe in forcefully and then exhale as hard as you can ten times. That will make you cough, but that's good. After that, breathe normally for ten minutes and then repeat. Pneumonia is like drowning. We have to get and keep the fluid out of your lungs."

Even though he was sick, Roscoe was curious. "What's in the drink?"

"Butterfly weed roots."

"Interesting. If I get better, will you tell me what you know about plants?"

"You'll get better. Let's both share."

Sally pleaded, "I don't know anything, but I want to learn."

"It's fine with me." Noah approved of anybody's desire to learn. Roscoe nodded his head.

Noah left to talk with those who weren't in the room. "Everybody needs to make sure Roscoe does his breathing. If he gets lightheaded, let him do a few less, but make sure he's exhaling forcefully. He also needs to have the butterfly weed tea three times a day, and the other tea I'm making twice a day."

Eli picked up the bags of flaxseeds. "Do you see anything?"

"Got it!" Ann pulled out a bowl. She handed it to Noah. "We will."

Noah twisted together a long roll of dried sage. It looked like a snake coiled in the bowl. They all went back to Roscoe. Noah lit the end of the coil. The aromatic smoke floated into the small room.

Sally entered with the garlic paste and handed it

to Stephanie. She returned to the kitchen to make Melvin's chicken and dumplings with one of Roscoe's food packets and plenty of extra garlic. Stephanie tied the garlic paste against Roscoe's chest.

With so much fluid in Roscoe's lungs, Noah feared that he would not survive the night. When the delicious smelling stew was ready, Noah made Roscoe get up. "Walk to the table and sit up while eating. It will help clear your lungs." Before Roscoe went back to his cot, Noah served him another cup of butterfly weed tea and a cup of mullein tea.

That night, Noah stayed in the room with Roscoe. He let Roscoe sleep only a short time. "Wake up. Sit up. Exhale hard." Roscoe's first deep breath caused horrible coughing, but the forceful lung contractions helped to clear his lungs. Noah again let Roscoe have only a short time of sleep. "Roscoe, drink this and then do your breathing. If you have another coughing spell, that's good."

Very late in the night, the medicine and breathing finally broke the mucus in Roscoe's lungs. The sound of Roscoe's coughs changed. Noah knew Roscoe was at the most dangerous stage. Roscoe had to clear his lungs, or he would drown in his own fluids. Roscoe would rather have slept, but Noah made him forcefully exhale the entire night.

Ann walked into the sick room with the morning sun. "How is he?"

Noah put his ear to Roscoe's chest and listened. "I think the worst is over. I'm going to bed. Give Roscoe his doses of tea and make him continue his breathing procedure every ten minutes."

Throughout the day, Roscoe coughed, coughed, coughed, and coughed. He struggled to breathe, but he tried to do as Noah had told him. His chest hurt so badly that he could barely stand it. He was exhausted, but he couldn't have rested even if anybody had let him. He felt starved for oxygen, and he was. Sally sat beside Roscoe. Roscoe used the tiny amount of air in his lungs to whisper, "I can't do this. Let me die."

Sally answered, "I will not let you die!" However, she did feel sorry for him. She knew Roscoe was suffering. When Noah woke later in the day, Sally asked, "Can we give Roscoe some willow tea for pain? I didn't want to give him anything except what you told us until I had asked you. I don't know if it would be safe with the tea he's drinking."

"We can't mix willow tea with garlic or mullein. It might cause bleeding in his stomach, and we wouldn't even know it."

"But his chest hurts so much from all the coughing. Isn't there anything we can do?"

"I hate to see him hurting, but we don't want to make things worse." He thought for a few minutes. "We could use the cedar poultice. It probably wouldn't help much, but it might help some."

"If I had cedar, I'd make it right now."

"I'll get some." Noah put on the thick, wool-lined, canvas coat that Jeremiah had given him when he had been building the ferry. Noah walked to the barn, climbed the ladder, put on snowshoes, and then stepped out of the loft onto the snow.

Sally snapped off and boiled the tips of the long

cedar branch that Noah brought back. She mashed them into a poultice and tied a cloth-full on Roscoe's chest. "This should help with the chest pain."

Roscoe wheezed, "You're an angel."

NINE

In Little Rock, the fourth day that Henry sat in the jail, three severely frostbitten scouts reported to Captain Cornish. "Did you follow Private Fenn out of town?"

The leader of the group started the report, "We saw him leave. We followed tracks goin' south til the snow covered 'em. We went all the way ta Pine Bluff. Nobody passed us goin' back ta Little Rock. We never saw who we was followin' ever again."

Another of the men stated his conclusion, "Musta been somebody else we saw leaving Little Rock."

"Did you see anybody at Bacon's Trading Post?"

"We seen one man movin' hay ta the barn. He looked like what you told us that Injin looks like. We didn't see no women, an there weren't no other men there neither."

The last man added, "Except Roscoe. We saw Roscoe shoveling snow."

"That will be all. Go to the infirmary." The captain was tired of dealing with the matter. He felt irritated by the waste of his time, and now, he had incapacitated soldiers. *Private Fenn didn't have frostbite or any sign of exposure; his horse didn't either. He was in*

Little Rock during drill and here two days later when they brought him from Amelia Logan's home. There is no way Henry could have gone to Pine Bluff, alerted anybody to hide, and gotten back in two days. I'll tell Judge Hall that Noah Swift Hawk was at Pine Bluff, but the others were not. I hope that will be the end of it.

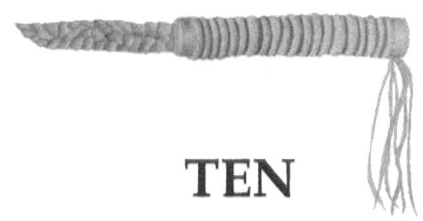

TEN

For days, Ann, Stephanie, Sally, Noah, and Eli cared for Roscoe and shoveled snow. When they finally cleared a path all the way to the river, they found the eagles hunting. Noah loved to watch them. Sometimes he saw the eagles arrive at their nest with fish, sometimes with ducks or small mammals, and many times with something too small to determine what they had captured. Noah and Eli joined the hunt. They chopped a hole through the river's icy edge and added fish to their food supply. They also killed ducks, which were plentiful and often close enough to the shore to easily shoot and retrieve.

Every night, they sat in the main room by the fire, read, and studied Eli's Bible. When Roscoe recovered enough, he and Sally cooked and experimented. Roscoe sat on the stool, coughed, wheezed, tried to breathe, and hurt, but he introduced Sally to the spices and herbs in his storerooms. Her favorite discovery was adding dill to bread. Everybody enjoyed the heavenly smell and the warm melt-in-your-mouth bread.

After two weeks at Pine Bluff, Eli brought up a need. "We've used most of the firewood that was stored in the barn. We need to chop more."

Noah asked, "Roscoe, where should we get wood?"

"Use the mules to pull some of the logs out from under the snow behind the smokehouse. You can chop and stack the wood inside the barn." Roscoe felt very bored with nothing to do all day but breathe and drink tea concoctions. "Walking to the barn will help me keep the fluid out of my lungs. Besides, I'm doing much better." Roscoe knew he would have been lying alone and dead if this family had not been there. He loved their attention, and he planned to do whatever Noah thought was best, but he hoped for release from confinement.

Noah put his ear next to Roscoe's chest and listened. "You are breathing better. You can come, but no working. So the air you breathe isn't too cold, and you don't breathe in any dirt, keep your mouth covered with your scarf."

In the barn, Stephanie asked, "What are the animal's names?"

Roscoe introduced each animal. "I call this donkey Little Jack because he's a miniature donkey and male donkeys are called jacks. I'm not very original, so I named the female miniature donkey Little Jenny because females are Jennies. This big female I call Big Jenny. The white donkey with gray spots is Spot. This brown one's name is Chocolate. The albino is Blanco. That's white in Spanish. The reason is obvious. This big donkey with the long cords of hair, I named Shaggy. I call Smiley, Smiley because the white marking around his mouth makes him look like he's smiling. This one's Honey. Not only is she the color of honey, but she has a very sweet nature. The gray donkey is QuickSilver. Even though he's big, he is really fast." Next, Roscoe touched each mule as he spoke its name. "These mules are Molly, Jumper, King, Rose, Hector, Blue, Chief, Diamond, and Ace."

Stephanie rubbed each of their necks as they were introduced. However, when Stephanie tried to touch the last one, the mule backed away. "That one is named Stubborn. I got it this fall. I don't know why I haven't put it down. She won't do anything for me. She's not worth the food she eats."

"She probably just needs special attention." Stephanie stood as close as Stubborn allowed her and looked at the animal.

Roscoe warned her, "It's best to leave her alone. She's been known to bite." He sauntered over to his next group of animals. "This goat is Billy because he's a male goat. This goat is white, but I can't give her the same name as Blanco, so she's Snowflake. I call this goat Bella. I think she is beautiful with her soft brown fur and black eyes. She gives the most milk when she's producing."

He walked to the last of the animals. "This goat is my favorite. I like the black and white stripes on her tan head. Her tan neck and shoulders make the white ring look like an upside-down harness around the bottom of her neck. The way her tan front fades into her black rump with the white stripes running down both sides is very lovely. She flicks her white tail all the time. To me, she seems fancy, so that's what I named her. Have you ever seen an animal so delightful to look at?"

"I think she's beautiful." Stephanie rubbed Fancy behind the ears but then moved back toward Stubborn. She stood close but ignored the mule.

Roscoe returned to the reason they had gone into the barn. "We should use King and Ace to pull the logs."

Noah walked to the harnesses. "They're huge. How much do these mules weigh?"

Eli and his father had usually gone to Fort Smith to purchase supplies when the army's new mules arrived. He had learned how to determine their weight by their height and girth. "I think King is 1,500 and Ace about 1,400."

Roscoe confirmed Eli's guesses. "Very good, Ace is 1,425 and King is right at 1,500."

By the time they had pulled a few logs into the barn, Stubborn no longer tried to move away and ignored Stephanie as much as Stephanie appeared to be ignoring the mule. Stephanie walked away from the mule to get a load of firewood then went back and stacked it beside Stubborn.

Roscoe coughed. Sally had designated herself as his nurse. She put down the wood in her arms. "I'm taking you to the house."

"I don't want to go, and I'm fine. It's not like before."

Noah encouraged Roscoe to do as Sally asked. "You don't need to be in the barn. You should go on back to the house."

Sally hadn't known Roscoe long, but she had become very attached, and she didn't want to lose him. "We want you to be all right."

Roscoe knew they genuinely cared about his well-being. He still grumbled as he went back into the house with Sally. She immediately made him a dose of butterfly weed tea.

As they lay in bed that night, Stephanie spoke with Eli. "Roscoe says Stubborn is mean, and she's not worth the food she eats, but she could be such a good helper. I think she only needs to know that somebody loves her. I think I can reach her. What do you think?"

Eli looked into his wife's gorgeous blue eyes. "You are the most loving and gentle person I know. If anybody can bring out the best in another, be it a person or a beast, it would be you, but be careful, and you need to ask Roscoe for permission."

"Thank you, darling." More than once, Stephanie shared her love with the man she not only loved but also appreciated.

At breakfast, Stephanie brought up the topic. "Noah, you got our horse, Dusty, to trust you after he had been beaten by the men in the Butterfield Gang. When Earl gave you Eyanosa, the horse took to you immediately. What did you do?"

"I treated Eyanosa as a friend, but also as his owner. I got Dusty to accept me by not coming directly at him. I made sure he saw me being kind to Arabella, and I also made sure he saw that Arabella trusted me."

"I have an idea. Roscoe, is it all right if I try to work with Stubborn?"

"You can try, but I've already tried and haven't gotten anywhere."

"I appreciate you giving me a chance."

Sally handed a spyglass to Stephanie. "Don't forget to go into the loft and make sure everything is safe before you come back from the barn."

Stephanie went to the barn. She made sure Stubborn saw her brush Eyanosa and scratch his rump, which was Eyanosa's favorite thing. Stephanie put the brush away. She put a small scoop of grain in a bucket and placed it where only Stubborn could reach it. It was also very close to the place where Stephanie planned to stack wood.

Eli went to the barn, mainly to make sure Stephanie remained safe. He also put wood on the fire in the blacksmith furnace in the barn. He melted snow and poured the water into the troughs then doled out hay and cracked corn. Before long, Noah came out and helped chop wood.

Stephanie ignored Stubborn as she stacked logs beside the mule. The mule stood as far away as it could. When they finished their work and left the barn, Stephanie left the bucket of oats.

Noah decided to ask for what he had hoped ever since he had discovered Roscoe's plant inventory. Roscoe's recovery had progressed well, and Noah knew Roscoe was bored with nothing to do. Noah walked into the trading post. "Roscoe, I still want to learn what you know about these plants, and I'll tell you everything I know too."

"I've been teaching Sally about food. I'd be happy to tell you what I know about my plants, but I suspect you know a lot more than I do."

"I have no idea what a person would do with quite a bit of what you have in your storerooms. I always want to learn everything I can."

Much to Noah's delight, Roscoe agreed. "Then we'll start tomorrow."

Late in the night, Noah woke. Ann was not in bed. He walked into the front room and found her crying. "What's wrong?"

"If you had come to Harmony a few years earlier, you could have saved my parents. We traded our cow to get Doc Gridley to come, but he didn't know anything. Mama and Papa were sick almost exactly like Roscoe. He said they had influenza and you said Roscoe has pneumonia, but it was the same. They couldn't breathe, they coughed and coughed, and they burned up with fever. I tried to save them. I really tried, but I let them die when all I needed to do was make them breathe right and give them your special tea, but I let them die." Ann cried harder.

Noah took Ann into his arms and tried to comfort her. "You didn't let them die. It was not your fault. I'm sure you did everything you could have. I'm sorry you didn't know about this treatment, but it doesn't save everybody either."

"I miss them, and you'll never even know them. You would have liked my parents, and they would have liked you."

Noah rocked Ann. "I know you miss them. I'm sure your parents were wonderful people because you, Stephanie, and Sally are wonderful."

"Thank you for saying that. I'm being a baby. I'm sorry."

"There's nothing to be sorry about. It's all right for you to miss your parents. There is nothing wrong with being sad that they died or crying about it. Come back into our room. I'll hold you and lament for them with you." They went back to the bedroom and lay on the bed. Noah held Ann and let her cry. "We can have a ceremony for them if you want. We can have it alone, or you can invite your sisters and Eli."

"What kind of ceremony?" Noah explained the complicated ritual. Ann wasn't sure. "I'll tell you in the morning." She continued to weep softly until she slipped into sleep in the loving, caring comfort of her husband's arms.

While they ate breakfast, Ann told the family what was in her heart. "I was thinking about Mama and Papa, how they died, and that we might have saved them with Noah's treatment. I want to lament their loss and the sadness of knowing we might have saved them. Noah and I are going to have a ceremony. If you would like to join us, you can, but if you don't want to, that's all right."

"What would we do?" Sally asked.

Noah explained the ceremony again. Stephanie filled their cups with tea. "Maybe Roscoe will let us use some tongs, but where will we get a Calumet, white paint, a soul bundle, or a flint knife?"

"We'll have to make them."

Sally scooped eggs onto her plate. "I want to be included."

Eli took the bowl of eggs. "I do too."

Roscoe sipped the tea he was glad wasn't medicine but was delicious English tea. "May I join?"

72

Noah told him, "That's up to the family of the deceased."

Stephanie consented, "If you want to, I don't mind."

"I don't either." Sally sweetened her tea.

Ann said, "Please join us."

Noah put down his cup. "Then we should all help to make the ceremonial items. We need to get some of the clay I saw at the river, three pieces of hardwood, an unused pair of moccasins, buckskin pants, spools of heavy red, yellow, black, white, green, and blue colored thread, and two unused rawhide strips."

Eli thought they shouldn't spend money on something they already owned. "Why can't we use the piggin strings we already have?"

Noah explained, "We shouldn't use anything that has been used in a violent way. We used them to tie up Gus and Roy. Also, I don't want the energy from those men involved at all."

Eli stabbed his last bite of breakfast with his fork. "I understand, and I agree completely. I'll buy them from the store."

Roscoe called out, "Write what you get in the book."

Eli bought the items from Roscoe's store. He opened the sales book and looked at the way Roscoe kept records. Roscoe had made a separate page for each item, with entries each time he restocked or made a sale. He didn't have a running record of daily sales or a balance sheet. *How does Roscoe know what he's got or write fast enough on a busy day?* He flipped to each page for each item and made the sales entry. *I can't believe Roscoe even made a separate sheet for threads by color.* "I could show you a way to keep your books that would let you know your overall status and make it easier to know what needs to be restocked."

After Eli's reorganization of the store, Roscoe was open to suggestions. He sounded wheezy as he said, "I'd like to hear what you suggest."

"You'll like my method." However, Eli didn't start on the books. Instead, he went to the barn and continued the never-ending process of splitting and chopping wood.

Noah stood up. "Roscoe, that cold air wasn't good for you. Please stay inside today."

Stephanie found the bucket of oats empty. She got another handful of grain and waited until Stubborn was looking before she put the food in the bucket. Then, Stephanie stacked wood in the same pile as the day before. Once again, Stubborn stayed as far away as she could and would not eat the grain with people around. This time, when they left the barn, Stephanie picked up the bucket and dumped the grain back into the bin. "If Stubborn won't come close to eat, she can't have it."

Noah split three long slender pieces of hardwood and handed them to Ann. "We'll use these to make the Calumet stem and the knife handle. I'm going to dig up some clay I saw." He got on Eyanosa and rode the path through the snow toward the talc hill and the river.

Sally came down from the loft. "All clear." They walked out of the barn. Inside the trading post, Eli went straight to Roscoe. "If you give me your books, I can do the whole thing." Eli liked the detail, clarity, and stability of numbers. He looked forward to doing the work. Years ago, Eli had gone through all the books for Yates Mercantile and had reorganized the data. He had shown the final product to his father.

Tom had looked at the books. "Eli, my son, this is a marvel! If I could, I would send you to college." Tom had meant it. He knew his son's mind was very sharp. He saw things in a different way. Tom thought Eli's method was a much better system and had immediately started keeping his records using Eli's accounting format.

Roscoe, however, didn't want anybody to know how much money he had accumulated over the years. His plan for knowing how much money he had made was that he knew the amount of money in the bag in his hiding place. "Show me your plan with this book." Roscoe pushed over the same book in which Eli had notated their purchases.

Ann put the wood Noah had given her in their room then went back into the front room and sat beside Stephanie. "I helped Papa run the farm, and then I did it without him. Now, I don't have a farm to run, anything to organize, to plan, or to execute. I don't know what to do."

Stephanie stood up. "Let's see what Roscoe has to read in his store."

Noah dug frozen yellow and white clay from the

riverbank and loaded it into duck cloth bags. To let the clay thaw, Noah got the large bowl he had used to burn sage. As he positioned the bowl on the hearth, Noah noticed that Ann and Stephanie were reading. He put the clay in the bowl, went into the store, and got a third book.

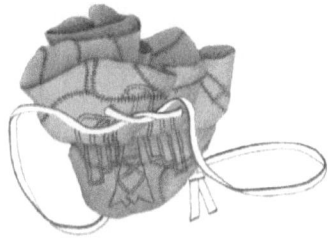

ELEVEN

Judge Hall didn't believe Captain Cornish. "Just because Noah Swift Hawk was the only man seen at Pine Bluff, doesn't mean the others aren't there. Nobody's going to take this court seriously if I don't enforce my sentences. If the men we sent don't find Ann in Harmony, you'll have to send your men back to Pine Bluff, and they will have to go into the trading post to look. I want to talk to the soldiers you sent to Pine Bluff."

I have way too many resources committed to this manhunt. I sure hope they find Ann in Harmony. Captain Cornish told Judge Hall, "I am not sending more troops out in this snow to double-check. We'll see what we need to do when my men get back from Harmony."

"If they take too long, you ARE going to send your men, and I want to talk to the soldiers who went to Pine Bluff, RIGHT NOW."

Captain Cornish didn't like Judge Hall ordering him around. "I'll send them over." He walked out of the building.

A short time later, three soldiers walked into Judge Hall's chambers. "Two of you, go sit in the courtroom." When only one man remained in the room, Judge Hall interrogated him, "During your mission to follow the man out of town, did you ever lose sight of him?"

"Yes, sir. Right off we did, but we saw his tracks."

"Was there more than one set of tracks?"

"Only one new set."

"Did anybody ever pass you going back toward Little Rock?"

"No, sir."

"And one of you was on lookout at all times?"

"No, sir. But there was snow an there weren't no tracks."

"What did you see at Bacon's Trading Post?"

"The day we got there, that man with them blue eyes went ta the barn. He musta given out food an water. Then he musta started a fire, cause I saw smoke come outta the forge chimney."

"You saw a forge?"

"No, sir. Everybody knows there's a forge at Bacon's Trading Post, an' I don't think he's got it in the house."

"Go on. What else did you see?"

"The man went back ta eat breakfast. I know cause I saw smoke come out the kitchen chimney before he got back in there. It wasn't long after that he come out again. Cause it was snowing, he moved all the hay in ta the barn –"

Judge Hall interrupted, "Did you talk to him? How do you know why he moved the hay?"

"Cause that's why I woulda done it. It was a good thing cause the next morning, the canyon was full a snow. Down in there, they was just about buried. It was the darndest thing! Lord Almighty that Indian climbed up on ta the trading post roof, put on snowshoes, stepped out on top a that snow, an walked ta the barn. He walked right in ta the loft. I ain't seen nothing like it in all my born days. He's a brave man. He could a gone down in there an died."

"That's all you saw?"

"No, sir. We saw Roscoe start shovelin' a path ta the barn. He hardly got anywhere before that Indian went back across the snow. When the Indian stepped on ta the trading post roof, we left."

"You saw Roscoe?"

"Sure did. He was shovelin'."

"All that work and you only saw the two men?"

"Yes, sir. That's all we ever saw."

"Go on back to the barracks." The judge walked into the courtroom and got each of the other men, one at a time. He asked the same questions and got the same answers. *Maybe the Indian is the only one at the trading post. Guess I'll wait for the report from Harmony.*

TWELVE

At Pine Bluff, Stephanie continued her pursuit of Stubborn. She made sure Stubborn saw her love on all the other animals and saw them come to her when she entered the barn. In addition, Stephanie only left the grain bucket out when she was working close to Stubborn.

Noah and Ann gathered the plants of power. Ann got out the willow bark they had brought to Pine Bluff and placed some in the woven reed bow they borrowed from the store. Roscoe contributed tobacco and sage to the mixture in the reed bowl.

After the easy part, Noah and Ann pulled carts over the talc hill and around the prominence to the pine forest. A cedar of the right size stood not far off the road. Unlike at Cadron Creek, the two of them didn't mind sawing down the cedar or dragging it down the hill to the snow-free road. Ann pulled the saw. "The smell reminds me of the cedars on the farm. I miss home."

"I wasn't there long, but I dreamed of your farm my whole life. I miss it too." Noah swung the axe. "I'll chop up the trunk and branches to use for the ceremonial fire. We'll add some of the branch tips to the bowl of plants for the mourning ceremony. The rest we'll add to Roscoe's store of plants."

Every day, in order to thoroughly ingrain the information into their minds, Roscoe, Noah, and Sally each repeated everything they had already said about the plants in the storerooms before they moved on to new plants. Not only did they learn from each other, but they also enjoyed the time spent together doing something that was important to all of them.

The one record book Roscoe had allowed Eli to see contained enough data for Eli to show Roscoe how his system worked. Eli explained, "This system is much easier to maintain and more informative."

"How did you come up with this?"

"I don't know. It just seems like this is the way to keep records."

"Thank you, Eli. I'm going to use your system from now on." Roscoe looked through the information. "I didn't realize that."

Stephanie wanted to know what her husband had done. "May I see what Eli did?" Roscoe patted the seat beside him. They looked through the ledger together while Roscoe explained to Stephanie the same information that Eli had shared with him. Stephanie said, "Really, who would have known?" After the second time she made the comment, the others also came over to look. Eli said, "You can tell which items are not worth selling because Roscoe is losing money on them, which items are earning him the biggest profit, how the prices for items varied over time, inventory levels, sales, expenses, losses, and overall profit."

Ann complimented her brother-in-law, "You do a

great job handling money, negotiating, and seeing the whole picture."

"That's my wonderful husband!" Stephanie put her hand on Eli's.

When the snow finally melted below the bottom of the windows, Noah put on a pair of snowshoes and circled the house. He unlocked the storm shutters then went back inside and opened the windows for Sally. Noah also wanted to move on with his plan to help Ann. "Family, we can start making the items we need for the ceremony. Let's start after tomorrow's morning meal."

In the morning, Noah got started. "First, I need to cleanse myself, and we need to purify the building before we make anything. I'd like to use the chapel."

"Go on." Sally waved him away.

"Please keep down the cover over the doorway." Noah went into the Chapel with a long rope of twisted sage and the clay dish with a hot ember inside. He positioned the bowl on the floor in front of the cross then crumbled a small section of sage on the glowing coal and ignited the portion still in his hand. He stood over the smoke that rose from the floor and spoke barely louder than thought, "Father God, purify me with the smoke of this fragrant plant. Remove everything negative or contrary to Your plan." He used the other part of the sage twist to pull the smoke up his body, inhaled a small amount and then exhaled out everything negative. "Cause the smoke of this sage to remove everything impure."

He drew some over his head. "Father, remove

fear, anger, worry, depression, and anything else negative. Make my every thought be in alignment with Yours." He waved the sage wand and brought the smoke to his eyes. "Open my eyes to the wonders You put before me. Cause me to see the signs You show me."

Next, he waved the smoke to his ears. "Father God, cleanse my ears that I may clearly hear the needs, gifts, sorrows, and joys of those around me and also everything You say to me." He drew the smoke into his mouth. "Cause my mouth to speak Your words of truth in love."

He pulled the smoke to his heart. "Purify my heart. Remove anger and all impurities so that I may faithfully and selflessly love You and all those You have placed in my life." He wafted the sage over his shoulders, arms, and hands. "Give me the strength to do everything You call me to do and to create with beauty and purity."

He then directed the smoke to his torso and back. "Make and keep all my desires pure." Finally, he directed the sage to his feet. "Connect my feet to Your will and not my own. Lead me to peace within my mind, peace with the living, and peace with the dead. God, hear my prayers."

Noah stubbed the sage wand out in the clay vessel and then opened an exit to the outside. He waved his arms in big circles and drew all the smoke to the window where it billowed out into the cold, carrying away all the negative energy and impurities. He forced the smoke from the room for many minutes until both he and the air in the chapel were clear, pure, and peaceful. He went into the main room. "Gather in a circle."

Noah allowed each direction to call its chosen. He then held the sage wand to the fire in the hearth to light it for the second step. He stood in the east and wafted the smoke over his body from head to toe. "Father God, put Your thoughts into my mind, Your words into my mouth, and Your spirit into my body." He turned to Roscoe who stood with him in the east. Noah waved the sage smoke toward Roscoe's head, over his arms, body, and back then down his legs to his feet. He added several puffs of the aromatic smoke toward Roscoe's face and chest. "Allow this sage to take away any impurity or negativity, to heal this body, to cleanse mind and spirit, and to make Roscoe present in this moment."

He moved clockwise to the south where Stephanie stood. As he waved the sage smoke over her, he spoke the words given to him. "Let this smoke cleanse body, soul, mind, and heart. Bring acceptance, love, and joy into this creation. In return, be filled with the same."

Eli stood in the southwest. Noah turned and directed the sage over his body. "Cleanse this mind. Cleanse this body. Cleanse this spirit. Remove anything negative. Fill this man with love, truth, peace, and grace. Let him be in this creation with strength and cunning and knowledge."

Noah turned clockwise again toward the northwest and Sally. "Allow this smoke to cleanse your mind, body, and spirit, and to fill your heart with love and joy. Come into this moment to create with beauty and purity." He felt called to add something. "Open these eyes to the spirit world, this mind to discernment, and this heart to fearless action."

Ann stood in the north. He wanted very much to take away the pain he knew she held in her thoughts and heart. "Cleanse this mind from all thoughts that are painful or negative." He waved the sage over her head and then several times toward her heart while he silently prayed for her beyond the present moment. *God, take away all the negative thoughts that tell Ann she failed or is less than what she wants to be.* Then he spoke aloud, "Purify this heart and use it as your conduit to bring love, joy, and comfort." He wafted more billows of smoke toward Ann's heart and again, prayed silently to his God for the woman he loved. *God, let this heart always see Your love. Let it always see my love and the love everybody else holds for her.* Noah wafted the smoke over Ann again. "Direct these arms and hands that they may serve You." He directed smoke over her body. "Cause this body to conceive all You give." *Give us the twenty children we desire.* He drew smoke over her legs and feet. "Let these legs and feet take this woman where You want her most." *God, take this woman to the place You have planned for her and let me go with her.* "Bring body, mind, heart, and soul into this moment to create in beauty and love."

Noah then told them, "Now, we go together to cleanse the house." He gave each of them a sage twist and lighted them from his own. Together, they smudged the center of each room, the corners, the windows, the door, the perimeter, and every place where any negativity or evil could hide. As they went, he repeated, "Cleanse this house. Let nothing negative or evil hide, slip into us, any object in this building, on the land around us, or into the river. Fill this house with creativity, peace, truth, comfort, love, and obedience." When they arrived back at the hearth, they offered the last bit of the sage to the fire to cleanse the fire, the hearth, and the flue. "Open the doors and windows. Drive the smoke, impurities, and negativity out." They fanned the smoke out until all was clear and pure.

THIRTEEN

"Now, we create. The colors symbolize the six powers of the universe. Red is for the east and knowledge. It's where the thunderbird lives, the place of the rising sun, and the beginning of life.

"Yellow is for the south; spring, bounty, growth, medicine, and healing. This is when we plant. The seeds grow into new life. It is the teenage years.

"Black is for the west where the sun goes down. It stands for the spirit world where the spirit helpers live. We seek spiritual wisdom and pray for help from spirit guides. It is mid-life.

"White is for the north; health, strength, endurance, truthfulness, and honesty. It is the place where the white blanket of snow covers Mother Earth. This is when we are grandfathers and grandmothers.

"Green is for Mother Earth of which rocks, minerals, trees, all plants, two-legged, four-legged, swimming, and winged creatures are an equal part. We should respect and protect Mother Earth.

"Blue is for Father Sky, who gives heat and life to everything on Mother Earth. It's where the Great Spirit lives. I believe the Great Spirit is God."

Stephanie asked for more information, "I want to

make a smudge bowl for the ceremony. What kind of decorations would be good?"

Noah drew some of the symbols. "We use the thunderbird, hope, morning star, crosses, medicine man eye, and the universe. Sometimes we put man entering the universe. He wanders as he tries to find the center. I believe that is where we find God. This is the symbol for families."

Stephanie stopped him. "Thank you, Noah. I know what I want to do."

Noah turned to Roscoe. "Would you make my medicine bag? If you don't want to, it's all right."

Roscoe had gone west many years before. He knew how sacred a medicine bag was to its owner. For Noah to ask him to make his was a high honor. "I'd be glad to make it."

It pleased Noah that Roscoe accepted. "I appreciate it very much. With your knowledge of plants, food, and medicine, it will have strong power." Noah handed Roscoe the large pair of buckskin pants that Eli had bought from the store.

Roscoe cut four rings off the top and the legs into fourths. He took one ring and a section of the leg. "There's enough for three more."

Ann took him up on the offer. "I'd like to make one. I'll take the parts now."

"Go ahead." As he walked to a table, Roscoe inserted a board into the leg section in his hand.

"I want to make one." Sally took a set.

Eli waited before he spoke, "Unless you want to, Stephanie, I'll make one."

"You go ahead." Stephanie handed Eli the last set of buckskin materials.

Sally held out her hand. "Give me one of those moccasins. I'll make half of the soul bundle."

Ann gave one to Sally. "Should we cut each into pieces and sew them together into a half-circle?"

"That's an excellent idea." Sally sat to take the shoe apart.

At the Williams Farm in Harmony, Noah had taught Eli how to knap arrowheads out of the nodules of chert they had plowed up from the cornfields. There at Pine Bluff, they had found chert in the talc piles at the base of the cliffs. Eli knapped a large shard to shape into a knife blade. He glanced at Noah. "I wondered why you took that charcoal out of the fireplace this morning. Why are you grinding it?"

Noah removed some congealed resin from a bag. "I'm going to melt and boil this pine sap with water, mix in this charcoal powder, and then use it to glue together these long pieces of wood that I'm going to whittle into the two halves of the pipe stem."

Before they ate the soup that filled the building with its mouth-watering aroma, they looked at what the others had created. Roscoe had one side of the medicine bag together. Sally and Ann had the two buckskin pieces sewn into half circles. Stephanie had built the smudge bowl. Noah had made the pipe stem, and Eli had made the handle of the knife.

Noah sat to eat. "We can have the ceremony whenever you want."

Ann meandered past their creations on her way

to the table. "I would like to have the ceremony tomorrow."

"When's the best time?" Eli asked.

"Considering the temperature outside, I think we should have it after the noon meal when the day is the warmest."

After dinner, Noah held out the wooden tube he had made and lovingly asked for Ann's help. "Wife, our men always make the stem and the bowl, but our women decorate the stem. Will you decorate ours?"

Ann took the pipe stem. "Of course, I'll decorate it, but I'd like to do it properly. Would you explain about the pipe?"

"The clay bowl is the earth, the people, and the female principle. They bring life. The bowl holds the eternal fire of the sun. The pipe stem is the male principle, all plants, and straightforwardness of mind, body, and speech. Sometimes we add horsehair to represent four-legged creatures or a feather for winged creatures. When the male and female parts join, the pipe is sacred and represents creation. The smoke perfumes the air. It touches and connects everything and carries our prayers to Heaven. The pipe is the bridge between man and the Great Spirit, who is God. He created the four directions, Mother Earth, and Father Sky. We offer tobacco to Mother Earth. We offer the pipe, the smoke of the herbs, and our prayers to God."

Stephanie picked up the undecorated buckskin that Ann had made. "Ann, would it be all right for me to work on this?"

"I can't get back to it, so I'd appreciate it."

Stephanie then spoke to Sally, "I want to embroider the universe, with a man at the entrance. Do you think that will complement the thunderbird you're sewing?"

Sally pushed her needle through the buckskin with a thimble. "That will look perfect."

Noah worked beside Ann. She leaned close and whispered, "May I use one of your turkey feathers? You kissed me the first time when we set the traps."

"That's why we have the women decorate the pipe. You think of the best things. I'll get you two of them. I don't know what number kiss this is, but here's another."

Ann took the feathers. "I'm going to cut hair from Eyanosa's tail."

"Let me do it. The tunnel of snow is only three feet high. I don't want to chance somebody being on the ridge, looking down here, and seeing you." *Especially since you prayed to let an arrow shoot through your heart if you should not have married me.*

Ann took the clump of Eyanosa's tail hair that Noah brought back. "Is there any particular order for the colored thread?"

"You can place them however you would like."

"I'm thinking red thread after the feathers, next to the yellow thread until the rawhide and horsehair. On the other side, the white thread then the black. I'm going to leave this area bare then wind the green thread until the rawhide at the other end."

Noah thought the pipe stem was going to be

beautiful, but he was curious. "Why this bare section?"

"I have an idea, but I have to speak with Eli."

Because of flying pieces of chert, Eli worked at a table far from the others as he shaped the blade. Ann walked over. "Eli, may I have a small piece of your alligator skin for the calumet?" She held out the pipe stem to show him how much she wanted.

"That's hardly anything. I'll get you some."

Ann sat beside Noah and felt how blessed she was to be able to touch him. She stroked the side of his face with the back of her fingers. "The alligator skin is for everything in the water. I'll have to use some glue."

Noah smiled at Ann. "I love you too." While Ann glued the alligator skin to the pipe, Noah mixed tallow, water, and white clay into a slurry in a bucket. After he had made the white paint, he started the pipe bowl in the shape of an eagle claw holding the earth. *Most people would make a bison, but this is the place of the eagles.* He used the yellow clay for the leg and claw. He made the talons with white clay mixed with ground charcoal to make the clay black and used a smaller amount of charcoal to make a gray earth. When he finished the pipe bowl, he put it and the smudge bowl into the fire to harden. *I need another pair of moccasins. I hate to ask for money.* "Ann, the pipe's bowl and stem need to be kept apart when not used. I thought maybe we could use another pair of moccasins to make pouches for them."

Ann could see that Noah didn't like asking. *I'll*

talk to Stephanie and Sally about dividing the money we have left. I'll give my part to Noah. "We'll need pouches too, won't we? Buy everything we need."

Noah appreciated Ann's response. Not only did she allow him to purchase the moccasins, she believed it was his decision to make. "Roscoe, I'm buying ten pairs of moccasins, more rawhide strips, and sinew for everybody. I'll put the money in the box or give it to you."

Roscoe remained engrossed in his work. He didn't want to put down the tools to take the money, and he knew Noah was trustworthy. "Just put it in the box." Noah allotted a rawhide strip, some sinew, and three individual moccasins to each of them, and two for the Calumet.

Sally took her share. "I understand what to do with sinew, but what are the moccasins for?"

Noah dissected a moccasin. "Take them apart, make holes around the top, and thread rawhide through them. Pull them tight, and you'll have a pouch."

Stephanie stitched the universe design but glanced at what Noah was making. "That looks too long and skinny."

"This one is going to be the pouch for the pipe stem. I'll make another for the bowl to protect and keep them apart when not in use. We also need to make one for the smudge bowl because it's beautiful, and I want to keep it safe."

Ann wrapped white thread around the pipe stem. "How many pouches should we make?"

"We usually make one each for tobacco, sage, cedar, and sweetgrass. We also carry a few beans, corn kernels, squash seeds, and a little cornmeal, but we use gut to hold those separately. We put them together in a doeskin pouch, so they don't break. You probably should roll the moccasins up and keep them, until you know how big each pouch needs to be."

Eli whittled the knife handle to fit the stone blade. "I think I'll make an alligator skin sheath for this."

Ann leaned closer and whispered, "Noah, I want to carry some red willow bark. Even if it hadn't taken away my pain, it was the best tea ever because you told me you loved me when you gave it to me."

Sally informed them, "I'm going to carry butterfly weed root because it saved Roscoe and some dill because it's my favorite spice and because Roscoe told me about it."

Roscoe put his tools down and walked over to Sally. "Come here."

Sally stood up. Roscoe put his arms around her. "You make me feel loved. If I had a granddaughter, I would want her to be just like you."

"And I'd want my grandfather to be you."

"You're a great young lady." Roscoe went back to work on Noah's bag. Sally went back to the Thunderbird.

Eli finished adjusting the handle. He inserted the chert blade into the groove and affixed it with the pine resin and charcoal glue. "I want to glue thin red, yellow, white, black, green, and blue ribbons along the side of the handle and let them dangle past the end. I'll wind rawhide over them, the handle, and the joining of the blade."

Roscoe flipped the board and buckskin. "Ribbon is a penny per foot."

"A foot of each color, except black, is enough. I don't know how much black it will take. I'm going to wind a black ribbon around the handle. After I've made it, I'll write it in your book, and put the money in your box."

At the end of the day, Roscoe had made the body of the bag. The section of the strap that would go around Noah's neck didn't have the edges sewn in, there was no tie-down for the adjustable-height top flap, and it was undecorated. "I want to work more on this later. Is it acceptable for tomorrow's ceremony?" Roscoe handed the bag to Noah.

"It's wonderful. I appreciate all your work."

When Ann had the pipe stem done, she brought it to Noah. "My husband, I've finished the pipe stem. Can we add more to it as we live?"

"We can. This is exquisite, just like you." Noah took the pipe. "What we have created is not just a thing. When the stem joins the bowl, it becomes a being." He whispered into Ann's ear, "Like the day when I'll join with you and create a new person."

Soon Eli brought over the finished knife. "Do you like it?"

"I do, and wrapping the black ribbon in with the rawhide on the handle is perfect because black is the color of the spirit world."

Sally brought Noah the soul bundle with both halves embroidered and joined. Noah accepted it. "This is also very wonderful and beautiful." He went to the fire and removed the hardened smudge bowl and the hardened pipe bowl. "We need to smudge these, a pair of tongs, the pipe stem, the pouches, the buckskin, the medicine bag, the knife, and the woven reed bowl full of willow, sage, cedar, and tobacco." Noah purified then placed the items in the reed bowl of herbs on the hearth and covered it with the buckskin for the soul bundle. "We're ready."

FOURTEEN

Noah walked to the river with the axe and two buckets. He made a fire pit, re-chopped the hole through the ice at the edge of the river, left the buckets, and then rejoined the others. After their chores, everybody took a bath to start purifying themselves. Since Noah wanted everybody to have a hot, tasty, nutritious meal before the ceremony in the cold, Roscoe served fish stew with potatoes and onions. Sally made hot, stewed apricots with maple sugar, freshly baked dill bread, and hot coffee. After dinner, everybody put on a layer of cotton socks, pants, and shirts, and then a warm woolen layer with buckskin pants and a buckskin shirt on top.

Roscoe told everybody, "Come into the store." He tried to hand Noah a point-blanket coat. "I want you to have something for saving my life."

Noah backed away. "We didn't help you for a reward."

"I know, which makes even more of a reason for me to give these to you. Please let me have the honor of giving you this gift."

"Well, then, all right. These are very appreciated."

Roscoe added to the gift. "All of you find a coat, a fur hat, and mukluks that fit."

From their nest, the eagles watched the six people

make their way to the river. The winter wind that usually rolled along the river had gone elsewhere and had left the air unusually still. Noah scooped two buckets of water from the river and carried them to the ceremonial pit. "Eli, keeper of the fire, start the fire. Girls, wedge the candlesticks into the ground. Lean the picture of your parents against them. Everybody, circle the fire." As they had the day before, each moved into the directional position that called them. Noah reached into his medicine bag, withdrew a handful of the plants of power, and threw it into the fire. Fragrant smoke rose into the air. He filled the smudging bowl with more from his medicine bag then with the tongs he retrieved and dropped in an ember from the fire. He circled the fire and fanned billows of the smoke from the bowl over each of them to complete the purifying of the people.

Noah put down the bowl. "We paint our faces the color of mourning." With the fingers of both his hands, Noah scooped some of the white clay and tallow mixture out of the wooden bucket. He smeared the paint of mourning on his forehead, down his temples and cheeks, and then over his chin. He then drew the color in from his cheeks over the bridge of his nose. Each of them took the bucket and applied the gooey whiteness. Roscoe passed the almost empty bucket back to Noah, who released the last of the paint of mourning to Mother Earth and sealed it with a sprinkle of the power plants. "Mother Earth, receive our offering. We ask for the souls of Emma Williams and Chris Williams."

Noah then brought forth the pipe stem and the pipe bowl. In his right hand, he pointed the pipe stem to the east. In his left hand, Noah held the pipe bowl. He joined the two, and the Calumet was born. He raised it to God; the Great Spirit who lives in Father Sky, then lowered the Calumet toward Mother Earth. "Our feet rest on Mother Earth. The pipe stem reaches into Father Sky. We are the bridge between the sacred above and the sacred below. Earth, sky, the two and the four-legged, the winged ones, swimmers, trees, and all plants are one. The pipe binds us together."

He sprinkled a pinch of the herbs on the ground, put a pinch in the pipe bowl, and raised the pipe to the East. "East, we thank you for each day you bring the sun and allow us to walk on Mother Earth."

He gave the East, and the pipe-bowl, power plants then repositioned and raised the pipe. "South, thank you for strength, healing, and new life in the spring."

Noah repeated the plant offerings and circled the fire. "West, we thank you for spiritual wisdom and the spirit helpers. Connect us to the spirit world. Help the souls of Chris and Emma Williams find us, so we may release them to God in Father Sky."

At the top of the circle, he said, "North, we thank you for endurance and health."

In the place where he had begun, he finished, "The circle to the spirit world is complete. God, in Father Sky, we ask You to hear us."

With the tongs, Noah again took a small glowing coal from the fire. He lit the pipe and then dropped the ceremonial ember into the smudging bowl. He drew in the sacred smoke then blew it out to God above. "I mourn the loss of Chris and Emma Williams. Take away what was not meant to be left behind." Noah passed the pipe to Ann.

"Help us accept the loss of Mama and Papa." Ann didn't say more because she didn't know what she was feeling about the passing of her parents, other than she was sad and wished they hadn't died. Ann inhaled the smoke of the herbs of power and sent her feelings to God, who knew her and what she felt even though she did not.

Sally took the pipe. "I mourn the loss of my parents, the family that was destroyed, and what might have been." She drew the smoke into her lungs and coughed as she passed the pipe to her sister.

"I mourn the loss of Papa and Mama, their comfort, and the security they provided." After what happened to Sally, Stephanie carefully drew the smoke into her mouth only then released it to carry her sadness into Heaven. She passed the pipe to her husband.

"I mourn the loss of Chris and Emma, the sadness it's brought to their daughters, and for all that is lost when parents aren't here." Eli silently added thoughts of his own dead mother as he took his turn.

As he had many years before when he had traveled west, Roscoe smoked the pipe. "I also mourn the loss of Chris and Emma Williams. I've never been around them, but I have met their daughters, and I know the world lost good people because they raised such fine, young women."

"Accept this offering of our words." Noah smoked the last of the herbs and sent what they had spoken to God. He separated the Calumet, placed each part in its separate pouch, and placed them into his medicine bag.

Noah drew the embroidered buckskin from the medicine bag along with more power herbs. He tossed the plants into the fire and held the folded buckskin in the smoke that rose from the fire. He lowered the buckskin to Mother Earth and up to each direction then opened it and placed it on the ground in front of him in the white tallow and herbs.

He laid a handful of power plants on the buckskin. "I give cedar and willow to the souls of Chris and Emma Williams to help them give offerings on their way to God in Heaven."

Noah retreated as Ann approached the buckskin. She placed dried beef with the plants of power. "I give meat to sustain these souls on their way to God." She went back to her place in the circle.

"I give fat, so these souls may feel satisfied as they go to God." Sally put beef suet with the other offerings.

Stephanie came forward and added apricots. "I give sweetness."

"I provide sustaining grain to the souls of the parents who have been taken from us." Eli went to the buckskin and gave cracked corn, beans, and squash seeds.

Roscoe stepped up to the soul bundle. "As a fragrant offering, I offer tobacco and sage."

"Receive our offering." Noah threw a handful of the herbs onto the fire and brought forth the ceremonial knife. He held the knife in the smoke, raised it to the sky, lowered it to the earth, and raised it to each of the four directions. "We have more words to speak. Hear us." He offered Ann the knife, resting on his palms.

Ann took the knife. What had been captive in her heart since her parents had died flowed out with tears that incised channels in the white paint on her face. "Papa, I'm sorry I wasn't as good a helper as you wanted. I tried my best. Now that we have Noah and Eli, I see why you were always disappointed. I could never do what they're capable of doing, but I did my very best for you." She held out the long hair on the side of her head. A few inches from her head, she drew the chert knife across the hair and left only straggling remains. "Take this offering and forgive me for not being the son you wanted." She deposited the hair on the buckskin.

"Mama, I was never the daughter you wanted either. Not like Stephanie and Sally. You put ribbons and ivory combs in their hair, but I never let you. I was dirty and sweaty and never had the time. I'm sorry I tried harder to please Papa than you." Ann cut a clump of hair from the other side of her head. "Take this offering and forgive me for not being the daughter you wanted." She set the hair on the buckskin.

"Then you both got sick. I tried to be your nurse. Even though the cure exists, I wasn't able to find it to save you. I failed you as a nurse and let you die." Ann cut free the hair in the back of her head. She placed the last handful of hair into the pile as a request for forgiveness. "I hope you saw something good in me before you died. I tried as hard as I could." She turned to Sally. With grief still written in the white paint on her face, she offered the knife.

Sally cut handfuls of her hair and placed it on Ann's. "I was mad at you for dying. I still wish you hadn't left me, but I have a different family now, and I've been forgetting to miss you. I promise even if I don't think about you all the time, I'll never forget you. I'll always love you, and I'll always be grateful for the time God let me have you." Sally offered the knife.

Stephanie held the speaking knife. "Mama and Papa, recognize this handkerchief and come to your soul bundle. Receive these offerings. I wish you all the best that the afterworld holds, but always remember your love for your daughters." She released what she felt was most precious: her mother's handkerchief with the apple seeds given to her by Smitty's wife.

Eli spoke of Chris and Emma as he repeatedly cut tufts of his already short hair. He laid them in the bundle and secretly placed a small roll of hide from the alligator that had tried to eat him. *And even though I don't remember her, I thank you for the mother who made me and cared for me for five years.* He presented the knife to Roscoe.

"I owe you my life because these girls came from you. Accept the essence of my life." Roscoe cut the palm of his hand and added drops of his blood.

Noah spoke last, "Chris and Emma, the love you shared brought forth these women and gave me the great gift of love. The love of Ann as my wife, Stephanie and Sally as my sisters, and because Eli loves Stephanie, you have given me the love of a brother. You made me a wonderful family, and I love them all. I would have loved you as parents, and I mourn that I will never get to know you personally, but I see you through your daughters, and I know you were good. When I thought I had lost this family because I'm part Indian, I decided that I would deny the white man in me. I hated the entire white race for what they had done. I planned to be entirely Indian and grow my hair long again as an Indian man should, but then God brought your daughters and Eli back to me. I give my Indian hair to you and accept what I am. I promise I will do everything in my power to love and protect this family as long as there is life in my body." Noah added his hair.

The soul bundle contained everything meant to be there. A single wind from the river rolled over the mourners and the items on the buckskin. It caused the pile to fall over and the family to think the souls of Chris and Emma Williams had gone into the soul bundle. Noah pulled the edges of the buckskin closed, tied it shut with one end of the long leather thong and then tied the other end to make the loop to circle the neck of the person who would bear the soul bundle.

"Water, take our sorrows with the souls of Emma and Chris Williams, and wash our sadness away." He dipped the bundle into one of the buckets of river water. "I mourn." Noah keened because Ann's parents had allowed her to believe something about herself that caused her pain and because her parents were gone and could never let her know how much they loved, appreciated, and valued her.

As Noah continued to wail, Ann received the bundle. "I mourn." She held it in the water and joined him for the loss of the parents she loved, for not being able to save them, and for not completing well what life had called her to do.

Sally took the soul bundle. "I mourn." She wept for herself and for Ann, who believed their parents couldn't have loved her because she thought she had failed them.

Stephanie dipped the bag. "I mourn." She cried tears because she would never place a child in the arms of her grandmother, send a child fishing with his grandfather, or ask her mother how she should care for her children when they were sick.

Eli shed tears for the loss of Emma and Chris, and for his mother, Hattie. "I mourn."

"I mourn." Roscoe left the soul bundle in the water as he let the sorrow of all his regrets surface and flow down his cheeks. Together, they shed tears for Emma, Chris, Hattie, and themselves who now had to continue through life without those they loved.

After many minutes, Noah picked up the bucket. "Join me by the river." He went to the frozen shore, removed the soul bundle, poured out part of the water, and instructed the river, "We give you our sorrows. Take them away." Each of them poured their pain and a portion of the water into the river. Noah turned to his family. "Who will be the first to carry the soul bundle?"

Ann stepped forward. "I'd like to carry it."

"Does anybody object?" Noah waited. Nobody spoke against her request.

"Ann, carry the soul bundle. Do not pick up or use a knife while you carry the souls of your parents. Live without strife and think of your parents all the time. Carry them until you're ready to let them go." Noah hung the soul bundle around his wife's neck.

"Come back to the fire." Noah poured the plants of power still in the smudge bowl into the fire. After the smoke of the burning plants dissipated into the air, Noah picked up the other bucket of water and poured it over the fire. "Fire, rest until we are ready to release the souls of Chris Williams and Emma Williams."

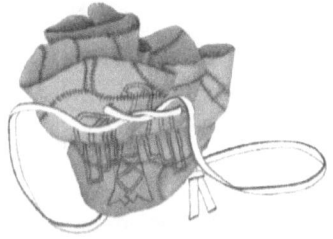

FIFTEEN

Around her neck, heart, and mind, Ann carried the soul bundle to their winter home in Pine Bluff. She stepped into the trading post. "I'd like to be alone for a while." Ann already believed she had let her parents die and that it was her fault that she and her sisters had almost starved. During the ceremony, she had realized she actually blamed herself for everything and also that she believed her parents must have thought she wasn't good enough. She was afraid she wasn't, and worst of all, she thought she never would be. As her family washed, Ann sat in the chapel. She continued to wear not only her white paint but also the monster of her mistaken beliefs that had her in a stranglehold.

Stephanie looked at Sally's scraggly hair. "Let me fix your hair."

"Make me beautiful." Sally handed Stephanie a pair of scissors.

Stephanie shaped what was left of Sally's, Eli's, and Noah's hair as they talked about their parents and other things that had brought them sorrow. In the sharing and acceptance, much of their pain floated away.

Eventually, Sally wanted to go to bed. Noah stood at the chapel door. "Ann?"

"Yes, husband?"

"Sally needs to go to sleep. Come to bed, my love. I won't talk with you if you don't want me to. I'll let you think without interfering."

Ann forced herself out of her reverie and trudged out of the chapel. "Goodnight, Sally. I love you to the moon and back." It struck Ann; *why did Mama always say that if she wasn't happy with me?* The question swirled in her mind even after she fell asleep.

When Ann woke, she had walked a million miles with the souls of her parents hanging heavy around her neck. Outside, the cold wind blew tiny, dry snowflakes into the canyon, but it was the coldness of her thoughts that closed in around Ann's heart.

Stephanie sat beside her sister at the table. "Ann, would you like to talk about Mama and Papa?"

Ann didn't know what she would say about them. She hadn't realized before the ceremony what had been living deep inside her. "Not really."

Stephanie hugged her sister. "I'm here if you change your mind."

After they ate, they scrutinized the ridge from the observation stations. The ridge appeared to be enemy free. Emotionally weighed down, Ann desperately needed to release the doubts that the souls of her parents represented. She stepped outside, gave Mother Earth a portion of her meal in exchange for the souls of her parents, and walked toward the barn. Sally joined her. She didn't give Ann the option to decline her opinion. "It's not true what you think."

"What are you talking about?"

"You think you didn't do things right or didn't do them well enough, and you think Papa and Mama felt you weren't good enough."

"Papa always said, 'We never get enough corn planted,' and, 'It takes too long to get the harvest in.' Every year, he said, 'If we'd been the first to bring our corn to market, we would have gotten more for it.' Whose fault do you think that was? Besides, I don't want to talk about it."

"It wasn't your fault. It was the circumstances, and you shouldn't tell yourself that you are so powerful that you alone caused everything that happened."

Ann defended herself, "That's not what I meant."

"Then how did you singlehandedly make everything go wrong?"

Sally's logic muddied up what Ann had thought was clear. "I don't know. Leave me alone." Ann threw down the bucket of cracked corn and stalked away.

Sally scraped the corn off the ground and back into the bucket. "Ann always tried so hard to please Papa, and I always thought she did."

"I always thought Ann was Papa's favorite. I tried to get her to talk about it." Stephanie helped salvage the corn.

Noah headed to the woodpile with an axe. "I also asked her if she wanted to talk, but she didn't."

"I heard Emma say she didn't know what they would do if they didn't have Ann. I always thought she was very grateful for Ann's help and proud of her. Maybe I should tell her." Eli drove a wedge with a sledgehammer.

"Maybe later. Right now, she's not going to hear you." Sally gave the corn to the chickens.

Stephanie never bothered Stubborn, never paid attention to her, and never tried to force her to do anything. She just placed the chopped wood so that the stack grew toward the mule and slowly squeezed them together. This morning, Stubborn touched Stephanie to get to the grain.

Ann quickly slipped into the barn, swung up onto Eyanosa, and galloped away from her family through the falling snow. It didn't matter how far she went; she couldn't leave her confusion behind. Out of nowhere, she remembered the date of Noah's birth. The day was almost upon them. The subject in her mind changed. She turned Eyanosa around.

Sally pushed a cartful of wood out of the barn just as Ann returned. Ann stopped to talk with her before she took the horse into the barn. "January twenty-seventh is Noah's birthday. I want us to celebrate."

"That's a marvelous idea! I'll ask Roscoe if we can fix a nice meal." Sally left to fill the wood box and confer with Roscoe about their favorite thing to do. Roscoe and Sally concocted their plan. As soon as she safely could, Sally secretly told Stephanie.

Stephanie passed the message on to Eli. "On Noah's birthday, some of us have to get Noah out of the trading post so the others can prepare."

"I can tell Noah I want help shooting live targets."

"Talk to Ann and see if that's acceptable."

After her frantic flight in the snow, Ann stood in the barn and brushed Eyanosa. Eli told her his plan. Ann replied, "I've only been able to practice since we've been here. I'd like a lesson too."

Eli wanted to keep Ann's mind out of the gloom she had been wallowing in, but he actually did want to practice. "Let's both go."

Ann agreed. For days, the snow fell continually. Every day, they shoveled the paths to the barn and the river. Ann, Stephanie, and Eli were close to the same height as Noah. In case somebody was watching, one of them would put on Noah's coat, cover his or her face with a scarf, and then take a turn shoveling.

The wind didn't blow hard enough to move much of the snow through the pine forest. Even so, the snow grew deep in the canyon. It also piled up in the woods. January 27th arrived without falling snow. Ann poured coffee into Noah's cup. "I need to practice with the bow and arrows. Since it's not snowing, would you take me hunting by the river?"

"I'd love to. As soon as we're done eating, I'll check the ridges."

"I'd like to come with you." Eli held out his cup toward Ann.

Ann answered as agreed, "That's fine with me."

The wind swept past the three of them as they walked along the frozen edge of the river. They stopped just beyond the prominence. In the cloudless blue sky, two small dots circled. Crouching in a thick clump of rushes, they watched a flock of wood ducks land on the river.

Eli drew back the bowstring, took aim, and then let the arrow fly into the closest duck. The arrow partially exited out the other side and skewered a second duck that had, with impeccable timing, swum beside the target. Eli exclaimed, "Two for one!"

Noah congratulated him, "Great aim and timing."

Eli crept onto the ice.

Ann stood on the shore with Noah. "I want to try when we see more." Ann glanced up. "Look at the eagles." With their talons locked together, they plummeted. "What are they doing?"

"My people have seen eagles do this many times. As far as I know, nobody really knows why. I think they're testing each other's courage. The braver one will not let go."

Eli knelt and reached for the skewered ducks. Noah called out, "Get the ducks fast!"

Eli pulled the ducks onto the ice. He jerked the arrow through both of them and then turned and saw Noah and Ann looking into the sky. He glanced up and then hastened to the shore. They sprinted up the riverside. Ann called out, "They need to let go!"

As if they heard her warning, the eagles separated. They soared to the heights, locked talons, and once more plunged closer and closer to the hard, unyielding earth. Five feet from impact, the eagles still held each other tight. Eli's jaws clenched, "They're cutting it too close."

At two feet, Noah exclaimed, "They won't be able to—" The outer edge of the river's ice shield shattered. Unconscious from the impact, the eagles floated toward the unbroken ice ahead. "They'll go under the ice and drown."

Noah, Eli, and Ann stepped onto the frozen river. It crackled. Ann stopped. "We shouldn't go out there." Ann and Eli turned back.

I have to get them. Eli just walked on the ice. Noah continued toward the eagles.

Splosh.

Noah dropped through the weakened ice up to his chest. The cold shocked his body. He sucked in his breath sharply. The wave pushed the birds farther away. Shivering and feeling dizzy, Noah hurried toward the eagles in the wintry water. He stepped in front of the eagles. His heart raced as he placed one foot back and braced for impact. The two large birds slammed him, but Noah stood firm. He pulled the eagles by their locked feet. "Eli, get them."

To spread out his weight, Eli slid out on his belly. He gently pulled the eagles onto the ice and then launched them, sliding toward the shore before he tried to pull Noah out. Several feet away, the ice split. The fissure inched toward them.

Noah ordered Eli, "Get off the ice." On his stomach, Eli dragged the eagles toward the shore. Noah waited until Eli was safely past the fracture before he pushed down on the ice to lift his body out of the frigid water. The edge shattered. *I have to get out. My body is going to shut down.* He shoved away broken ice and prayed the next section would support him.

Ann stood on the shore. "Don't give up! You can make it!"

Noah tried again but snapped off another section of ice. He slurred, "I'm tired...I'll ...just ...rest ...a little."

Ann commanded her husband, "Noah, come here now! I need you!"

Noah could barely think, but Ann needed him. He pushed against the ice and tried to move toward her voice. Something blocked him. *Can't ...go.*

He turned and walked into the river. Ann screamed, "Noah, not that way! Turn back! Come to me!" As Eli pulled the eagles onto the solid land, Ann made a decision. "Noah's been in the water too long. He's not thinking right. I'm going out to get him."

"I'll go. Keep trying to get Noah to come back this way." Eli prayed, "Please let what's left of the ice be solid enough." Once again, Eli slid toward the frozen edge.

Ann shrieked, "Noah, they've got me! They're taking me away! Stop them!" Nobody was taking Ann away from Noah again. He changed direction and struggled toward his wife, who called to him from miles away. "This way, help me!"

Noah needed to save Ann, but it required more energy than he had. *I'll ...go... later.... I'll......... sleep ...for...* As Noah leaned forward to put his head down,

Eli gripped him under the arms. Several minutes after Noah had dropped into the life-stealing water, Eli pulled him out. Ann knew she had to get Noah out of the wind and into the warmest place available. As Eli dragged Noah's body, Ann started to make a hollow where it would be much warmer than the freezing wind.

The eagles and Noah lay frozen on the shore. Ann didn't think saving the eagles was worth Noah's life. As she dug in the snow, she told her unconscious husband, "Now, the eagles and you are all going to die."

The arctic wind was quickly freezing Noah's wet clothes with him inside. Ann finished the burrow. She took off her coat and laid it inside. "Eli, pull him over here and take off his clothes." She crawled in. "Help me keep the coat under us." Ann pulled her naked husband into the snow den. "Run as fast as you can. Get lots of dry, warm clothes." Eli removed his coat, gloves, hat, and scarf. He threw them all into the hole, grabbed the dead ducks, and ran.

Ann wrapped Eli's coat around Noah and then stripped as fast as she could. "Husband, don't you die on me!"

Ann put her dry wool clothes under them. She prayed that Noah would survive as she took off her socks. She put the socks on Noah's feet and then pulled Eli's hat over them before she jerked her boots back on. Next, she wrapped all four of their legs together with her pants and the scarfs then decided to take off her boots and put gloves on her feet instead.

She opened up the coat around Noah, lay beside him, and pulled both coats around them. Inside the coat cocoon, Ann slipped one arm under Noah's neck and rolled his icy body tight against her warm skin.

Noah's rigid body lay unresponsive against her. She couldn't feel him breathing. "Please live." Arms that had always encircled her with love and passion lay cold across her side and dropped lifeless behind her. She pulled the coats tighter to draw his arm against her back.

Ann squeezed Noah against her body and crushed the soul bundle between them. She relaxed her arms and then drew him vigorously against her again. As hard as she could, she repeatedly squeezed Noah until she felt him breathe then tightly held the man she loved and prayed, "God, don't let Noah die." Noah's body drew every bit of heat from Ann. When his body no longer felt completely frigid, Ann's feet did. She was afraid her toes were frostbitten, but she was going to warm Noah even if her toes fell off.

Noah's blood finally warmed enough to bring his mind back. He opened his eyes. All he saw was white. He didn't understand. "What are we doing?"

"I'm trying to warm you."

Noah felt Ann's skin against his. "Are we naked?" He wrapped his arms closer.

"You almost froze. My skin had to be against yours to warm you. There was no other way."

"I did? Where are we?"

"We're in a hollow in the snow, which is why I hope Eli will be back very soon with lots of clothes. My feet are freezing."

Noah felt socks on his feet. "Do I have all the socks?"

"Yes, I have gloves on my feet, but they don't cover them well."

"We're going to rearrange." Noah twisted in the small space and removed a pair of socks. He put them on Ann's feet and put the gloves back over them. He kept one pair of socks and the hat on his feet. He lay down again, snuggled as close to Ann as he could, and pulled the coats around them.

Ann asked, "Do you think the eagles have frozen?"

"The eagles?" Noah tried to remember what had happened to the eagles.

Ann explained, but she also wanted an explanation, "Why did you do it?"

"I don't remember, but the eagles would only have had a chance out of the water. It obviously wasn't a good choice. I guess I did it because I feel those eagles are my sign that everything is well. I hope they didn't die."

"Then, I understand. You were saving us."

Ann gave Noah a long, loving kiss. He held her close to continue to warm his body. His heart was already warm because Ann understood, and she didn't condemn him. "Ann, I have to tell you something. I think I died!"

"You were so cold, and you weren't breathing, so maybe. But why do you think you died?"

"I went along the Milky Way until I got to a brilliant white space. I saw your parents there. I know it was your parents because they looked like your picture. They told me, 'It's not your time to be here.' I'm sorry that I didn't want to come back to you, but I felt so happy and content. I didn't want to leave and told them I wanted to stay.

"What they told me was so strange. They said, 'Noah, you have to go back to save our first-born grandchild. You have to stop her'. Isn't that strange? Anyway, they also said, 'Tell Stephanie, we always knew why she didn't have her peppermint when we got home from the store and that she's forgiven. Let Sally know that she doesn't need the silver brush to be beautiful. Say to Ann that we were always proud of her, and tell only her that she is the jewel set in this family. Tell her she's carried us long enough and it's your turn to take us. Noah, it's also your turn to love and protect them'. I promised I would, and then I woke up here with you."

Tears filled Ann's eyes. "They said that?"

"That's what I remember."

Ann reasoned in her mind. *Noah couldn't have known anything about the peppermint. Only Eli, Stephanie, and I know about the peppermint. He really was with my parents!* "I don't like it that you died to bring this message, but I don't know how I will ever be able to repay you or let you know how much it means to me." Still weeping tears of relief, she took the leather thong from her neck and looped it around Noah's neck.

"I wouldn't have chosen to die, but I'm very blessed to have traveled to the spirit world and back.

Remember that you said you wished I could have met your parents, that I would have liked them, and they would have liked me? Now, I have met them, and we do like each other. More importantly, they let you know how they really felt about you."

If Ann could have, she would have absorbed herself into Noah, but she still would not have been close enough.

After what seemed like a very long time, Eli returned with two packs of clothes. He feared he would be too late, and had run as fast as he could for much longer than he had thought possible. He panted from the long run, "I'm back."

Ann whispered, "I'm enjoying holding your luscious naked body, but I guess we better get more socks on our feet."

Eli leaned over, put his hands on his knees to rest, and looked into the snow den. He laughed.

"What's so funny?" Ann asked.

The other three arrived, squatted down, and looked into the cubbyhole. There lay Ann and Noah with gloves sticking up at their feet, their legs all wrapped together with the pants and scarfs, the coats around the two of them facing each other with their heads turned to look at their family, peering into the hole.

Eli explained, "You're a two-headed, hand-footed, one-legged monster."

Sally confirmed Eli's assessment, "You do look kinda funny all wrapped up with the gloves on your feet."

Roscoe smiled with the others, but he had been

worried. Until this family had arrived, Roscoe had lived alone at Pine Bluff for twenty years with nobody to care about him. He was lonely, especially in the winter. He wished he had a family, but Roscoe knew he was the only one to blame for his loneliness.

Every time the chance to have a family had come along he had decided to walk away. The last woman he had loved, he left when he started Bacon's Trading Post. She didn't want to live so far away from people, but mostly, she didn't want to leave her family. He had left her behind and gone alone to Pine Bluff.

At first, Roscoe had been happy. He owned a successful business, and he felt proud of what he had built. The years passed, and he started thinking about dying alone. If he died during the winter, it would be months before anybody would know he had passed. No matter when he died, nobody would care.

He believed he was now with people who did care about him, and he didn't want to lose them. He wanted very much for this family to be what they seemed to be. However, since he knew Noah was all right, and he had never seen an eagle up close, he walked over to look at them.

"Are there socks in there?" Noah asked.

"Yep." Stephanie pushed the packs into the cavity.

Ann told them, "I'm so glad you brought lots of socks. We both have very cold feet. If it had been much longer, we might not have toes."

"We'll come out in a minute." Noah pulled in the packs.

Noah still felt cold. Ann asked, "Are you sure you're warm enough?"

"Not that I want to stop holding you, but I think I am."

Soon, they both wore plenty of layers of dry clothes and many socks. Noah put on a pair of Harry's boots. He walked to Eli, put his arms around him, and held on. "Thank you for saving me again!"

Eli was very glad Noah hadn't died. He hugged him back. "I didn't do it alone. You were walking into the river. Ann got you to come back to the edge of the ice. I wouldn't have been able to get to you if she hadn't, and she kept you from freezing after I got you out of the water."

"I'm very grateful for what both of you did!"

Noah let go of Eli and walked to the eagles. He put his hand on one of them. It was breathing, barely. He checked the other. It also breathed. He stroked their heads. It gave him an eerie feeling to touch a living thunderbird. They were icy, but the oils on their feathers had kept the water from penetrating all the way to their bodies. As he caressed the eagles, he believed he felt the difference between the male and the female energies of thunderbirds. "Maybe we should put them in the snow cubby hole."

Ann saw Noah touching the eagles. She didn't like it. "If they wake up while you're fiddling with them, they could hurt you."

"I'll pull them on my frozen coat. I'll be further back and can get away quickly." Noah didn't remember anything about what had happened, but he believed what Ann had told him. He had scared Ann too many times, and he wanted to respect her feelings, so he waited.

Ann didn't want Noah to almost freeze to death, and then be clawed by eagles on his birthday, or ever, but she knew these eagles were especially significant to him. "Be careful and be ready to get away."

Noah unlocked the eagles' feet and put the birds on the coat. He told them, "Ann says I almost froze to pull you out of the river."

"Don't you remember?" Eli asked.

"I recall leaving home this morning. After that, only one thing until I woke up in the cubbyhole with Ann's arms around me." Noah pushed the eagles close together inside the hole and then tucked dry flannel shirts from the packs around them.

"Since I almost died for them, I'd like to wait here for a little while to see if they recover."

Roscoe didn't want to get sick again. "I'm going home."

Stephanie had things to do with Roscoe. "Now that I know Noah is going to be fine and I've seen the eagles, I'm also going home."

"I'll stay with you." Ann wanted to be sure Noah was all right, and she wanted to witness the fate of the eagles because they represented the family's safety in Noah's mind.

"I'll stay too if that's all right?" Since she was supposed to be helping to get Noah's party ready, Sally looked at Roscoe and Stephanie for the answer.

Noah replied, "I'd love for you to stay."

Stephanie and Roscoe nodded their heads.

Eli joined his wife. "I'll go home."

Noah walked to the river's edge where the ice was broken to pieces. "That's where it happened?" he asked.

"Yes," Ann replied.

Sally stood with her arm around Noah's waist and looked at the river. "You weren't very far out."

Ann hugged Noah's other side. "It doesn't matter if it's only two inches if you can't get out."

Noah had his arms around both girls, so he squeezed them tightly. "I'm very glad and grateful that Eli pulled me out from wherever I was."

"Me too." Sally hugged him back.

The three of them walked up and down the river's edge, close to the eagles. Each time they walked past the snow cubbyhole, one of them looked in. "This time, I'll see if they're still alive." Noah walked toward the flannel-shirt-lined nest. The girls followed behind him.

One of the eagles had woken and sat inside the hollow. It saw Noah approach and screeched. Sally froze where she stood. "You don't need to check that one."

Ann whispered, "I think it's protecting the other one."

"It must not be dead, or its mate would have left." Only ten feet away, Noah stood still and watched the eagles. The eagle sat silently and let him. Several minutes later, the other eagle sat up and tried to orient itself in the uniform whiteness that surrounded it.

Noah whispered, "That one must be the female; it's bigger."

The female eagle stood up, the male stretched its head forward, held its wings out, and walked out of the snowy nest screeching. Noah, Ann, and Sally backed up. The male eagle walked a few more feet toward them then stood between them and its mate, dragging out the flannel shirts with its beak. The female dropped them then jumped into the air and flew off, holding the flapping shirts in its talons. When the male saw its mate safely in the nest, it flew away.

Sally commented, "A shirt sleeve hanging over the edge of an eagle's nest looks hysterical." It seemed as if the eagle heard because it pulled the sleeve into the nest with its beak.

Noah looked up at the nest. "He let us stay so close. Do you think he knows we saved them?"

"I believe they do," said Sally.

Ann took Noah's hand. "So do I."

Noah happily agreed, "I do too."

Sally asked, "I'm ready to go home. Are you?" Both girls looked at Noah for the answer.

"Sure." Noah walked over and looked into the cubbyhole. "There are feathers in here." He reached in. "This feather must have gotten bent when they slammed into the water. The eagle must have pulled it out, along with the matching one from the other wing."

"Would they really pull out their own feathers?" Sally looked at the feathers as they walked home.

Noah explained, "It has to, so its flight will be smooth and balanced. If it can't fly right, it can't hunt, and it will starve."

"I didn't know that. May I hold them?" Sally held out her hand.

Noah gave Sally the feathers. "It must have been the male. I didn't see the female pull them out."

Ann joked with Noah, "I think you made a 'flannel shirt for eagle feathers' trade."

Noah said, "It looks that way." However, he believed it was a gift for saving them, and he felt highly honored.

Sally handed Noah back the feathers and then hurried ahead. To notify those in the building that they were back, she opened the door with lots of noise.

When Noah stepped inside, everybody yelled, "Happy Birthday!"

"I didn't know you even knew that it's my birthday."

Ann reminded him, "You told me at Sally's party."

"You are a sneaky woman. I'm going to have to remember that." Noah drew Ann up to his side. He looked at the five people in the room, his family. He felt very blessed.

Sally started a game. "Guess what the eagles gave Noah?"

Eli guessed, "A peck in the leg.

"Nope."

Even though he saw the feathers in Noah's hand,

Roscoe went along with the game. "The evil-eye-stare."

"No. Stephanie, what's your guess?"

Stephanie tried to think of something that would be cute, but not the obvious answer. "A fish."

Sally raised Noah's hand that held the feathers. "No, you sillies. It's feathers!"

Roscoe walked toward the kitchen. "Tell us how you got them after we get this food on the table."

Ann, Sally, and Noah took off their coats to help.

Sally exclaimed, "Noah, you have the soul bundle!"

"I'll tell you in a minute."

"Course one." Roscoe placed four orange quarters on each plate.

For the sake of their health, Noah encouraged his family, "We better eat all of these."

Sally wanted the important information. "Noah, how is it that you have the soul bundle?"

Ann needed to know beyond the shadow of her doubt that the message from her parents had been real. "Before Noah says anything, I want to know something. Stephanie and Eli, did either of you ever tell anybody about Eli taking the peppermint?"

Eli replied, "I've never told anybody about my life of crime."

"What!?" Sally exclaimed.

Ann replied, "Be patient, Sally."

Stephanie confirmed her silence on the topic of concern. "Me neither."

With much love and awe, Ann accepted the

implication. "Then it actually happened. Tell them the incredible news."

"I wasn't just cold; I was dead."

Sally again said, "What!?"

Noah explained while they ate orange wedges. "I went to a very bright place. Chris and Emma were there. They looked like this." Noah walked to the mantel and held up the picture of their parents. "Your parents said they knew why Stephanie didn't have her peppermint candy and she is forgiven. Emma told me to tell Sally that she doesn't need the silver brush to be beautiful. I'm supposed to tell Ann they were always proud of her, and tell you all that your parents loved you exactly as you are and were proud of you. I was also told to tell Ann that she had carried them long enough, and it was time for me to take them. I woke up in the snow with Ann. I told her what happened, and she put the soul bundle around my neck."

"That's why I wanted to know about the peppermint. Noah would not have known about that. He must have talked to Mama and Papa in the afterworld."

"What happened with the peppermint?" Sally asked.

"So, I guess I finally have to confess. When we were little, I snatched Stephanie's peppermint and ran away with it, so I could eat it. I thought it wasn't fair that she had it when she had disobeyed her father, and I was never allowed to just take anything."

Stephanie continued the story, "I wasn't

127

supposed to eat the candy until we got home, but I took one out of the bag and sneaked away with it to eat it right away. Then, I didn't let Ann tell Papa or Mama that Eli had taken it because I had disobeyed Papa. Honestly, I haven't ever told anybody."

Eli assured them, "Me neither."

Tears ran down Ann's cheeks as she explained, "That's why I gave Noah the soul bundle. Mama and Papa were proud of me, and they appreciated me. I was a good girl, and I helped them. They told Noah that I was supposed to give their souls to him, so I did, and I'm happy about it."

The message was what Stephanie needed to hear as well. "They were proud of all of us. I'm glad they told you, Noah. Papa never told us anything like that. I always thought he only loved Ann."

It was Ann's turn to be shocked. "What?"

Stephanie explained, "We all worked on the farm, but whenever anything important happened, Papa always wanted you."

Ann stood up, walked around the table, and sat on the bench next to her sister. She took Stephanie in her arms. "I'm so sorry you believed that. Now, we all know that Papa was proud of us and loved us."

Stephanie hugged her sister back. "I'm glad to know that he loved and was proud of me as well. Both of them must have loved us. They found a way to tell us from the other side of the veil."

Eli saw through Ann and Stephanie how important fathers are in the lives of their daughters, and he knew it was the same for sons. "When we have children, I'm going to tell them every day how much I love them and how proud I am of them."

Noah laid his last orange peel on his plate. "Me too."

Sally notified her brothers-in-law of what they needed to do for her, "And you better tell my husband when I have one."

Noah assured her, "I will."

Eli also swore to pass on the critical information, "I promise."

The conversation made Roscoe think. "I guess it was a good thing I never had children. Even though I would have loved them, I wouldn't have told them. I would not have realized they wouldn't just know it. That's probably what happened with your father."

Ann stood up, "Probably."

"I didn't tell Ann about this because I didn't know who she was or what it has to do with us, but there was another woman there with Chris and Emma. She said, 'Tell Theodore, I made the right decision in time.' I don't know anybody named Theodore."

Eli jumped up. "It's me! I'm Eli Theodore Yates. It worked!" He danced a jig. "I'm sorry. I know it was for Chris and Emma. Please forgive me. I have a braid of my mother's hair. I keep it in this watch." He opened the pocket watch and showed them the small braid of hair. "I put a little bit of it in the alligator skin. I'm sorry, but I thought she was in Hell. I thought if there was any chance to save her that I needed to try. I'm sure I shouldn't have messed with the ceremony, but she's not in Hell. She accepted God. We never knew. It's been horrible for Pop, thinking Ma was in eternal torture. It's also been horrible for me."

Noah enlightened Eli, "You could have told us you wanted to include your mother. It would have been all right."

Stephanie conveyed her feelings about drawing Hattie. "No harm was done. Now we have your mother, and I'm very happy about it."

"Exactly. There's nothing to be sorry about," Ann assured Eli that everything was good.

Sally stated, "All is well as far as I'm concerned."

"Thank you. I can't tell you how much it means to me. And thank you, God, for not giving up on my mother, even to the last second."

Roscoe told them what the next course of the birthday meal was going to be. At the bottom of their bowls, Stephanie had previously placed a piece of the pumpernickel bread that Roscoe and Sally had baked. "Now, we have Onion Soup. Put some cheese in your soup." Roscoe ladled soup into Noah's bowl. "Tell us how you got the eagle feathers."

Sally piped up and told the story, "After you left, we walked up and down the river. Each time we went past, we glanced at the eagles until the last time, when Noah went to look. One was sitting in the hole. It screamed at us, so we stopped. The eagle looked at us, we looked back at it, and I have to tell you, eagles are not good at staring contests. It blinked all the time. I won right away."

Roscoe told his protégé, "You've got strong bragging rights now that you've stared down an eagle."

"I believe you're right." Sally took her soup.

Ann held out her bowl. "The male eagle stayed and protected his mate, but he let us stand there and look. When she woke up, he came out screeching and stood between her and us until she flew away."

Sally stirred her soup, so it would cool enough to eat. "And she took your flannel shirts."

"I swear that really is how we lost your shirts." Noah tasted his first-ever spoonful of onion soup. "Mmm, this is good."

Roscoe declared, "If I didn't know about all the other strange things that have happen to you folks, I wouldn't believe that story in a million years, but in this case, I do."

"I don't know why I did it, but I looked into the hole and found these." Noah held up the feathers that he had lain on the table beside him.

Ann offered to make amends for losing the shirts. "I'll make you more shirts if you let me use some flannel material from the store."

"Go ahead and use the bolt of blue flannel. Nobody seems to like it. It has sat on the shelf for a long time. Make as many as you want. You can use the whole bolt."

"Thank you. I'll show you the one I think you're talking about before I do anything."

Stephanie told Ann, "I'll help you."

Sally offered, "I will too."

Roscoe felt he was part of a family, and he liked

it. "I'll end up with nice new shirts, instead of those old worn-out shirts. The best part is that I'll know you women made them for me. That will make them extra nice."

They finished their soup. Roscoe stacked the empty bowls. "Now, we'll have stewed tomatoes with lima beans and dumplings, and I roasted the ducks Eli shot today. We also steamed potatoes until tender, and we made gravy."

Roscoe, Sally, and Stephanie brought in the doings. Eli carried in the platter with the roasted ducks. After they finished the main course, Roscoe brought out a cake that was light and marvelously fluffy.

"This is delicious!" Ann tried to fit the cake into her stomach.

Noah ate his last bite of cake. "Thank you, everybody. This meal was some pumpkins."

Roscoe offered a gift to the man who had saved him from another lonely winter. "Noah, pick something you want from the store as a birthday present."

"I'd like some dried beans, corn kernels, and squash seeds, plus a little cornmeal and tallow."

"You can have it, but that's nothing. Take something else."

"I'd like enough for everybody."

"Noah, you are very unusual. If that's what you want, you can surely have it."

After dinner, Ann and Roscoe went to get the bolt of material. Ann stroked the cloth. "This is beautiful flannel. I don't know why nobody has wanted it."

"You'll need thread and sewing supplies, and Noah wanted just about nothing for a birthday present, so take these." Roscoe handed Ann several spools of thread and three sewing kits.

Ann took everything to the main room and placed it on one of the other tables. "We'll start tomorrow." She walked over to Noah and whispered, "Tonight, I want to make sure my husband is completely warm."

He answered back, "I think I'll need a lot of warming." He looked into Ann's face. He saw that she wanted his love, and he needed to show her all the passion that filled his heart. "Goodnight, everybody."

SIXTEEN

Ann had carried the soul bundle for four days. Therefore, after his fourth day of thinking about and harboring Chris, Emma, and Hattie, Noah gave the bundle to the second oldest daughter. After her four days, Stephanie took it to Sally. Sally waved her hand. "I don't want to be next. I want to be last, and I want to release them on the anniversary of our parents' death."

"Let's talk it over with the others." Stephanie led Sally to the main room where the others sat by the fire, reading.

To get their attention, Sally said, "Family." Everybody looked her way. "We think it would be good to release the souls on February fourteenth. Papa and Mama died on that day two years ago. What do you think?"

Ann replied, "I think that's perfect. Noah, would that work?"

Noah counted on his fingers and then answered, "That's an excellent day to have the ceremony, but we've been carrying the soul bundle for four days. February fourteenth is only nine days away. There are still three of you left, and Hattie's also there. What do you think, Eli?"

"You can skip me," Roscoe offered.

Noah spoke up, "I think that's unacceptable. Everybody involved with drawing the souls ought to carry it, and you gave your blood. You should—"

Sally interrupted, "Noah, you said we could carry them for only one day if we wanted. So I think Eli, Roscoe, and I should each take them for three days."

"That's fine with me," Eli agreed to the plan.

Roscoe was happy to be included, "All right."

"February fourteenth it is." Noah resumed reading.

Stephanie took the bundle to Eli. Eli asked, "Don't you want to be next, Sally?"

"No, I want to be the last. I want Papa and Mama to be released by their child."

Noah contemplated. *Sally wants to be the gatekeeper to the spirit world. I wonder if ...*

"Then, I'm ready to take them." Eli took the bundle and hung his mother's soul around his neck. Even if it was only for a few days, Eli was glad that he had his mother resting against his heart. He was even happier that she would be going to God. His mind released the belief that had upset him and his father for most of Eli's life; the belief that his mother was in Hell, just as his father had told him.

That night when they went into their room, Noah told Ann, "Last time, my feet were cold. We can't feel that we need to get our feet warm when we release the souls. If the souls feel that we need something, they might not go."

"The wool blankets are very warm. We could cut up one and make inserts for the mukluks. If we wear socks and the inserts inside the mukluks, our feet should be warm, and we can try them out first."

"That's good. Can we make them in time?"

"It should be easy to cut a big rectangle, remove a wedge from each side at the ankle, sew up the seam, round out the front, and add a piece over the top."

"I'd like to make them in our room privately. I don't want to interfere with the carrying of the souls."

"I have one of our small blankets, the thread Roscoe gave us, and my sewing kit in here. The color of the thread doesn't match, but I don't think that will matter since they'll be inside the mukluks. Do you want to start now?"

"Yes, let's start." Noah held both of Ann's hands. "Have I told you lately how much I love you and how wonderful I think you are?"

"I remember you telling me something like that last night and this morning."

"Just making sure you know." They used their own feet as models for all the inserts, cut out all twenty-four pieces from the one blanket, and sewed together one set each before they went to sleep.

Roscoe carried Hattie, Chris, and Emma. "I feel them here in my heart. I feel peaceful, loved, and loving, like I'm a part of the family."

When Sally carried the soul bundle, she came to believe that her parents were happy that the warmth and love of a family again surrounded their daughters. She thought her parents gave her

136

permission to love her current family because they knew it didn't mean she didn't love them.

February thirteenth arrived. Noah wanted to double-check. "If all of you are sure you're ready, tomorrow we'll let your parents go. It won't be a long ceremony. I don't need to explain in advance unless you want me to."

Ann walked over and kissed Noah on the top of his head. "I trust you." The rest of the family also agreed they would just follow along.

"I tried to get this finished before tomorrow, and I did." Roscoe handed Noah the completed medicine bag. Close to the bottom of the bag, at the front, was a loop. At the other end, a long rawhide string could tie down the top at any length. The pouch also could be rolled up and tied with the same strip of leather. On the top flap, Roscoe had sewn the design for a family with three men and three women.

"Thank you, Roscoe. It's beautiful and perfect."

Sally held up her bag. "I've got mine almost done."

Eli disclosed the status of his bag, "Mine isn't decorated at all."

Ann confessed, "Mine is still the pieces I carried into our room."

"My bag will be enough for the ceremony tomorrow. Tonight, we need to rest well. I know we're running out of food, but we need to have a satisfying meal in the morning. If the souls feel an unfulfilled desire in any of us or any longing from us, they might not make the journey."

The next morning, Roscoe served the last of the bacon, eggs, bread, and honey, along with coffee. Noah took a swallow of coffee and then saw Ann come out of their bedroom. "My love, will you bring our gifts?" Ann arrived at the table with the six sets of blanket inserts that she and Noah had made. She gave a set to each of them.

Noah explained, "Dress in many layers of thick clothes, wear your blanket coats, fur hats, scarfs, gloves, warm wool socks, and these inserts for your mukluks. Remember, you must be completely warm."

When they had finished the satisfying meal and had all dressed as Noah directed, they walked to the river protected from the cold wind that tried to chill them and cause a desire for warmth. Noah pushed a bucket through the thin layer of ice that had developed in his fishing hole and then pulled up water from the river. Eli laid the cedar logs and started the fire.

Noah drew a handful of the plants of power from the medicine bag. He threw some of the sage, cedar, tobacco, and red willow bark into the fire and put some of the herbs into the smudging bowl. With the tongs, he removed a hot ember from the purified fire and dropped it into the bowl. He used his good eagle feather, drew the smoke over his body, and purified himself.

Of her own accord, Sally again stood in the west. Noah, therefore, believed that the spirit world had called her to service. He smudged her all the way down to her feet. "Be purified of all negativity and

138

brought into this moment in purity." He worked clockwise around the circle, said the same thing, and smudged each of them until he returned to Sally in the west. "Keeper of the souls, come forward." Sally walked into the circle and stood before Noah next to the fire. "Keeper of the souls, are you willing to release the souls of Chris Williams, Emma Williams, and Hattie Yates?"

"I'm ready to release them."

"Family, will you release the souls of Chris Williams, Emma Williams, and Hattie Yates?"

They all replied, "We release them."

"Keeper of the Souls, release the souls to me." Sally raised the rawhide string over her head and handed the soul bundle to Noah. He hung it around his neck and then fed more of the plants of power to the fire.

Weeks before, Noah had ground beef jerky, mixed it with currants and tallow, and then tied the mixture into a piece of duck cloth. He brought out the pouch of pemmican. "Those who are saying goodbye must eat to acknowledge that you can go through life without these people who you love." He held out a small piece of the pemmican. "Sally, receive nourishment by my hand, and release Chris Williams, Emma Williams, and Hattie Yates from responsibility to provide for you."

"I take nourishment from your hand. I release Mama, Papa, and Hattie from the responsibility." Sally put the food into her mouth and ate.

Noah circled the fire, asked the same question,

and gave a small piece of the pemmican to each of them. He ate the last morsel of the symbolic food. "Chris Williams, Emma Williams, and Hattie Yates, I release you from the responsibility to provide for your children, Roscoe, or me, and I pledge to share that responsibility with Ann, Stephanie, Sally, Eli, and Roscoe."

He removed the two pipe halves from his medicine bag, joined them, and raised the Calumet to God in Father Sky. He threw another handful of the herbs onto the fire. "Father Sky, prepare the way for the souls of Chris Williams, Emma Williams, and Hattie Yates and allow them to pass through you as they go to God." He sprinkled herbs on the ground and put the first pinch of the plants of power into the bowl before he lowered the pipe toward Mother Earth. "Mother Earth, thank you for nourishing the souls of Chris Williams, Emma Williams, and Hattie Yates during the years they walked here. Today, we ask you to release them."

Noah raised the pipe to the west. "West, send the Holy Spirit to guide the souls of Chris Williams, Emma Williams, and Hattie Yates to God, the Great Spirit."

In the north, he offered the plants and added to the pipe. "North, cover the souls of Chris Williams, Emma Williams, and Hattie Yates with the sacrifice and righteousness of Jesus and give their souls the strength and endurance to stand before the justice of our mighty God."

He said to the east, "East, assure the souls of

Chris Williams, Emma Williams, and Hattie Yates with the knowledge that they go to the Great Mystery, so they are willing to give up the sun. Thunderbirds, clear the path of any hindrance with your mighty talons."

Noah placed one last pinch of herbs into the pipe and raised it to the south. "South, show the souls of Chris Williams, Emma Williams, and Hattie Yates the bounty on Mother Earth that will nourish their children, so their souls will feel freed from any obligation to the living."

Noah turned back to the west, took a stick from the fire, and used it to light the herbs in the pipe. He puffed the smoke out to the west. "The circle to the spirit world is open." He passed the pipe to Sally, "Smoke the pipe and send your prayers for these souls to God in Father Sky."

Sally drew in the smoke, this time being sure that it did not get into her lungs. "God, receive the souls of Papa, Mama, and Hattie Yates. See Jesus when You judge them and allow them into Heaven and Your presence."

Stephanie smoked the pipe. "God, take these souls of my parents and Hattie Yates. Allow them to look down on us, to see all of us and those to come, and with us be happy. When we go astray, let them help us back to whatever path You have called us to walk."

Eli sent his prayer, "Holy Spirit, thank You for never giving up on my mother and for causing her spirit to open the door. Jesus, thank You for stepping into my mother's heart. Father God, thank You for Your plan of salvation that brings peace between You and us who believe. I thank all of You for letting me know that You will receive my mother. Let her come to You with the souls of Chris Williams and Emma Williams."

Ann drew the smoke in and exhaled three times. "I ask You, God, to take the precious souls of Chris Williams and Emma Williams. I thank You for giving them to me as my parents. Tell them that I know they loved me and that they were proud of me. I ask You to take the precious soul of Hattie Yates. I thank You for her life and that You gave her to Tom who loved her exactly as she was. Let Hattie know that Tom was always proud of her and in love with her. I know this because Tom told me so, and I want Hattie to know how thankful I am for Eli. He is a good man, a wonderful husband to my sister, and a wonderful brother-in-law to Sally and me."

Roscoe smoked a puff. "Souls of Chris and Emma Williams and Hattie Yates, be free to go home to God knowing that your children are loved by me and all of us here in this circle and that we will do everything we can to provide everything they need."

Noah consumed the last of the herbs in the bowl. "Souls of Chris Williams and Emma Williams and Hattie Yates, thank you for meeting me in the spirit world and sending me back to Mother Earth with your messages. I know you didn't mean to cause your children pain. I thank you for your children and our memories of you that we'll forever hold dear." Noah disconnected the pipe bowl from the stem. He placed them in their pouches.

Noah withdrew another handful of the herbs and added it to the fire. "Keeper of the soul bundle, take the souls to the center of the universe." He held the pouch in the smoke that rose from the fire. He raised it to God, lowered it to Mother Earth, raised it to the north, then the east, next to the south, and last he raised it to the spirit world in the west. "Mother Earth, release the souls of Chris Williams, Emma Williams, and Hattie Yates." Noah untied the bundle. "God, receive these souls." He opened the soul bundle in the fire's smoke rising into Father Sky.

"Anybody who would like to keep some of the hair from the soul bundle, come forward."

After everybody had taken what he or she wanted, Noah dropped the buckskin and everything left inside into the fire. "Fire, sever the bond between Mother Earth and the souls of Chris Williams, Emma Williams, and Hattie Yates, so that they may fly to God."

Sally told her parents, "Goodbye, Mama. Goodbye, Papa."

Eli watched the soul bundle burn. "Be happy in Heaven, Ma."

Noah told those around the fire, "Think of Chris Williams, Emma Williams, and Hattie Yates flying along the Milky Way to the center of the universe and joining God."

As the soul bundle was consumed, Noah allowed his family to meditate, reflect, and think of freedom and happiness for their parents. When it was gone, Noah picked up the bucket of water and poured it on the fire. "Water, cause your brother fire to rest." Noah informed everybody, "They're released. We can go home."

"They're gone. I'm sure of it." Sally started toward the talc hill.

Eli followed. "Thank you, Noah."

"You're welcome."

"Husband, why did you always say the whole names and not just 'these souls'?"

"Because I wanted to be sure Mother Earth, Father Sky, and God knew which souls we were asking to be released. I didn't want to lose anybody I want to keep here."

Stephanie thought about what Noah had said. "That was a very intelligent plan."

"Noah, my love, you are a wise and helpful man. You've given us a wonderful gift that I appreciate more than I can tell you."

Noah remembered what Sally had dreamed right after Gus had destroyed their farm. "I'm glad to be able to help, and I believe, just as Sally dreamed, that we are a strong and powerful family, just like the eagles."

SEVENTEEN

At Pine Bluff, as they had done for Noah, the eagles at the river validated Sally's belief that her family was safe and strong. She watched the eagles and tried to learn from them how to live.

As Sally and Noah watched the eagles, Stephanie worked with the mule. One day Stephanie didn't put out any grain. Stubborn pushed the bucket over with her nose. Stephanie scooped some into the pail, stood still, and held out the food. Stubborn cautiously came over and ate while Stephanie held the bucket. After a few more days of holding the bucket while Stubborn ate, Stephanie put the oats in her hand and offered it to her favorite mule. Stubborn's lips tickled her palm as it took the food. Stephanie had won Stubborn's acceptance. She hoped to gain her assistance as well.

When they weren't doing chores, they worked on their medicine bags, braided the hair from the soul bundle, sewed the flannel shirts, or read books from Roscoe's store, all while enjoying each other's company. By the end of February, the shirts were ready. The women decided to give the newly sewn blue flannel shirts as a special event and brought them to breakfast.

145

Sally leaned over, kissed Roscoe on the top of his head, and gave him two shirts. "These are to replace those that line the eagles' nest. Stephanie made one, and I made the other. We all want to say thank you for everything you've done for us and for being a wonderful part of this family." Sally then gave one to Stephanie. "I made this for you because, even after we lost all our animals, you've taken the chance and loved an animal again, and you even picked the meanest one."

Next, Ann gave one to Noah, "I sewed this shirt for the most wonderful man in the world. When you wear it, it will cover you with all the love, respect, admiration, and appreciation I have in my heart for you, and I hope it will remind you not to take any more detours into the afterworld." Ann handed one to Sally, "Since you only have the winter clothes that belonged to Harry and are only able to keep them from falling off with suspenders, but mostly because I love you to the moon and back, I made one that fits you."

Stephanie placed a shirt in Eli's hands. "Every stitch holds a prayer for you, for our lives together, and for all the children we will have. As you know, I think you are the man who is the most wonderful in the world." She handed one to Ann, "This shirt also holds a prayer on every stitch for you and Noah, who is also a wonderful man, and for long, peaceful, unmolested lives together with many children."

Ann stood up. "Everybody, put on your shirt then come back." They all did as told and then sat at

146

the table in their new blue flannel shirts as one happy, matching family while they ate boiled oats and drank hot coffee.

After eating, Ann finished making her bow. Since they needed meat, Noah took her to hunt and look at the eagles. They searched along the river for hours but didn't see a single animal suitable for food. Noah still thought it was a good day. He was with Ann, and the eagles had grabbed fish not far from where Ann practiced shooting a target drawn in the snow. Noah complimented Ann, "You're doing great. You're always hitting the mark."

While Ann practiced, Noah watched the eagles eat not far up the river. "Too bad we can't get the eagles to fish for us. Nothing has been coming to the fishing hole. It's probably the only way we'd get any."

A white rabbit hopped into view but tried to remain camouflaged against the snow. "Try to shoot it," Noah whispered.

Ann quickly pulled an arrow, nocked it, pulled the string, and released. The rabbit bolted away with the fur shaved off its back. "Oh, foot! I missed. You should have shot it." Ann plowed through the snow to retrieve the arrow.

"We'll be all right without meat. I love eating oatmeal. Besides, even though you missed, that was an excellent shot. You did the whole thing in one smooth action. You'll get one soon."

After Ann returned with the arrow, they walked the river's edge toward home. Despite the fact that they had been eating animal feed for days, they enjoyed being in what seemed to be a perfect place. They crested the talc hill only to find a huge elk blocking the corridor through the snow. Noah halted. "It must have come here to eat. That's probably the only plant life not buried under the snow."

"I'm sure it won't let us pass."

"This is a great chance for you to shoot an elk."

"It's too far away."

"We'll sneak closer then you can shoot it."

"What if it charges us?"

"It can't turn around in the narrow passage."

"The snow melted a lot this week."

"It's still four feet deep. I don't think it will turn around when it has a clear path ahead. You can do it."

"How am I going to kill it? I won't be able to get a shot at its heart or lungs. Shooting it in the rear will only make it mad."

"But that should make it run forward. When it gets to the clearing at the trading post where there's more room, it'll turn. When it does, shoot it again."

"Get ready too. I think it's going to take both of us. We can't let it get away. We need the food."

Noah pulled an arrow, handed it to Ann, and drew another. They stalked the elk until close to the end of the path. Ann sent her arrow into its rump. The elk jumped, kicked to eliminate what had caused pain, and then, in a mindless panic, it charged ahead.

The trading post door splintered. Antlers ripped off its head as the elk rammed through the wood. Inside, Eli, Stephanie, Sally, and Roscoe bolted into the kitchen. "What in tarnation!" Roscoe peeked back into the room. A huge head frantically twisted.

Ann and Noah rounded the bend in the path. Noah exclaimed, "That is not something a person would ever expect to see!"

Ahead, wedged tightly in the doorway, the elk's hind end thrashed. "Now, what do we do?"

"Come on." Noah ran to the kitchen window. "Ann needs to come in through the window. Let her shoot it."

Roscoe opened the window, Noah pushed Ann up, and Eli pulled her in.

"If I kill it right there, it will be stuck in the doorway."

"Shoot it," Eli ordered.

Ann paused. She contemplated the possibilities and consequences. Roscoe told her, "We'll get it out when we cut it up."

The elk started to back out. Sally yelled, frantically, "It's getting free!"

Noah ran to the front as Eli forcefully commanded, "Ann, shoot it!"

Ann's arrow went into the monstrous elk's chest exactly where Noah had told her she would hit its heart. The animal jerked back in pain and was free. As it ran toward the passage out, Noah shot the elk in the lung, but it persisted onwards. Ann dashed out the front door. She and Noah raced behind it.

Noah yelled, "It won't go far!"

Eli, Stephanie, and Sally grabbed their coats. Roscoe dashed into the kitchen. "I'm getting my butcher knives. Get your carts."

The elk's lung didn't provide enough air for the

animal to keep its legs moving. The massive body crashed to the ground. Ann's arrow snapped as it jammed into the beast's heart.

Ann tried to pay respect as Noah always had, "Elk spirit, forgive us for taking one of your herd. We thank you for giving us this elk for food. We will honor its mighty strength when its flesh gives strength to our bodies. I'll acknowledge its sacrifice by making a remembrance from its antlers." Ann looked at Noah. "I hope I said the right thing."

"What matters is the respect in your heart when taking the life of an animal that has as much right to live as you do."

"I didn't ask for permission first. Do you think that's why it smashed up the trading post? I didn't ask the rabbit either. That's probably why I missed."

Noah didn't want Ann to think it was her fault that the elk had damaged the trading post, because it wasn't. He told her the truth. "Sometimes the hunt isn't easy, and unexpected things happen."

When the others got to the fallen elk, Noah and Ann already had their coats off as they disemboweled the animal. Noah pulled his arrow through the elk and then out through the open abdomen. He saw Roscoe with his knives. "You think we can get it to the barn without cutting it up? It will taste better if we can let the blood drain out."

Eli arrived with their carts. "I'll tan the hide."

It amazed Roscoe to discover yet another talent in the family. "You know how to tan?"

Stephanie bragged about the skills and

accomplishments of her husband. "Eli is the one who tanned that alligator skin. He also tanned a cougar and a deer hide that were burned up with our farm."

Eli was proud of Stephanie and gave credit where it was due. "Stephanie is the one who killed the alligator. I'm exceptionally glad that she's an excellent marksman."

Noah wanted to make gut containers for the corn, beans, squash, and cornmeal he had received for his birthday. "Eli, can we tan some of the intestines?"

"I've never done that, but we can try." *It would be interesting to try something like that.* He started thinking about how he could tan intestines.

Noah pulled Ann's broken arrow through the elk's heart. "This elk has been provided by the Huntress Ann Williams." He looked at the broken arrowhead then put his hand back inside. "Found it." Noah brought out the other fragment of the arrowhead. He held the parts toward Ann. "I think you should keep the arrowhead."

"You helped kill it. You should have half."

"My arrow slowed it down. Your arrow killed it, but I'll keep half."

Roscoe considered how to accomplish moving the elk to the barn. "I have poles in the barn. We can use them to rig up something with the mule packs and get a couple of mules to pull it."

Eli looked at the length of the carcass. "Even hanging from the very top of the barn, it's barely going to fit."

Ann proposed, "If we can tie these carts together

and get the elk on them, we should be able to pull it with mules."

"Maybe, let's go to the barn and see what we can figure out." Roscoe walked toward the barn. They got the fourth cart, four long poles, three long ropes, Ace and King, and their harnesses. Back at the elk, they lashed two long poles to the handles of the carts that they had placed end to end. Then, they slid the other two poles under the elk and lashed the carcass to the poles. The six of them unsuccessfully tried to raise the thousand-pound elk onto the carts.

Eli looked at everything they had with them. "Maybe we can lay the carts on their side next to the elk, lash the elk to the carts, and then tip the carts back up. They might pull the elk up with them."

Noah replied, "Let's try."

They tied the carts to the elk's back. Noah, Ann, and Sally got at one end of the top pole. Eli, Stephanie, and Roscoe stood at the other end. Noah coordinated, "On three. You ready?"

"Ready," the others all replied.

Noah called the count, "One two three pull!" They pulled with all their strength. The elk came up. As it approached the zenith, Noah yelled, "Shift to the top of the pole!" It went past the tipping point. He hollered, "Don't let it crash! Pull back!" They pulled against the forward momentum, trying to keep the contraption from coming down hard and breaking to pieces. The makeshift vehicle slammed against the ground.

Eli called out, "Yahoo! It's still in one piece!"

Ann danced a jig. "We did it!"

"It looks so funny with its legs in the air." Sally laughed hysterically. They all joined her.

When Noah finally stopped laughing, he slid the elk's innards into the carts. "I guess if this works, it doesn't matter how ridiculous it looks."

Roscoe responded, "Let's get this do-hickey attached to the mules." He tied the front end of the poles to King's harness. "These carts are very well built. It's amazing that they stayed together."

Roscoe put Ace into his harness and attached him in front of King then commanded his mules, "Come." Ace walked behind Roscoe, King went where Ace went, and the carts rolled forward.

Stephanie followed them. "I hope it continues to stay together."

Ann picked up the broken arrow and her arrowhead fragment. "I do too."

The lashed together poles, carts, and elk made a stable vehicle that they pulled to the turn at the front of the trading post. It was too long, so they dug away the corner of snow. When they had rounded off the bend enough, they maneuvered around the corner and easily traveled the final run.

Inside the barn, the other five untied the elk from the carts while Roscoe unharnessed his mules. Using the double pulley, Noah, Eli, and Ann pulled the elk, still attached to the poles, into a hanging position. They propped the poles against the rafters to help hold it up.

Ann felt proud. "Noah, together, you and I killed this elk with only three arrows."

Stephanie looked at the elk. Its head touched the ground, and its rump went almost all the way to the roof. "That's a big animal."

"We'll get lots of meat." Sally scattered cracked corn to feed the chickens.

Roscoe suggested a slight change in their hunting technique. "Next time, try not to run the animal through the front door."

Ann replied, "I'm sorry. I don't know why it did that. I guess we need to figure out what to do about the door."

As they walked to the trading post, Eli told them his idea, "We can make a temporary door by putting one of the tables on end against the opening, and then we can move other tables over to hold it there."

Noah agreed, "We don't have time to make a door tonight. I think that's the best plan."

"I'm very sorry, Roscoe. Don't be mad." Ann cleaned up the shattered remains of the door.

"I'm not mad. It's just something that happened. One thing's for sure, you all certainly keep things exciting."

Sally and Stephanie carried the broken boards to the fireplace to burn for heat. Noah and Eli moved the heaviest table to the door, raised it up, and then pushed the other three tables against it. The girls stuffed blankets from the store into the gaps to keep out as much cold air as possible. With the door temporarily patched, Noah, Eli, Stephanie, Sally, and Ann climbed out the kitchen window and started toward the barn to clean elk guts.

Roscoe poked his head out. "Bring me some ribs! I promise, they'll taste great this fresh."

EIGHTEEN

Noah detached the elk's skin and then broke a section of ribs loose from the spine. While he and Eli stood under the elk, Stephanie, Ann, and Sally cut the flesh that held the bones. That part of the carcass fell into the arms of the men. They laid the hunk of meat on a tarp. Then with axes, they chopped the ribs into pieces. Sally helped lug the bloody elk remains. "This is probably more than he meant."

Noah knocked on the kitchen window. "Is this too much?"

Roscoe looked at the five people, each holding a large section of ribs. *One piece would have been enough. They must be very hungry.* "I'll make some for later too. Pass it all in here."

As Roscoe took the meat to the butcher counter, Noah remained by the window, "Thank you for cooking this for us."

Eli had decided on the best way to proceed. "A length of intestines six-foot-long is the most we can easily handle and thirty feet should be plenty." He cut and then handed a section to each of them. "We have to clean the intestines inside and outside very, and I mean very, very, very, well." Eli brought a ten-gallon washtub to the middle of the barn. "Squeeze the contents into the tub."

Sally turned her head away as she pushed out feces. "This is so nasty!"

Eli tried not to breathe. "Get as much out as you can, and then we'll dump it in the river. I know we all wish we didn't have to deal with it, but the part we need is the inside."

They gagged as they extruded the mess and tried to listen to Eli. "We have to get this thin membrane. Slit the outer layer several inches down. Be careful you don't cut the inner part. Hold the portion we want while somebody else grabs the waste material and pulls it off."

Eli slit the tissue he wanted to remove from his emptied section then held the membrane he wanted to keep as Noah peeled the flesh back. Noah held the inside-out portion. "Too bad this isn't the part we need to use."

Eli waved toward the tub of nastiness. "Toss it. Girls, do the same with the other pieces while Noah and I take away this poop."

Noah offered, "Unless somebody else would like to help Eli?"

Ann spoke up, "You're not getting out of smelling that stuff. You're the one who wants tanned intestines. Since I don't want to ruin any of these pieces and have to do the first step again, Eli should supervise. I'll help you."

Close to the edge of the river, Noah chopped through the ice. They dumped the mess through the hole and then washed the tub in the icy water. After they returned, Eli moved on. "We need several containers of water to wash these, and we need to light some lanterns. We should be sure we get the intestines completely clean. Turn the pieces inside out, wash them thoroughly, change the water often, and repeat several times."

When the pieces were clean, Eli looked up from his tub. "Last, we need to fill these with very salty water to draw out the moisture."

"I'll get salt." Sally left the barn but quickly returned with the requested ingredient that Roscoe had passed through the window.

Eli examined the tubes of salt-water filled intestines on the tarp inside an empty stall. "Perfect!"

"I hope I never do that again." Sally closed the barn door.

They washed the elk innards from their bodies then ate the elk's ribs that Roscoe had barbequed in a delicious tangy sauce.

That night, like every night at Roscoe's home, Noah and Ann lay together in bed as Noah prayed, "Father God, Jesus, and Holy Spirit, I thank you for twice giving me Ann, a woman who loves and respects all of me. She never turns away from my Indian ways. Today, Ann walked in our ways because she wanted to. I never asked her to do that. She just did it. You could not have given me a better wife. Lead me, so I will be the husband she needs and deserves."

"My husband, don't ever doubt that I love the part of you that is Indian. That's what makes you so unique, interesting, competent, and desirable. You respect nature and life. I always have as well, but I like the way you do it. I want to walk in your ways. Teach me how."

"I will, but only do or believe what seems right to you. Agreed?"

"Yes, my love."

"Right now, I want to show you how an Indian man loves his wife."

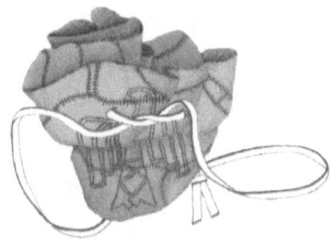

NINETEEN

After their morning chores, Stephanie worked with Stubborn. Recently, she had been able to walk up to Stubborn anytime she wanted to brush her, pat her, or hug her neck. Today, Stephanie decided to get Stubborn comfortable if she approached with a pack. She walked toward the animal while carrying one. Stubborn didn't object. Stephanie gave her extra hugs and rubbed Stubborn behind her ears. Stubborn not only allowed Stephanie to touch her, but she also took Stephanie's attention as a reward.

Roscoe put out hay. "Stubborn has come a long way."

Stephanie returned the pack to the tack room. "But she isn't to the point of being a work animal."

"You'll accomplish it." Needing to make a new door, Eli rummaged through the boards that Roscoe had stored in the barn.

"Stubborn isn't upset at all. I'm going to try to hold the pack against her side." Stephanie retrieved the pack again and walked toward Stubborn. Everybody turned to watch. Stephanie immediately changed direction and moved away from the mule. "Don't do that. You'll give her the idea that something's wrong."

159

Everybody returned to work. Several minutes later, Stephanie walked to Stubborn with the pack. As she hugged the mule, she held the bag against her side. Again, Stubborn remained content. Stephanie slid the pack up Stubborn's side and laid it on her back. Stubborn didn't flinch. "You're such a good girl." Stephanie scratched her chest but didn't try to secure the pack. After a short time, she took it off and walked away.

Noah and Eli sawed and shaped boards to make a new door. Ann, Stephanie, and Sally chopped the log the men had dragged into the barn. They worked with their usual procedure and rotated through chopping, splitting, moving, and stacking firewood. Every hour, Stephanie exited the process for a few minutes, carried the mule pack to Stubborn, and laid it on her back.

Eli and Noah finished their fourth round of shaving the top inner corner of the new door with the carpenter's plane. Eli put down the tool. "We're going to test the door again." He and Noah carried the door out of the barn with Roscoe right behind them. Stephanie carried the mule pack to Stubborn and put it straight on her back without the preceding hugs. Stubborn remained happy. After the third time, Stephanie secured the girth, which caused no adverse reaction.

When the men came back with the door, Ann asked, "Did it fit?

Noah lowered his end. "It did. We're going to attach the hinges."

Roscoe walked into the barn behind Noah and Eli. "You've got the pack strapped on!"

Stephanie told them her plan, "I'm going to leave it on her all night. I want her to get used to wearing a pack for a long time."

"In only two months, you've accomplished what I haven't done in all the months I've owned her, so do what you want."

Stephanie rubbed her favorite mule in its favorite place, right behind her ears. "She just needs extra love, patience, and acceptance."

Ann called out, "Stop messing with that mule and come help. We need to get this wood into the house." Stephanie kissed the side of Stubborn's head and then helped load wood into the carts.

When he and Noah had all four hinges attached, Eli picked up his end of the door. "We're going to attach it if everything is right."

"I want to watch." Ann followed with a cart.

Stephanie, Sally, and Roscoe also pulled a cart of logs to the trading post. Noah placed the bottom of the door in the hole. Eli stepped to the inside. "Push it up."

Noah raised the door into the jam. "How does it look?"

"Perfect. What about that side?"

"Exactly right."

"I'm swinging it open, so we can screw the hinges to the frame." Eli rotated the door. Noah held it while Eli screwed it on. Eli stepped back. "Try it again."

Noah closed the door. "It fits snugly."

Roscoe opened and closed the door several times. "This door fits better than the last one, and it's heavier too. I like it."

Ann tested the door. "Great work."

Stephanie tried it next. "It's nicer than the one the elk destroyed."

"Let me try it." Sally swung the door back and forth. "Very nice. I have the best brothers ever."

Even though it had been much warmer the last several days, Roscoe wanted the building to be toasty before bedtime. "Let's get that wood in here and warm this place up."

While Roscoe started the fires, the others filled the wood storage areas inside the trading post. Then Roscoe and Sally cooked supper, and Ann read Eli's Bible aloud.

Noah put a helping of boiled oats originally designated as mule feed, corn that Roscoe owned to feed the chickens but had cooked for supper, and elk ribs on his plate. "I've been wondering how much time we have before we should leave."

Sally stated what they all felt, "I'll hate to go."

Roscoe blurted out, "I don't want you to leave!"

Ann picked elk meat off a rib. "They'll be coming soon. Henry told us they would. We have to go."

"Then, I want to go with you."

Eli mixed his oats and corn and hoped it would make the food more enjoyable. "But you have this trading post."

Roscoe replied, "What's a place if there's nobody

there that you care about? I know I've only known you for a few months, but I feel like you're my family. Let me come with you. I don't want to die here alone and unloved."

"It's probably going to be a hard and dangerous trip. Plus, we could get caught and then you'd be involved." Noah picked up a rib and gnawed.

Sally mixed her barbequed elk into her boiled oats. "I want Roscoe to come with us."

"What about the animals?" Stephanie asked.

Roscoe believed there was only one logical option. "We'll take them with us. We'll use them to pack out as much as we can take."

Ann mixed her elk, oats, and corn into a conglomeration of mush. "It's all right with me for you to come, but I want you to understand that Noah and I will have to go a long way, and some of us may only go to Harmony."

Roscoe stirred his oats to put off taking another bite. "That's another reason why I should go. I know the way across the plains to Raton Pass."

"We should start getting ready." Eli forced himself to finish his meal.

To verify that he was not going to lose the family he had taken into his heart and adopted, or maybe the family that had adopted him, Roscoe stated, "Then, we all go together."

Noah confirmed, "We go together."

"Do you think we can take everything?" asked Ann.

"How much can the animals carry?" Sally pondered.

Eli knew the answer. "I went with Pop to Fort Smith several times when the new mules had just arrived. The traders said that mules can carry twenty-five percent of their weight. If I can use some paper and a pencil, I can figure out how much weight we can put on each animal."

"I think we should separate everything into three groups. The things we have to take, what we want to take, and what we'll leave behind." Roscoe went to get the requested items.

Stephanie wanted to be sure none of the animals suffered. "First, we have to bring enough animal food to last until the grass is up then they can graze."

"Let's clean up the dishes then we can go to the store and sort." Roscoe gave Eli the paper and a pencil.

As they separated Roscoe's merchandise, he informed them, "I want somebody worthy to have this place. What about Melvin or Henry?"

Noah carried six spyglasses to the 'take with us' area. "I don't think they have money to buy it, and I don't know how we could safely get in touch with them."

"I'd rather give it to somebody who deserves it than sell it to a person who doesn't." Roscoe carried an armful of books to the 'leave behind' area of the store.

Sally placed snowshoes on the shelf with the other things they needed. "How would you give it to one of them without anybody realizing what's happening?"

164

"We don't need to find the answer right now." Ann set goggles with lenses of green glass next to the snowshoes.

Stephanie carried first aid kits to the same section of the store. "We need to protect and feed the animals. There's still a lot of snow, and the wind is blowing. They won't last long without shelter."

"What can we do?" Noah asked.

Roscoe considered the possibilities, "The biggest thing I have is a Prussian Military Tent, but I doubt they would all fit inside."

Ann picked up a pack of wool socks. "How big is it?"

"It's twenty feet across, ten feet tall at the center, and eight feet tall at the outer edge."

"Let me think about it." Ann took a pencil and some paper to the table and sat beside Eli.

Since Eli was the one calculating what they could pack out, Roscoe told him, "We each need a survival pack. You already own most of the items for a survival pack."

Eli stopped ciphering. "What's in a survival pack?"

"It's everything in one pack that one person needs to survive for three weeks, except shelter and weapons. It weighs thirty-nine pounds. It's sixteen more pounds if you add one rifle, two pistols, a belt with a pouch that contains twenty rounds of ammunition, a gun worm, a package of flint caps, and a powder horn full of powder. That's fifty-five pounds so far. The shelter is eight pounds. That makes sixty-three pounds. Animal traps are ten pounds each. With one animal trap, the total weight is seventy-three pounds."

Eli tapped his pencil on the side of his jaw. "That's a lot of weight for the women to carry all day."

"We don't have to take six of everything. The shelters are tarps that can snap together. We can make a ten-by-ten cube with six. With less of them, we can make a different configuration and still fit inside. Also, we don't need six animal traps or that many weapons."

Noah stood in the middle of the store and surveyed what remained to be sorted. "You probably won't convince the girls to cut back on weapons." He looked at Ann, "Could we?"

Stephanie answered, "Not after what happened at our house."

Roscoe felt confused, "I thought your house was burned down."

Sally looked at Roscoe, "It was. Before that, it was shot up by the same people who later burned it down. You've never seen so much firepower as they let loose."

"I was with them when that happened. Sally's telling you the truth." Eli went back to figuring how much each animal could carry.

Roscoe suggested alternatives, "Since we'll be bringing so many weapons, we can cut out weight in tools and cook pans. We also don't need six medicine kits, plus we'll be wearing most of the clothes."

"Show us what's in a survival pack? We don't want to duplicate items or leave out anything we need."

Roscoe picked up an already assembled survival pack. He named each item as he placed it on the table. "An india rubber poncho with a long neck and head tube that has a drawstring to pull it closed, and also a pair of india rubber gloves with wool liners. A short winter overcoat and a fur hat with earflops. Buckskin pants and shirt, one flannel shirt, two pairs of wool and cotton socks, two long cotton unmentionables, one pair of wool pants, one wool shirt, suspenders, and four silk handkerchiefs.

"For sleeping: one pillow and two one-point blankets. The survival pack also includes a sewing kit, a first aid kit, a hunting knife in a sheath with a pouch for the small whetstone that's included, a compass, a spyglass, and goggles. There's also a hygiene kit with two washcloths, one towel, a toothbrush, a comb, a hairbrush, and a bar of soap.

"The eating kit has one tin plate, cup, knife, fork, and spoon. A tin pot with a wire handle and a skillet lid with a handle, a fire hook, a corked glass bottle with fifty matches, and an india rubber canteen. In addition, twenty-one individual meal packs, salt, pepper, sugar, coffee, tea, dried apples, dried apricots, and dried beef. So you don't have to make a fire, you eat the dried fruit and dried meat for the mid-day meal. The other seven meals, you hunt, catch, or go without."

Eli hoped all that food existed. "How many do you already have made up? Is all that food here?"

"Only this one."

"What's in your survival shelter?" Eli asked.

Roscoe retrieved a shelter pack. He put the parts on the table with the other items. "It has an india rubber impregnated duck cloth tarp with snaps on all four sides, twelve four-foot poles with tin sleeves to join them, six tie-down ropes with pegs, all inside this india rubber bag. The bag is big enough for your pillow and blankets as well. You can configure the tarp and poles in different ways, or you can snap them together with other tarps. You have enough space inside for yourself and your supplies."

"How did you come up with this?" Eli asked.

"Most of my customers have been travelers. Some were on foot or had an animal, but nothing else. They couldn't carry a lot, but needed to go a long way before resupplying."

Ann said, "On the run like us."

"I don't ask. I also have an optional toolkit that has a spade, a hatchet with a hammer end, and fifty-feet of three-quarter-inch hemp rope. The tools weigh twelve pounds."

Eli stood up. "We'll probably need to use snowshoes, but they'll be under our feet. May I use your weights? I want to weigh some of these things individually."

"Sure." Roscoe went to get the weights.

When he got back, Ann shared her plan to ration food to each animal and fit the animals into the Prussian tent. "We could make a divider out of duck cloth that would fit inside the tent. At the center,

168

would be a six-foot circle. If we suspend it from the top, the animals can't push it over. It could be secured into the ground with stakes, so they can't go under it either. We divide it into four quadrants. Each of the goats would be in its own section with a feed sack.

"Attached to the outside of the goat pen would be twenty-one dividers to separate Eyanosa, every mule, and every donkey into its own area with a food bag. They would have their heads toward the goat pen and their rears toward the tent wall. That way, the bigger ones would fit inside because their heads can go over the goat area. We make the dividers high, and we secure them at the rear by tying them to the tent wall. That way, they wouldn't be able to reach each other's food."

Since it was Roscoe's tent and duck cloth, and all but one of the animals belonged to Roscoe, Noah asked, "What do you think, Roscoe?"

"I don't think there's any other possibility. How long will it take to make the divider?" Roscoe got all the duck cloth and several rolls of strong thread.

"Two weeks or maybe less," Ann guessed.

Sally added, "If I help, and we work on it all day, it will take less time."

"What about the chickens?" Stephanie asked.

Ann offered a grisly plan, "I don't think we can keep them warm enough to take them. We should start eating them."

Roscoe didn't hesitate. "That would be kinder than letting them freeze or starve when we leave. Also, I would like to eat some chicken meat."

Eli put the tin pot with handles, the lid, and the spit on the scales. "I hope the trip won't be too hard with all this snow on the ground."

Noah looked at the items on the table. "You want me to make six sets?"

"Everybody, claim a spot at a table and bring whatever items you already own to your place. We'll add what's still needed. I know you don't have these." Roscoe gave each of them an empty pack. "Since we're leaving soon, we already have enough wood. Don't waste time chopping any more. Instead, plan, make the tent divider, and pack."

They got what they had brought with them to Pine Bluff. For each of them, Roscoe added the missing parts. Minus the food, tools, animal traps, cooking pots, and the shelters, everybody had a complete pack ready to go when they went to bed.

TWENTY

The following week, the girls worked on the animal tent's divider while the men butchered the elk. Since they still had plenty of coffee beans, Eli ground a sack of them. He opened the elk intestines, let out most of the water, added coffee grounds, and then resealed them. While they smoked the elk meat, he moved them into the smokehouse, but he buried the intestine tubes under coffee grounds.

Eli had previously scraped the elk's hide clean of flesh and fat, and he had wrapped it in salt. Now, he opened it up, washed it, and hung it to be smoked with everything else.

Meanwhile, Noah and Roscoe looked over all the plants and spices they wanted to take. Noah made a suggestion, "We can make cloth bags and not add very much weight."

Roscoe thought about it. "We could use some of that duck cloth. It would be strong, and we can write what's inside on the bag."

"I'll find out if there's going to be any extra material." Noah went to the front room. "Are you going to need all the duck cloth? We thought we could make bags for the plants and spices."

Ann stopped sewing. "We've made all twenty-one of the long dividers and the nineteen-foot section for the goat corral. We still need four three-and-a-half-foot-long pieces for the goat dividers. The material doesn't need to be wide for the feedbags, so we should be able to make all twenty-five from the same bolt. We'll also need material to hang the divider from the top and tie it to the tent wall, but we have enough scraps for that, so I think we'll only need two more bolts. We don't need the last one."

"Great." Noah appropriated the material, a sewing kit, and a spool of the strongest thread. As they made bags, Noah and Roscoe reviewed what they knew about the plants. They left what would be easy to replace, but packed the items that would not.

When the supply wagons had come that fall, Roscoe had returned the perishables that he hadn't sold that summer and had bought more of what he needed for the winter. He had stocked the store with only enough food to feed one person until spring when the resupply wagons would bring fresh goods. Even though they had eaten lots of wild game, the food was almost entirely gone. They had eaten all the chickens, except the three best egg producers. The one set of Roscoe's survival food packets and most of the elk meat was slated for use during the trip to Little Rock where they could resupply. Unknown to any of the others, Roscoe had also put aside the ingredients he needed to make a birthday meal for Ann on March tenth.

Roscoe asked, "How is the divider coming? We should leave before the resupply wagons arrive."

"It's almost done. We can finish it tonight if we work late."

Noah asked, "When do they normally get here? I don't want anybody to find us, but I'd like to wait until after Ann's birthday tomorrow."

Roscoe paced. "They're usually here by now. I think they're late because there's still so much snow. We should go on March eleventh to be safe."

"I've got the loads figured out for everything we want to take. We can pack today and then load the animals the morning we leave." Eli got the papers with his calculations.

Stephanie asked, "Did you include Stubborn? She'll do anything I ask. Several times, I've had a heavy pack on her all day. She's been happy to do it, and since she's a big mule, she can carry a heavy load."

"But she'll only do it for you," Eli replied.

"It doesn't matter. I'll be there. Also, I've meant to bring up something; Stubborn needs a new name."

Noah joked, "Maybe we should call her Partially Stubborn."

"I want to call her Redeemed."

Ann said, "I like that."

"I do too," Roscoe accepted the name.

Sally stopped sewing for a second. "Then, Redeemed it is."

"I'll add items and figure out a pack for Redeemed. Except for our tent, the tarps, the tools, and the cooking equipment that we'll pull in our carts, we'll carry everything that's ours in the packs

Roscoe gave us." Eli looked over his lists one more time. "Here's what to put in each side of the animals' packs. I notated if they need a support board in the bottom to distribute the weight. Animals normally should be able to carry twenty-five percent of their weight. However, since ours will have to plow through snow, I made it twenty percent. First, they have to carry enough of their food to get to Little Rock. The smallest goats can't even carry all the food they'll need. I distributed the rest of their food among the others. Then I added the items Roscoe wants in the order of the importance he assigned. Pack so the load is stable, evenly distributed, and won't shift. Here's what we should put in each pack."

Eli gave each of them a list before he went to get the intestines ready. He emptied the water but kept all the moist coffee grounds inside. *It's a good thing Roscoe had so much coffee; its tannin is a good preservative.* He placed each on a separate strip of leftover duck cloth with some of the wet coffee grounds also on the outside. Then he added salt, rolled it up, folded the ends in, and tied it with a rawhide string. He tied up the elk hide the same way and placed them all into a bag. By the early afternoon, they had packed everything they planned to take, including all the smoked elk meat. Then, they ate the last of the barbecued elk ribs together with oats.

Noah wanted to climb the tree and look inside the eagles' nest, and he hadn't seen them around for days. However, he didn't want to tell Ann his plan because he didn't want to scare her. He got up from the table. "I have some things to do. I'll be back before dark."

Ann knew Noah was probably planning to do something she wouldn't like, but she'd come to believe that he was capable of doing just about everything on the planet. However, she didn't want to worry, so she didn't ask about his plans. "Enjoy yourself, my husband."

Since she sat at the table, Noah leaned over and kissed Ann on the cheek. "I'm so blessed to be married to you."

After they cleaned up from their mid-day meal, Ann bundled up. "I want to get some things before we leave. I'll be back soon." Ann assumed she would have to chop ice from the spot they kept open for fishing, so she got an axe and walked the passageway through the dwindling snow. She didn't know the depth of the water or if she could reach to the bottom. She hoped she could get six small, beautiful river stones on the first try.

Ann walked up the hill to the river as Noah took off his coat and started up the tree. Ann stopped, searched through the talc, and gathered six small jagged stones she thought were perfect. She resumed her expedition to the river as Noah arrived at the top of the tree. He scooched along the branch out to the eagle's nest. Noah heard ice shatter, looked down, and saw Ann at the river's edge. *I can't let Ann see me up here.* He climbed into the nest. *This is not going to be good if the eagles come back. It's one thing for them to let me be several yards away. It's an entirely different thing to be in their nest.*

He watched Ann take off her coat then kneel and insert her bare arm into the icy water all the way to her armpit. *What is she doing?* Noah could not imagine why Ann would reach into the hole. She brought her arm out of the water, looked at something in her hand, and then repeated the procedure.

Noah felt irritated. *She shouldn't be getting her arm that cold.* It occurred to him that a person laying in an eagle's nest ought to understand about taking risks to accomplish a task. Even so, he felt more and more concerned and upset each time he watched Ann plunge her arm into the freezing water. On top of that, she didn't have on her coat.

He was about to get out of the nest, climb down the tree, and make her stop. Ann looked at the latest batch of whatever she had brought up from the river, picked something out, and dumped the rest. When she stood up and put her coat back on, Noah felt very relieved that she had stopped the ridiculously dangerous behavior for which he could image no possible justification. *Maybe I should be thinking about what justification Ann would find acceptable for me to climb into an eagle's nest.*

As Noah thought about that, Ann looked up at the eagle's nest. She waved and then calmly walked the rest of the way to the talc hill and went over to the other side. Noah thought, *what just happened? Ann couldn't possibly have known I'm here.*

As he tried to think it through, he started the task for which he had come to the nest. He looked at the conglomeration of items that sat on top of the flannel shirts. To make the nest more comfortable, the eagles had pulled out handfuls of down along with small white and dark brown feathers. He found sixteen talons, one of which was extremely weathered. *I think this might have been from the first eagle that lived in this nest.* He counted twenty-three wing feathers as well. "That's how old I am."

The eagles had also left three wood duck wings with all the feathers still attached, one equally intact kestrel wing, five duck skulls, one shrew skull, many fish and other unidentifiable bones, and six buttons pulled loose from the flannel shirts. Under the shirts, he felt more remains from the eagles' lives. Noah was about to move the shirts and look then thought, *some of these are so old. The eagles must have pulled them up from below. I'll only take what's on top of the shirts.*

Noah pulled his medicine bag out from under his shirts, put in the items he believed the eagles had left for him, then stood up in the nest, and held the pouch up into the sky. "Thunderbirds, I thank you for these gifts." To rejoin his family on Mother Earth, he tucked the bag between his wool and buckskin shirts and then climbed down the tree that stood high, but dead, in Father Sky.

Noah walked through the front door of the trading post. Six one-ounce-sized bags of blue flannel rested on the table. Ann spoke very serenely, "Hello, my husband. I'm glad you're home. What did you find up there?"

"You knew I was there? How did you know?" Noah didn't understand how she could have known.

"I didn't know. I thought you would probably want to go up there. You just told me that I was correct."

"I keep forgetting how clever you are. Are you mad at me?"

Ann told him what she honestly felt, "No. If you hadn't gone up there, you would have spent your life wondering. But I was worried."

Ann never ceased to amaze Noah. "I don't think I can tell you how much I love you." He walked to Ann. "Come here." He took her into his arms and held her close for the longest time. When he let her go, he said, "Let me show you what I have!"

"All right, I've also been curious about what's up there."

"Where is everybody? What are the blue flannel pouches?" Noah took his bag to the same table.

"Everybody else is in the barn loading the carts." Ann touched the little packages. "I stayed in here to make these. I'll tell you about them when everybody is back. Roscoe feels that we need to get everything ready. He thinks we need to go now. Maybe we shouldn't wait until after my birthday. It doesn't matter if we're here or not. Maybe we should go ahead and leave first thing in the morning."

"I want us to be here to celebrate the day God brought my beautiful wife into this world. Besides, what's one day?"

Noah took off his medicine bag. "Maybe I should get something to put under these things and not put them directly on the table. They aren't very clean."

"I'll get something." Ann quickly came back with a sheet.

Noah carefully laid out his treasures as he stated his thoughts, "These things were on top of the shirts. I didn't look at or take anything from below, but I could feel that there was a lot more under there. I got the idea that the things that were on top of the shirts were there for us to take, but not the rest. Some of these are ancient. The eagles had to have brought them up from below. That's why I think they wanted to give these specific things to us."

"May I touch them?" Ann asked.

"Of course. I think they were given to all of us."

"This talon looks very, very old." Ann picked it up.

"I know. I thought that it might be from the first eagle that lived there. I can tell that it's very old and these two feathers are as well." Noah handed them to Ann. "See the little holes in them where some bug has eaten them, or maybe the weather did it?"

"And six buttons. Those are crazy birds. It's so funny that they would do that. I hope you left the shirts undisturbed."

"I did. The shirts belong to the eagles now."

As Ann and Noah looked through everything that Noah had gathered from the eagle nest, the rest of the family came into their winter home.

Sally hurried over to look. "What do you have?"

Ann said, "My very brave husband climbed to the eagle's nest and got these."

Sally looked at one of the eagle claws.

"You can hold it." Noah handed the talon to Sally. The others took off their coats and came to the table. Sally carried the ancient talon with her as she went to hang up her coat.

"May we touch any of it?" Eli asked.

Noah replied, "Touch and pick up anything you want, but be careful." Noah scooted over so Sally could sit beside him. "We can divide everything between whoever wants any of it."

Roscoe walked toward the kitchen. "I only want one talon, a little bit of the eagle down, and one of the eagle wing feathers."

Noah told him, "You can have more."

"That's all I want, and I'm going to take apart another pair of buckskin pants to make myself a medicine bag. There will be buckskin left over. Stephanie, you can make yourself one too, and we can divide the rest of it between us."

Stephanie looked over the items. "I'm not sure I want to make one."

Sally asked, "Why not?"

Stephanie replied, "Maybe God wants us to stay purer."

"What does that mean?" Ann asked.

"I mean, not mix Indian things into our worship. No offense is intended to you, Noah."

Ann stopped looking at the bones and glared at Stephanie. "So, what is the proper format?"

Stephanie replied, "I've never been to a church. I don't know what the correct way is."

Ann stated her opinion, "Suit yourself, sister. We

180

believe that God is the creator and sustainer of everything. That Jesus is the incarnation of God in human form, born of the Virgin Mary. He lived a perfect life and then died to save us from the penalty of our sins. After Jesus had overcome death, God the Father resurrected him on the third day, and now Jesus sits at the right hand of God in Heaven and intercedes for us. Beyond that, what you wrap around it is your choice. You don't have to choose this way, but I do."

Stephanie asked her brother-in-law, "Is that what you believe, Noah?"

Noah assured her, "Completely!"

"Then, why aren't we having a church service on the Sabbath?"

Ann felt even more offended. "So now we have to have a church service, or we don't love God? We've never been to one in our entire lives."

Stephanie quoted the Bible, "Hebrew 10:25 says, 'Let us not give up the habit of meeting, as some are doing. Instead, let us encourage one another all the more since you see that the Day of the Lord is coming nearer.'"

Ann argued with her sister, "I don't think that means we have to have a church service. We meet and read the Bible every single day."

Eli decided to stay out of the conversation. *I should have talked with Stephanie before I made a medicine bag.*

Noah interjected, "I think Stephanie is right. We should have been having a service, and we have a chapel right here. I'm sorry we never did that. I wish you had brought this up long ago."

Stephanie looked at her brother-in-law for a trace that he wasn't sincere, but she didn't see one. "I'll think about making a medicine bag. I do want some of this because I know the eagles are connected to us."

Ann felt perturbed that Stephanie insinuated that Noah didn't love and worship God and that he was trying to corrupt them, but she didn't want to be upset. With no apparent reason for the conversation to have brought her to her gifts, Ann said, "This brings me to these blue flannel bags."

"What are they?" Sally inquired.

Ann opened one of the bags. "To me, this place is magic. I don't want to forget the cliffs that have surrounded us. I've felt safely protected in the womb of this mountain." She took out a small, sharp-edged stone. "This stone is from the talc pile we've walked over many times. It's the mountains."

Ann put it on the table and then took out a small smooth stone. "The river has been our provider. From it, we have received food in the form of ducks, geese, and fish. It carried Noah to the spirit world, so he could bring us a message from our parents. To me, and I think to Eli, that message altered my life. This stone I took from the river this morning. It's the river. The blue flannel is our family. All six of us joined here at Pine Bluff. I want you each to have one." Ann gave all five members of her family a little blue flannel bag pulled together by a thin blue ribbon threaded through holes at the top.

"Ann, that's so beautiful. I feel the same way. Thank you." Sally held hers to her heart.

Eli voiced his feelings, "Ma's message sent through Noah has changed me. It freed me from an immense sadness, and it will for my father as well. Thank you, Ann, this is a very thoughtful gift."

Roscoe added his appreciation, "I felt for many years that this place is the womb of the mountain. However, for the last several years, I've felt it was my prison. Thank you for resurrecting my belief in the goodness of this place and for counting me as a member of this family."

Stephanie felt contrite. "Thank you for reminding me that Noah's beliefs have been a gift to us. This little package will always remind me of what we received here. I found out that our father loved us, you and Sally know it as well, and Eli knows his mother is safely in Heaven. Thank you, Ann."

Noah held the little bag. With his thumb, he stroked the smooth stone through the cloth. "Ann, you being my wife is my greatest gift here below, and there's nothing I want more as I walk on Mother Earth. This gift further proves what a treasure you are.

"It's here where I received you and this whole family back again. The river was my gateway to cross into the spirit world. Death holds no fear for me. I am completely sure my God will take me when I die.

"When I watched you getting these stones from the river, I thought there was no possible justification for taking off your coat and repeatedly plunging your arm into the freezing river. Now I see that your reason was good. I know what you did to retrieve these stones, and it means even more to me. Thank you."

With her talent to take everybody, without offense, from one state of mind to another, Sally brought the conversation back to the eagle's treasures. "I want to decide what I want from this pile." She placed the ancient talon on the table. "This belongs to Noah."

"I agree." Ann pushed the claw over.

Sally continued, "I would like to have two talons, two eagle wing feathers, and for some reason, I want the shrew skull. Is it all right with everybody for me to have the skull?"

"It absolutely is all right. If the shrew skull has spoken to you, you should have it." Noah handed Sally the animal's head bone.

Before she picked anything, Stephanie asked, "Is there anything else you want?"

Sally appropriated the items she had named. "No."

Stephanie made her request, "Then I would like to have two talons. I want this duck skull and a bunch of these bones. I want to use duck bones to make a necklace, but I don't know which ones are duck bones, so I'll use whichever will fit together. May I take them all and give you back those I don't use?"

Noah gave his permission, "It's fine with me. Did you know that bird bones are hollow?"

"I didn't. That will help me find the duck bones,

and they'll be much easier to use than I thought. What about the rest of you, may I take all these bones?" Nobody opposed, so Stephanie took them all.

Eli asked, "Noah or Ann, either of you want to go next?"

Ann replied, "No."

"You're next, Eli." Noah wanted Eli to have the biggest selection possible.

"I also want two talons and two wing feathers from the eagles because the eagles have been part of our family, and I helped to save them too."

Noah assured Eli, "Yes, you did."

"Not like you did, Noah, but I pulled them onto the ice and over to the shore. The eagles took the shirts and gave you the feathers. I think they gave the buttons from the shirts back to me. It seems strange for them to do that. I have no idea why buttons matter, but somehow I think they do. I would also like twelve of these small feathers. Six of each color, so I have two for each button. I think I'm supposed to attach them to the outside of my medicine bag, but only if it doesn't upset my wonderful wife. And last, I want two duck wings for the two I shot before the eagles plunged from the sky into the river."

Noah turned to Ann. "My wife, you're next."

"Those eagles have been our sign that we're safe, but they've been gone for days. I think trouble is coming, and we need to get going. Saving those eagles almost took you from me. However, I believe it was God's design. He wanted you to go into His world. He knew He would send you back. He did not do that only to give you the gift of entering His domain, but He did it to heal me, really all of us. Those eagles crashed into the river because God told them to risk their lives for us. God knew we would save them. They were willing to do it, and so were we. I feel I should give something to them, not take from them. You keep the rest."

Noah held Ann's hands. "I want you to have some of it."

"Maybe someday, not now."

"If that's what you want, I'll carry the things they sent to you until you're ready to receive them."

"Thank you."

"I have something else for everybody." Noah went to his room and came back with six small pieces of cedar. "When I saw which arrowhead was on the arrow that got broken when Ann killed the elk, I realized that was the arrow I had made at your farm the night it burned down. I thought you would all like to have a piece." Noah handed each of them, including Roscoe, a portion of the arrow shaft he had smoothed at each end.

Roscoe took his piece. "Much obliged. Now, we all have a part of the Williams Farm. This is a special treasure."

"You're welcome, Roscoe. Which pair of buckskin pants were you going to cut up? Would it be all right for me to make some pouches for these items tonight?"

"I'll get it." Roscoe went to the store and got the largest pair of buckskin pants he had. He also got all the sinew, all the rawhide strings, and narrow rolls of red, white, yellow, black, blue, and green ribbons. "I want two rings from the top, this broad." He held up three fingers together. "Give me the bottom quarter of both pant legs. Split the rest as you see fit. If you cut it for us, I would appreciate it."

"I will. Thank you." Noah went into his room and got the sewing kit Roscoe had given to Ann.

"Sally, let's cook together." Roscoe went into the kitchen.

Noah cut the pants as instructed and put the parts Roscoe wanted to the side. Ann whispered into Noah's ear, "My love, I don't need any more buckskin right now. You use my share."

"Thank you. I love you too," Noah kissed her cheek. "The other three of you want some?"

Stephanie listed what she wanted. "I only want a piece big enough for these items. I'll keep the necklace in it after I make it. I also want to have some sinew, a length of each color of ribbon, and some of the rawhide strings."

Sally called out from the kitchen, "Same with me."

Noah asked, "Roscoe, do you want some for your things?"

"No, I'm going to be fine as is."

"What about you, Eli? If you want to work together, I can show you the best way to protect these objects."

"I'd love to. I appreciate that."

While the eagle's gifts lay spread over the other

table, they ate the dinner Roscoe and Sally prepared, which was elk, oats, corn, and coffee, again. After the meal, Ann used a needle to weave the ends of the hair from the soul bundle a long way back into the other end of the braid and made the hair into one very long continuous circle. She twisted it over once to make it a double necklace and put it on. "Goodnight, family." She kissed Noah on the cheek and went to their room. After Ann left, Roscoe went back into the kitchen to his cot for the night. The other four made containers for their eagle gifts.

Noah explained how to protect the wings, "It's best if you don't pull or push a wing or feather directly into or out of a bag or a pouch because one way or the other, you're pushing against the directions of the feathers. You take a piece of buckskin large enough to fit around your item and cut a rectangle out of each corner. Next, make the bottom and top flaps long enough to stay inside when folded over the wing or feather with the quill down into the bottom. Then, you fold the side flaps over. You can make a tie-down to keep it closed if you want. You can store wings from the same kind of bird together. It's best not to put different kinds together. Same with skulls, but it's usually better to wrap each one separately, so they don't break each other. You can put the talon directly into your medicine bag, or you can make a pouch."

Stephanie made a small bag. "I'm going to use a blue ribbon and a green ribbon that each pulls through to the opposite side because the bones came from the water, the sky, and the earth." Stephanie pushed her bag of bones across the table along with her blue flannel Pine Bluff pouch with her piece of the arrow inside. "Eli, may I put these in your bag? I'm ready to go to bed."

"I'll carry them for you. I'm not finished. I'm going to stay up."

Stephanie leaned over and placed a kiss on the side of Eli's neck. "I love you."

With the awl from her sewing kit, Sally punched holes around the top of a buckskin circle. "Because a shrew lives in the ground, and green is the color for Mother Earth, I'm going to use a green ribbon to tie it closed." Then, she punched holes close to the edge of the flaps of her feather-envelope. "For this, I'll use a blue ribbon because it's the color of the sky."

She placed the skull in its bag and the feather in its envelope. She put them, along with the blue flannel bag, the piece of the arrow shaft, and the talon, into her medicine bag. "Goodnight, brothers."

Sally took her medicine bag with her to the chapel. She had watched Ann work on her braid and had done the same with the hair she had taken from the soul bundle, but she had made a long braid, not a loop. She put it into her bag, crawled into her bed, and went to sleep, happy.

Noah said, "Let's talk about the trip."

"Good idea. I hope the journey won't be too hard on the women, Roscoe, or the animals."

"The snow is hard and sharp from melting and refreezing. We need to protect the animals' legs and feet from cutting and from the cold, and we shouldn't travel very long before we stop each day."

Eli cut a rectangle for his kestrel wing. "We could wrap their legs and the bottoms of their feet with a piece of a blanket, put some of the duck cloth we have left around that, and then tie it all on with rawhide."

"It may look strange, but ribbons would be softer than rawhide."

"The red ribbon is widest. The others may not be strong enough."

"All right, and we'll have to melt snow to get all the water we'll need. Can we add more weight?"

"We can melt snow in the two ten-gallon washtubs we've already packed. If we give them water each night and again in the morning, that should be enough for the animals to drink."

Noah stopped what he was doing. "The worst part is going to be getting through Little Rock."

"Maybe we should split into groups."

"I don't want to separate and take a chance of not being able to get together again. I don't want to lose any of you."

Eli replied, "After the rest of you are on the west side of town, I could try to find Melvin or Henry. It should be safe for me alone."

"Stephanie would never forgive me if something happened, and I wouldn't either."

"There's no reason I shouldn't be allowed in Little Rock."

"I don't want to take any chances. Let's see

what's going on when we get there. There's no sense in guessing."

Eli had all his eagle gifts protected, he was tired, and he wanted to lie next to the woman he loved. "Are you done?"

"Yes, I appreciate you staying up and talking this over with me."

"I've wanted to talk with you too, but I didn't want to upset the women."

"Smart man. I'll see you in the morning. Goodnight, brother." Noah tiptoed into the bedroom.

Ann thrashed on the bed and moaned, "No."

Noah called to her softly, "Ann, wake up." She continued to call out in distress.

"Wake up." Noah shook Ann's shoulder.

Ann opened her eyes. "Noah!" She sat up and threw her arms around his neck. "They found us and took you away again!"

"It was only a dream. I'm here with you." Noah held Ann as her body shook with fear. "I'm here."

"I need your love. I'm afraid this will be our last night together."

TWENTY ONE

In the very early hours of Ann's birthday, while everybody else slept, Roscoe woke. *This is the perfect time to make it.* He got out of his cot, closed the kitchen door, and stoked the fire in his stove.

Roscoe had saved an egg here and an egg there until he had enough for all of them. He cooked two sunny-side-up eggs for each of them, along with a pot of oatmeal devoid of flax seeds or currants or any other tasty addition. He wished he had something better, but he didn't.

Noah lay with Ann in his arms. "Do I smell eggs?"

Ann snuggled closer. Then she smelled the air. "I smell eggs too!"

Noah was never in a hurry to move away from Ann, but they were all hungry from stretching the food, and none of them wanted to eat another bowl of boiled oats. "Let's go see."

"I hope it is eggs." Ann jumped out of bed.

Ann must be as sick of oats as I am. Noah followed her and found Eli and Stephanie in the kitchen, talking with Roscoe.

They heard Sally in the chapel. "Is that eggs?"

With a smile on her face, Stephanie came out of the kitchen carrying two plates of eggs that looked like a bright, beautiful, sunny morning. Eli followed behind her with two more plates. Stephanie called out, "Sally, come to breakfast!"

Roscoe came into the room and put two more plates of eggs on the table. "Happy Birthday, Ann! Be right back." He went into the kitchen. To their dismay, he returned with a pot of oatmeal. "Two eggs aren't enough. You still have to eat some oatmeal."

"This is great!" Ann forced down her oatmeal, so she could savor the eggs and not ruin her enjoyment, knowing she still had to eat boiled oats.

Roscoe washed dishes with Sally. "I'm going to walk around outside and say goodbye. I don't want to stay here, but in many ways, I'm going to miss this place."

Sally asked, "May I come?"

"I'd like for you to come, but we shouldn't leave multiple sets of tracks."

They all loved the place. Sally wanted to go, but she knew he was right. Roscoe bundled up, put on snowshoes, and walked the canyon on top of the remaining three feet of snow.

Since it was Ann's day, Sally asked, "What do you want to do today, Ann?"

Ann couldn't think of anything. "We've got everything packed, and there's not anything to do, so let's do something we never do: nothing."

"I don't know how to do nothing," Sally replied.

Eli added, "Me neither."

"Today is our first lesson. However, since it's my birthday, I'm going to take a long, hot bath with lavender." Ann got a towel and a package of lavender flowers from the things to leave behind in the store.

The others sat beside the fire and looked into the flames. They talked about how much they liked Pine Bluff, about all the things they had done since they had arrived, and the beautiful mornings when the sun rose over the river.

Ann rejoined them smelling like a garden. Stephanie stood up. "I'm going to do the same."

"I thought some of you might want to take a bath. I left the water in the tub, and the lavender in there. You can add more, and there's a pot of boiling water on the stove."

A few hours later, everybody had taken a lavender bath except Roscoe. Roscoe opened the door and came in with the last three chickens as dead as a chicken with a wrung neck could be.

Roscoe looked nervous. "I'm going to cook your birthday meal now. The supply wagons have always been here days before now. Last night, the wind along the river cleared most of the snow off the road."

Sally was very bored with learning how to do nothing. "I'll help."

"Not this time. It's a surprise for everybody."

Disappointedly, Sally plopped back into the chair and went back to doing nothing. "All right."

Stephanie figured out something to do. "I'm going to check my pack."

Eli thought he had spent enough time engaging

in the day's assignment and decided he also needed to make sure everything was packed correctly. "I better do the same."

Everybody, except Roscoe, emptied their packs, made sure that they had what they were supposed to have, then repacked. Again, they sat by the fire and watched the flames. "I'm going to get a spool of red thread and another sewing kit. I'll work on my medicine bag." Ann went to the leave-behind-items.

Sally called out, "Bring me green thread."

Eli added, "Sewing kit and white, please."

Noah said, "Yellow."

In case they finished with one and wanted a different color, Ann brought a spool of each of the six colors and four sewing kits. They sewed designs on their bags while Stephanie, who still did not want a medicine bag, read the Bible aloud, and Roscoe cooked.

Roscoe finally called out, "Sit at the table and don't look!"

Sally sat at the table with her eyes closed. "I'm excited. I can't wait to see what Roscoe made."

They sat at the table and listened to Roscoe put things on the table. Stephanie said, "You know it's going to be chickens."

When everything was ready, Roscoe said, "Open your eyes!"

On the table sat bowls of stewed chicken in gravy, baked sweet potatoes, lima beans, a tin of butter, and a light, fluffy cake like the one Roscoe had made for Noah's birthday.

Ann exclaimed, "Oh, my word!"

With appreciation, Sally said, "I don't think I've ever seen a meal that looked so incredibly delicious, and there's no oats or corn!"

"Thank you, Roscoe. This is a wonderful surprise! I didn't know we had anything left." Ann went over and hugged Roscoe.

Like a wolf about to catch its prey, the saliva had built in their mouths. Eli tried to hurry things along, so he could get to the eating part. "Sit down, Roscoe. Let's say the blessing."

The aroma of the buttered lima beans filled Noah's nostrils. "Father God in Heaven, Creator and Provider of everything, Jesus, Your son, who came to live as a man on Mother Earth to be our example and redeemer, and Holy Spirit who lives in us to guide us and who takes our needs before the Father and the Son, we come before You to thank You for this meal. We know that all this flowed first from You. We are truly grateful for this meal and for Roscoe who planned and accomplished this marvelous feast. Bless this food to the nourishment of our bodies and us to Your service, in the name of Jesus, Amen."

Everybody said, "Amen," then scooped food onto his or her plate.

Noah put a ladle of lima beans on his plate and then passed them on. He savored a bite. "This is so good."

Sally already had a sweet potato on her plate when she took the beans from Noah.

Ann spooned out the chicken that had been

stewed until it was tender then covered in thick, savory gravy. She asked, "When did you make the cake?"

"I made it this morning. I was afraid everybody would smell it cooking even with the door closed. I guess closing the door worked because everybody smelled the eggs after I opened the door."

After they had crammed in every morsel of the delicious food, Roscoe picked up his knife and cut six slices of cake. Stephanie declined, "I'm so full my stomach hurts. I can't eat cake right now."

"Me neither. I loved the meal, but I'm stuffed. I have to lie down." Ann made sure she would still get her piece, "I'm going to eat my cake later. Don't take it away."

Sally echoed the feelings, "Me too."

Eli, Roscoe, and Noah ate their cake immediately. Noah didn't admit that the amount of food he had eaten had stretched his stomach to the limit or that he needed to lie down like the women. "I should stay with Ann on her birthday."

Roscoe and Eli also wanted to lie down, so they left the dishes on the table while everybody slept. Roscoe was the first awake. He cleaned up and took the rest of the cake into the kitchen, but left the three plates with the slices on the table.

Even though he wanted to go with his new family, Pine Bluff had been Roscoe's home for twenty years. He wanted to absorb all the memories he could. Since it was the last day he would be there to admire it, Roscoe looked out the window at the opening to the river. A few bumps grew up from the talc hill. *No, not today!* A minute later, he knew for sure. The resupply wagons had arrived. Frantically, but not loudly, he called out, "Wake up!" He knocked on the door to Ann and Noah's room, "Wake up!" then the wall of the store and the chapel, "Wake up! Everybody get up!

"What's wrong?" Noah asked from behind the door.

"They're here! Get into your traveling clothes, NOW! You'll have to go out the kitchen window. There's a duck cave in the cliff on the left where you can hide until they've gone. Look under the ledge as you go along. I'll keep them in the kitchen as long as I can, so you can get across the field. I can see that they're all coming, so there shouldn't be anybody over there to see you go out."

Inside the room, Noah and Ann got into their warm clothes. Noah asked, "How do you know about the duck cave?"

"I've lived here for twenty years, of course I know."

Sally walked into the room. "I'm not going into a cave."

Ann made the bed and removed any indication that anybody had been there. She spoke through the door, "You have to, Sally. I know it was terrible when you lost your lantern in the cave back home. In that cave, there was not a single speck of light, and it was very frightening, but this cave is not dark inside. It's a little cave, not an endless crack into the mountain. It's right on the surface, and there's a big opening in the back."

Sally's eyes grew large. "I'm not doing it. I can't." She rapidly sucked down deep breaths.

Stephanie told her forcefully, "Yes, you can!"

Eli pulled the feather mattresses out of the chapel toward the stack in the store where he had already placed his own.

Sally raised her hand to her throat. "I can't breathe."

Eli dropped the mattresses and caught Sally as she fainted. "She's not going to be able to go into the cave."

Ann shoved all the sewing materials into her medicine bag and turned to Roscoe, "I don't have time to put them back."

"That's fine. Just get them out of here." Roscoe pulled the chairs away from the fire and positioned them around the tables.

Noah and Ann took Sally's mattresses, pillows, and blankets to the store. Noah ordered, "Everybody, check in your area. Be sure you've got everything."

"What are we going to do about Sally?" Eli carried Sally to the hearth, sat, and held her unconscious body while Noah, Ann, and Stephanie searched for evidence. "Except the three pieces of cake on the table, everything will be gone when we leave with our packs."

Ann told them definitively, "We are not leaving without Sally."

Noah panicked, "Even if they don't know us,

they'll tell somebody about us, and then they'll surely come looking for us."

Ann offered, "I'll stay. Two women shouldn't raise any alarms."

Stephanie challenged the idea, "You think two young women with Roscoe wouldn't raise any curiosity?"

"You're right. It would. I retract the suggestion."

Eli still held Sally in his lap. "I'll stay with her. We're Roscoe's niece and nephew. We came to take him to live with our family."

Roscoe felt frantic. "You have to do that; she's unconscious. You have to go now, and that's a good idea."

Ann agreed, "I guess that would be best."

"I could stay." Stephanie leaned over and kissed Eli.

Eli rejected that option, "They'll think Ann and Noah ran away together and left us. I love you, and I want you around me always, but today, I want you to go without me."

"Thank you for taking care of Sally." Stephanie kissed Eli again.

"I also appreciate you looking after Sally." Ann picked up a plate as she went past the table. "I'm taking my birthday cake with me." Ann, Noah, and Stephanie climbed out the kitchen window. Roscoe passed them their packs and the three plates of cake then closed the window. Eli lay Sally in Ann's bed and then threw two mattresses back into the corner of the storeroom with a pillow and a blanket.

Ann, Stephanie, and Noah stuffed cake into their mouths with their fingers. Ann whispered, "This is superb," then heard the men step onto the front porch and knock on the door.

"Russell, you're finally here! Everybody come on in. Meet my family. You'll have to excuse my niece. You know how young girls are; always napping."

Eli saw Noah, Stephanie, and Ann in the field and quickly spoke the first name after his father's name that popped into his head, "I'm James. Pleased to meet you."

Roscoe thought quickly. "I've got a proposition for you. Come into the kitchen. I'll make coffee."

Russell followed Roscoe. The rest of the men stayed in the front room. Even though they were facing away from the window, Roscoe called out from the kitchen, "I need to talk this over with all of you!" When he had all the men safely contained in the kitchen, he shut the door.

"What's going on?" Russell asked.

"This has been a good business. You know how much I buy from you every year, but I've been here for a long time. I'm getting old, and I'm here alone, so I wrote to my brother and asked if I could live with him and his family. He sent his children to get me."

Russell probed, "Why would he send a young girl? That seems awfully dangerous."

"I guess I made it seem like I was ill and feeble in my letter. My brother thought I needed a woman to take care of me."

"So what do you want to talk to us about?" Russell asked.

After he had the men in the kitchen, it occurred to Roscoe that either Russell or his partner, Arnold, would be a worthy person to own the trading post. They would have the money to purchase it, and they would know how to run it. "I want you to buy the trading post."

Russell declined, "I've got my business delivering supplies."

Arnold immediately spoke up, "My girl told me if I don't marry her and settle down, she's moving on to somebody else. I could sell out my half of the business to buy this place. Then, I could get married and settle down without having to be a farmer."

"I've made a good amount of money selling hay. People depend on getting hay here, but I have never once plowed or planted. I've hired men to cut and bale it. I don't know if you'd call that farming or not."

"Nope, let's go look at what you have." Arnold walked to the door.

Roscoe knew he hadn't kept them in the kitchen long enough. He stood in front of the door. "You can't go out there."

"Why not?"

"Becaaaaaause, I have cake! You haven't had your coffee and cake!"

"I'm all for that. You make a good cake. Maybe you would give me the recipe for Marybelle." Arnold took the first slice Roscoe cut.

Roscoe passed cake to the men and explained his plan for the transfer of supplies and property. He insisted, "First, you need to look at everything in the storerooms."

Russell and Arnold were both curious because Roscoe had never allowed anybody to take supplies directly into the storerooms. They had always put everything on the tables in the front room.

Roscoe opened the first door. Arnold joked, "I always thought you were keeping bodies back here." Arnold looked into the clay containers on the shelves. "What's all this?"

"Plants."

"A lot of them are empty. What kind of plants?"

"They're spices, medicine, and things like that."

"I wouldn't know what to do with them. Take it all out of here, except standard spices like pepper and salt."

"I can't take more than we've already got packed." *How dull your food must be.* "Maybe Marybelle will know how to use them."

Arnold always looked for an opportunity to negotiate to his advantage, "Maybe we can trade for some of these supplies."

"What are you proposing?" Roscoe slowly opened the door to each of the storerooms that he had emptied to feed six people all winter.

Russell realized that Roscoe must have been rationing food while waiting on him. "I didn't know you cut it so close. I'm sorry we're late."

Arnold spoke up, "How about I give you one or two of the wagons as part of your payment? Then, we can go through everything and decide what's here that I'm buying and what you're taking. We'll use standard prices for the goods. How much do you want for the trading post, all the outbuildings, equipment, and the land?"

Roscoe stood in the storeroom and haggled over the price a long time before he opened the door to the room with the bathtub. Lavender lay scattered across the floor. *A bath is one of the things these girls love. It smelled like a garden when we were eating. I should have known.*

Arnold made fun, "Roscoe, I didn't know you like to smell pretty."

Nancy was the name of Roscoe's grandmother, who had raised him. Her name popped into his head. "I've told Nancy to clean up."

Roscoe had kept everybody in the kitchen, but he had no further way to stall. He hoped Noah, Ann, and Stephanie had made it out of the canyon. Roscoe opened the door and saw them on the far side of the talc barrier. He ambled through the door as their heads sunk out of view.

When the group of men came into the front room, Sally was conscious and wore a dress from his store. Roscoe assumed Eli had told her the plan and seen to getting her appropriately dressed.

"Nancy, I've told you to clean up any lavender you spill. If you don't, I won't let you use it. Go clean it up."

"Yes, Uncle, I was going to do it. I just didn't get to it yet. I'm sorry," she apologized and then left the room. Eli had told her why they had stayed in the trading post. She knew Eli's name was James. They had not known if Roscoe had told the men a name for her or not. Now, they knew her name was Nancy.

Eli, now James, thought about how to keep Sally, now Nancy, safe around so many men. He decided she should sleep in the bedroom. He made a big show of moving his mattress in front of her door. He hoped they would all get the message to stay away. When she got back, James told Nancy, "Be sure you take a chamber pot because nobody is going in or out this door after we go to bed for the night." James was going to keep Nancy safe with every ounce of his strength.

Roscoe told James and Nancy, "Arnold is going to buy the trading post. We've got to go through everything." He turned to Arnold and said, "James is a real sharp tack. He's going to help." Years ago, Roscoe had realized that Arnold would whirl things around so fast that he never knew what was what. Roscoe was very good at this himself, but he knew James was better at remembering, calculating, and deciphering than any of them. He also knew that James would be accurate and make sure they both got a fair deal.

"I'm glad to do so." They started to segregate and notated everything into Arnold's four lists.

List 1: Items Roscoe wanted to buy from Arnold, which they would move from Arnold's wagon to Roscoe's wagon and deduct the value from the amount due to Roscoe. Roscoe made the list. Arnold looked it over to verify that he had all the items.

List 2: Items Arnold would buy which they moved to a corner of the store as Arnold notated how many of each.

List 3: Items to trade like for like. None of them wanted to carry something out to the wagon and then take the same thing back to the trading post, so they recorded the type and quantity of each item and moved those items to a different corner of the store. Later, they would move the supplies directly from wagon to wagon.

List 4: Items Roscoe was removing from the trading post that they had not already packed.

James watched and corrected several mistakes. *A man in this business should be more accurate, and these are all in Arnold's favor.* He took over keeping the lists.

Russell and Arnold's men helped load everything that Roscoe wanted to take. Nancy strapped a load onto Redeemed. She called out, "Look what Redeemed is doing. Redeemed really is redeemed."

James loaded King's pack with a saddler toolset. *I'm glad we're bringing these. Now, we'll have the tools I need to work on the elk hide, harnesses, bridles, or other leather items.* He then filled up the cart harnessed to King with the personal blacksmith and carpenter tools that Roscoe had decided to take since they now had two covered Conestoga wagons.

Roscoe loaded Ace and then went back into the trading post. Everybody else hauled provisions to the wagon. James propped his cart against the back of the wagon.

Arnold took hold of the cart. "These carts belong to the trading post."

James replied, "Actually, I made them. They belong to me."

"I can't run this place without the carts."

As soon as Roscoe got the two big pots of ham and split pea soup cooking and the white potatoes baking, he took Ace to the wagons.

Nancy saw Roscoe coming over the rise and ran to him. "Arnold says the carts are staying with the trading post, but E, ahh, James doesn't want to let him have them because we made them."

"Arnold, I never said the carts were part of the deal. James and Nancy own the carts."

James stood in the wagon, holding the handles. Arnold stood on the ground holding the bucket of the cart. "I need the carts. These are the best I've ever seen, and I want them."

"Then you'll have to buy them from James. They don't belong to me."

Arnold had made owning the carts into a matter of honor, and all the men were watching intently. "How much do you want?"

James liked the compliment. Still, he wanted to keep the carts. *There's no way he's going to pay a ridiculously high price.* "Ten dollars apiece."

Arnold pulled out his bag and counted out forty dollars. James stood flabbergasted. *If he's going to give me that much, he's bought them. I'm not letting pride make me that stupid.* "I'm letting go." He released the cart handles and held out his hand for the money.

Arnold stated forcefully, "Men, take this cart to the barn."

All his men left with Arnold's new possession. James, Nancy, and Roscoe put Ace's pack and the items from the other cart into the wagon. James unhitched the cart and rolled it to its new owner. "Here you go."

"Thank you." Arnold pulled the cart up the hill then disappeared down the other side.

James looked toward the cave. "I should run over and tell them what's happening."

Nancy didn't want to take the risk of revealing Noah and her sisters. She felt awful that she had acted the way she had, and had fainted of all things. She wanted to make amends. "You might think they won't be back for a long time, but somebody might return too soon. Let's wait until tonight then I'll sneak over and tell them."

"You don't know where it is," James replied.

Nancy used the logic of which she was so good. "I assume it's where the ducks are always disappearing."

James countered, "It's dangerous for you out here alone at night."

"The eagles are back. They'll warn me."

James looked up. "That's them, all right. I've seen them so often and so close, I know them individually. See how far down the white feathers come? And look at the shape of the bottom edge on the big one."

Nancy added, "And she's rearranging the shirts. I'm not taking no for an answer. You'll be guarding my door the whole night. I'll climb out the window."

"When you put your mind to something, there's no way around it, is there?" Roscoe put his arm across Nancy's shoulder.

"Exactly, an eagle couldn't stare me down, and nobody is going to talk me down either."

Roscoe started back to the trading post. "I believe you."

The whole group ate ham, split pea soup, and potatoes. Arnold told Russell, "I'm going to leave somebody here while I go with Roscoe to Little Rock to complete the transaction."

Roscoe wanted to kick himself. *I'm going to have to ride to Little Rock with Nancy and James and leave Stephanie, Ann, and Noah to get there on their own. I sent our beautiful, lavender-smelling, birthday-girl into a smelly duck cave, and now I have to abandon them.*

Nancy also realized the problem. "Uncle Roscoe, I don't want to leave yet. Let's wait a few days before we go."

Arnold insisted, "I don't have time to wait around. We have to go in the morning."

James couldn't just leave his wife. "I don't want to ride with Arnold."

Arnold snapped, "Be a man, James, not a whiny baby! I bought those carts fair and square."

Actually, James didn't want to be around Arnold. However, he had a bigger concern. He had seen the way the men had looked Nancy over that afternoon, and he didn't want any of them to be around her. George buzzed around Nancy incessantly. "George is the best person to watch this place. He's smart enough to handle the trading post alone. What do you say, George?"

While everybody looked at George, Nancy

slipped a potato into her pocket. George thought it would be an honor to take care of the trading post. "Arnold, I'll take very good care of everything until you get back."

James stood up. He tapped on his tin cup. Everybody looked at him. "Congratulations to everybody…" James droned on.

Nancy slipped a tin of butter and one more potato into her pocket, but nothing else was close. Even though James had the men distracted, Nancy didn't get very much using that method of food gathering. After dinner, she saw an opportunity to access all the remaining food. "I'll take the pots and dishes to the kitchen and clean up while all of you finish packing."

Nancy's beautiful heart-shaped face and lips drew George like a fly to honey. "I'll help." That winter, Sally had transformed into a young woman who looked very different than she had the previous fall at Cadron Creek. During the mourning ceremony, she had cut her long, sun-bleached chestnut-colored hair. The short, curly hair that now framed her face was much darker and redder. The most significant change was the hourglass shape of a woman that she had acquired. All winter, Sally had worn the baggy trousers and shirts that had belonged to Harry. None of the family had noticed that she had changed. Now that she had on a dress, the fact that Nancy was a very attractive young lady came clearly to everybody's attention.

George and Nancy carried everything from the

table to the kitchen. Nancy had plans, and she couldn't care less about George. "Thank you, but cleaning is women's work." She sent him out and closed the door behind him. Nancy poured all the pea soup into her india rubber canteen and rolled up the remaining potatoes in a clean dishtowel.

By lantern light, the others continued to move items and record the transactions. When all the men went to the barn to divide the hay and oats, Nancy slipped the food into her bedroom.

Animal food filled one of Roscoe's wagons. His other held everything else he was taking.

Russell and Arnold argued insistently over how much of the supplies each of them owned. Late in the night, they reached an agreement.

Russell owned a wagon full of hay and oats not acquired at his expense, but his other wagons were much lighter, and two wagons no longer belonged to him, but Russell French became the sole owner of the resupply business.

Arnold Buzmann would own the fully stocked trading post when they transferred the deed in Little Rock. However, Arnold got to keep only enough hay for the four mules that would be his. Russell and Arnold wrote the document of transfer of ownership.

All the men slept in the trading post as Roscoe, Nancy, and James hoped. James lay on his mattresses in front of Nancy's bedroom door. Roscoe lay on his cot in the kitchen. All the other men slept on the floor because Arnold didn't want his mattresses to get dirty.

Nancy waited until she heard nothing but snoring before she rolled up a blanket and placed it against the bottom of the door. She slid out the window then shoved a large screwdriver under the bottom edge of the window, so she could pry the window open when she got back. Nancy ran across the field and over the hill. She climbed into the wagon and got their only buffalo hide. She wrapped it around her shoulders then hurried to the place she thought was the duck cave. She still was not going in, so she called into the entrance, "Ann? Stephanie? Noah?"

Inside three blankets and a tarp, Ann lay on the rock ledge with Stephanie and Noah. *Sally?* Ann pulled together her mind, groggy with sleep. "I dreamed that Sally was here."

Sally called again, "Ann? Stephanie?"

"I think she's outside," Stephanie whispered.

Ann was about to answer when Noah put his hand over her mouth. "It may be a trap. Don't say a word or make any noise." He slipped out the back then ran as fast as he could plow through the snow.

Sally didn't know why they didn't answer. She didn't know the depth of the tunnel, but she thought they should be able to hear her. She tried to look in, but it was pitch-black inside. She couldn't see anything. Sally pleaded, "Ann, Stephanie, Noah, do you hear me? I have to talk to you, and I have food."

Stephanie whispered, "It doesn't sound like a trap, and she's getting upset."

"Noah said, 'Don't do anything.'"

As if his hair was on fire, Noah charged down the hill through the snow. When he got to the snow-free road, he became a rushing wind all the way to the prominence. He stopped and peeked around the corner.

A buffalo calf walked away from him until it reached the end of the ledge of the towering stone cliff. It turned and came back toward him. Noah crept forward. *That buffalo looks like it has only two legs.* As a shadow cast by the half-moon, he slid along the cliff wall until he saw the details of the buffalo's body. *Those are human legs.* He realized a human body was wrapped in a buffalo hide. It reared up. Noah saw the creature's face. It leaned forward again and followed along the ledge.

Noah called, "Sally!" He ran to her.

Filled with relief, Sally held onto her brother-in-law. "Noah! Thank God. I didn't know what to do. I have to talk with you. I didn't know where you were or if I was at the right place. I've been looking forever, but I can only find the one hole. I was afraid I wouldn't find you."

"I'm sorry I caused you distress. I had to be sure you were alone."

Noah called into the cave, "It's safe. You can come out."

Ann pulled herself through the hole. She wrapped her arms around Noah and Sally. "Sally, I'm sorry I didn't come right out. Please forgive me."

"I'm sorry too. I caused this because I was afraid, and I fainted like a little child. I'll try not to be afraid."

Stephanie came out and joined the hug. "I'm also sorry."

"I brought you food." Sally stepped back and pulled out the canteen of soup, the potatoes, and the tin of butter then held out the buffalo skin. "I was afraid you'd freeze, so I brought you this."

Stephanie had been sleeping on the outside. All they had between them and the ledge was the tarp and the blankets. Not only was it cold, but it was also hard as a rock, literally. "Thank you. We need this!" She took it gratefully.

Ann opened the canteen and tasted the soup. "It's pea soup, and it's delicious." It wasn't very hot, so she took a big mouthful, swallowed the soup, and then chewed the ham pieces. Stephanie did the same before giving the soup to Noah. Sally related what had happened since they had climbed out of the kitchen window. "Roscoe sold Bacon's Trading Post to one of the men who came. Now, we have to ride to Little Rock with them to transfer ownership because Eli and I are pretending to be his nephew and niece, James and Nancy Bacon. The horrible part is that we don't have a way to take you."

Ann told her sister, "Don't worry. You and Eli go with them. We'll get there fine."

Stephanie felt upset. "Why didn't Eli come? Is he willing to let me walk to Little Rock without even talking to me?"

"Stephanie, Eli wanted to come, but I'm the one who is supposed to be in the room. He's sleeping in front of the door on a mattress to protect me and to give me time to come here and get back. It wouldn't have worked any other way. He feels horrible. He wanted to come, but I convinced him that it had to be me. He's extremely upset. He said he wouldn't have volunteered to stay if he had known you would have to walk to Little Rock without him. He told me that he was sorry if that hurt my feelings, but that you were his priority, and he didn't want to do anything that might allow harm to come to you. I told him I understood and that he hadn't hurt my feelings."

Stephanie was proud of Eli, sort of. He had found a way to protect Sally, and to send warmth, food, and a message. Stephanie wanted Sally to reassure Eli. She also wanted to reassure herself. "Tell Eli we'll be fine."

In his mind, Noah went over what they had and what they needed. "We need some items we don't have, and we have things we don't need."

"Bring what you don't want to take and come to the wagon. We're ready to leave in the morning. Everything is already divided and packed, so nobody is going to look at what's in there."

"I'll pass out our packs. Can you help us find snowshoes, a hatchet, rope, gunpowder, and wadding for the rifle and pistols, and some ammunition?"

"I know exactly where everything is."

They hurried to the wagon. Sally gathered the things they needed. Noah, Ann, and Stephanie removed everything from their packs except the ponchos, canteens, cooking sets, matches, and the green glass goggles.

Noah added a spyglass, a compass, fifty-foot of rope, a lot of dried elk meat, apricots, all twenty-one of Roscoe's survival food packs, ammunition, and powder.

Ann added a large three-point blanket, hatchet, spade, and a pistol.

Stephanie moved the first aid kit to her pack and then put in another tarp with its ropes, but left the poles in the wagon.

They also got three sets of snowshoes. Back in the cave, they had Noah's rifle, knife, bow and arrows, a tarp with poles, ropes and pegs, and the three small blankets and pillows.

Once they had everything repacked, Noah said, "We're set now, and you need to get back. You've been away far too long. Thank you for the food, for telling us what's happening, and for helping us get the right supplies."

Sally hugged her family. "All three of us love all three of you, all the way to the moon and back, and we're sorry about this. We'll meet you at the Oakland Cemetery shed."

Ann looked Sally in the eyes. "You do understand how much I love you and that nothing you do or don't do will ever change that, right?"

"I'm still sorry, but thank you."

Stephanie added, "Tell Eli that I love him."

Noah knew Eli would be extremely upset about this turn of events, so he sent a message, "Tell Eli he brought my wife and family safely to me, and I'll bring his wife and family safely to him."

"Get going." Ann shooed Sally toward the talc hill.

Over her shoulder, Sally called back, "I love you."

Sally hurried to the trading post. As Nancy, she arrived at the window, pried it open, and pulled herself in not long before the sun peeked over the horizon. She slipped under the covers and fell asleep. All night, Eli had lain awake and worried. Worried about Stephanie traveling without him, worried about not being able to tell her he was sorry, worried about Nancy being out in the night alone, worried about Nancy getting back in time, and about everything else. When he finally heard Nancy in the room, he breathed a sigh of relief, thanked God, and fell asleep.

When Noah, Ann, and Stephanie arrived back at the duck hole, Ann expressed her displeasure, "I don't want to slide through that mess again."

"You can go the long way around with me. I have to do something about the track I made coming out."

Stephanie felt too tired to care. "I don't think adding another layer of duck poop to my coat will make a difference."

"I guess you're right. I'll go in here."

"I need the buffalo hide to wipe out my tracks."

Stephanie handed Noah the hide then went in. Ann passed in the packs and then also went in through the hole. They took off their nasty coats and reconfigured the sleeping area with the new blankets.

Far into the pines, Noah knocked the snow into his tracks and rubbed the hide across the top to smooth it out. It was not a very good concealment, but he figured nobody would be looking, so it would be good enough. When he thought he had erased the trail far enough that nobody on the road could see it, he walked the rest of the way without bothering. The girls stood up to put the hide down then all three wrapped up together, nice and warm in all the blankets.

TWENTY TWO

Roscoe woke early and slid several loaves of bread into the oven. He heard Nancy climb in the window and did something he'd never done before. *God, if You are there and You helped her, thank You. Help Noah, Ann, and Stephanie get to Little Rock safely. Bring us all back together.* While everybody slept, Roscoe removed a brick from the back of the kitchen stove at the floor. He reached into the hole and pulled out a bag.

Inside the pouch, he had twenty years of profits and a ring. Roscoe didn't make a profit every year, especially early on. However, on this day, as he ended his life as the owner of Bacon's Trading Post, he had seven thousand, seven hundred and fifty dollars in the bag. He decided not to tell Arnold about the hiding place. If Arnold knew there was a secret hiding place, he would realize Roscoe had more than the money in the strongbox. Roscoe didn't think Arnold would try to steal from him, but anybody who did want to rob him would only know about his money box.

Roscoe took out the ring. *Maybe I'll give it to Sally; though not as an engagement ring like Margret.* He thought about the girl who he had wanted to wear the ring back when he had been Sally's age. She was the reason he had never had a family. As much as he had tried, he had never been able to make himself completely want a family without her. That was why he understood Sally. The woman he had loved had been five years older than him. She had always wanted Roscoe around and been nice to him, until the end. She had frequently come to the farm and gotten him to go riding, or walking in the meadow, or whatever it was that she had wanted to do that day. He thought she felt the same way he did, and he had the ring that had been given to him when his mother died. He had never met the woman who had given birth to him. He felt that his granny was his real mother, but his birth mother had left him the ring. He had it in his pocket the day he turned fifteen. That was the day he had asked Margret to marry him.

She had laughed at him. "Roscoe, you're a child. You don't even know what love is." She never came for him again, but she was wrong about him not knowing what love was. He had loved her. As he looked back on it, he realized that she was the one who hadn't known about love. He put the emerald ring back into the pouch then pushed the bag to the bottom of his satchel of necessaries. *I'll make sure I'm the only person who carries this satchel when we leave in the morning.*

The aroma of baking bread floated out of the kitchen into the nostrils of the men in the front room. The smell opened their eyes. Sally and Eli, now known as Nancy and James, had only been asleep half of an hour, but the aroma also brought them back into the world of the conscious. Roscoe took the freshly baked bread from the oven then fried eggs to go with the bacon and the stewed apples that he had already cooked. He put out butter and honey, along with hot coffee. Roscoe was doing what he liked, and to make it even better; he was cooking with Arnold's ingredients. After the meal, he took the dishes to the kitchen for the last time.

Nancy offered, "I'll help." The eggs and apples were gone, but there was still quite a lot of fried bacon, which she wrapped in a clean dishtowel. "I'll eat this later as a snack." Then, she put loaves of bread into a duck cloth bag until it was full. There was still a loaf and a half left. She got another duck cloth bag, dropped in those last two pieces of bread, and placed the bacon in on top. Loudly, she told Roscoe, "I love coffee. I hate to pour it out. Plus, the warm container under my clothes will feel wonderful when we're out in the cold." She poured the remaining coffee into her canteen.

Nancy watched Roscoe lovingly caress the dishes with the dishtowel and then stack them away. She thought, *maybe Roscoe will miss this place less if he has his familiar pots and pans around him.* "Why don't you tell Arnold that you're taking all your cookware?"

Roscoe's face lit up. "That would weigh a ton, but I'll take a few things!" He placed on the counter: all the cooking utensils, his favorite coffee pot, and the dinged up tin coffee cup in which he'd drunk his coffee every day since the first day he had arrived there and had taken it off the shelf in pristine condition. He also decided he would take his favorite Dutch oven.

Roscoe called into the front room, "Arnold, I'm taking some of the kitchen items. You and James come write it down. We'll adjust the final amount."

As he retrieved more paper and another pencil, James carefully and premeditatedly placed his Bible on the shelf in the store. Arnold followed James to the kitchen to record the inventory Roscoe planned to remove. Arnold looked at the counter. "It's going to take a long time to notate everything. Do you need to take so much?"

"I'm used to cooking with all of it. I don't want to always be thinking that I wish I had brought some thingamajigger or do-hickey."

James notated the items on list four. "It's going to be too heavy to carry the satchel to the wagon. Arnold, may we borrow a cart to take these to the wagon?"

Arnold was not giving Roscoe anything. "Not yet. We haven't figured out the cost of all this."

Roscoe placed the last spatula and knife from the kitchen drawer into his bag. "We've got the list. We can negotiate as we go. James, get a cart."

James quickly returned to the kitchen. Roscoe put the bag with all the kitchen utensils into the cart and then rolled it to the front room where they added their personal bags and packs. Due to Roscoe's kitchen items, nobody noticed the weight of Roscoe's money in his bag of necessaries.

After everybody had exited Bacon's Trading Post, James glanced at his Bible to verify that it was still in the store and then pulled the door closed. Nancy hitched the cart to Redeemed. Roscoe, James, and Nancy led all twenty-five of their animals on their last trip across the canyon.

Roscoe put the bag of utensils and his satchel with the money into the wagon before he climbed in. "Pass me the rest of our things." They handed Roscoe the last of their possessions, along with the breakfast items that Nancy had packed, and then took the cart back to Arnold. While nobody was looking, Roscoe carefully packed his money out of sight but put the cooking items in clear view. He noticed that the buffalo hide was gone, as well as three sets of snowshoes. *I better leave the food sack and canteen of coffee at the very back of the wagon.*

Arnold instructed George, "Put the cart in the barn. Take what you need out of the store, but keep a record, and get everything properly organized."

Everybody else mounted a wagon or prepared to walk, except James. He sat on Eyanosa beside Russell's wagon. Russell flicked the whip on the rump of his lead mule. "Forward, ho."

Nancy looked toward the trading post. "Goodbye, Pine Bluff." Roscoe chose not to look. He had said goodbye the day before.

Five minutes beyond the back entrance into the duck cave, Eli exclaimed, "Oh no! I forgot my Bible. I have to go back to get it."

Russell frowned. "We're not waiting. You'll find us on the road when you catch up."

Nancy knew James would find a way to say goodbye to Stephanie. She had packed breakfast for

James to take to those in the duck cave, and she piloted her wagon at the back end of the caravan. She spoke softly as James slowly passed. "James, sneak out the bag of food and the canteen of coffee at the back of the wagon. Bring back the containers."

James made a symbol of a heart with his fingers in front of his real heart. He rode to the rear, snatched the food bags that Roscoe had made easily accessible, quickly put them in front of him in his lap, and urged Eyanosa into a run.

When James got to the slope up to the duck cave, he veered into the pines. He jumped off Eyanosa. "It's Eli, don't shoot me." He raised the door of vines.

Eli hurried to Stephanie. She flew across the cave. "You came!"

"I couldn't leave without seeing you." Eli held Stephanie in his arms. "I'm" -kiss- "sorry." -kiss-"I don't" -kiss- "want to" -kiss- "go with the wagons" -kiss- "while you trek" -kiss- "through the snow." -kiss- "I'm very sorry."-kiss- "Don't be mad at me." -kiss- "Forgive me" -kiss- "please." -kiss-

Eli was the man Stephanie thought he was. She would walk through the snow all the way to the moon and back to be with him. "Now that you've come to see me, it's all right."

Eli handed over the bags. "This is for you."

Ann took a swallow. "Coffee. It's still warm!"

Noah looked into the bag. "Bacon and bread. How did you get away from the others?"

"I left the Bible in the store, so I'd have to come back for it. I can't take too long." Eli continued to hold

Stephanie. "I love you very, very much. You know that, don't you?"

"Now that you came, I'm sure of it. I love you so much too. Do you know it?" Stephanie held Eli tight and cherished the minutes she would get to hold him.

"Yes." Eli kissed her again. "I'm worried about you."

"Did Sally give you my message?" Noah asked.

"We never had a chance to be alone."

"I'll bring your wife and family safely to you like you brought my wife and family safely to me." Noah held up the vines and brought Eyanosa into the cave.

"Thank you, Noah! I believe you." Eli appreciated Noah reminding him about that. He didn't feel quite so horrible.

Noah rubbed Eyanosa's neck. "Be a good fellow for Eli. I'll see you again in a few days." Noah scratched Eyanosa behind the ears.

"I'm going through the duck hole, and I'll come back through going the other way. That will save me thirty minutes. Wait for me to come back. Please?"

"We will, darling. Wear my coat to go through the hole." Stephanie was not going anywhere if Eli was coming back. Eli kissed her again, took off his coat, put on his wife's coat, wrapped his own inside, and slid out the hole. When he got to the other side, he removed the coat that was completely covered in filth and laid it in the hole. He put his coat back on and dashed at top speed to the trading post.

Noah put the whole loaf of bread into his pack to take with them. They opened up the tin of butter that

Sally had given them the night before, broke the half loaf into three pieces, and put one on each plate, along with a third of the bacon. Ann scraped some of her bacon back onto Noah's plate. "You need more than I do, my love."

James knocked on the trading post door. George stopped moving the goods stacked on the table, the floor, in the corners, and everywhere else. He opened the door.

James swept past him, "Forgot my Bible." He snatched the book and dashed past George on his way out, "Can't stay. Good luck to you and Arnold."

As James raced across the field, George hollered, "Thank you!"

This was important to him. James ran the same way as he had when he had fetched dry clothes for Noah. Every minute he saved during the trip, he could spend with the woman he loved. James made the hour-long walking trip from the duck cave to the trading post door and back to the cave in half the time. He put the soiled coat over his clean coat. Then, because he did not want them to be startled, he spoke as he crawled into the cave, "I'm back!"

Stephanie told him, "Eli, we've been calculating while you've been gone. We think you can stay forty minutes if you want to."

"I was also calculating. I saved fifteen minutes by going through this cave both ways, and because I ran so fast, I saved thirty minutes crossing the canyon and back. I raced here on Eyanosa, and I'll make up time going back, so I can stay an hour if you let me. I don't want to leave sooner, but I won't hold you up if it will keep you from getting to a safe place for the night."

Noah assured Eli, "I'll find us a safe place. Don't worry about that."

So that Stephanie could lean against him, and he could keep his arms around her, Eli sat on the bedding behind her. The four of them talked about what to do to safely sneak through Little Rock and give Roscoe enough time to complete the sale of Bacon's Trading Post. The hour passed too quickly. Eli looked at his pocket watch to be sure he stayed every minute he could. He put the empty food bag and canteen inside his coat and then led Eyanosa out of the cave.

Stephanie walked out with him. "Thank you for coming to see me, my darling. I love you, and don't worry; we'll be fine."

"I love you too. There's nothing more important to me than you. Come to me safely in Little Rock." Eli kissed his wife properly and passionately then rode down the hill. He called back, "I love you all!" Stephanie stood outside until he was out of view and then went back into the cave. Noah held out Stephanie's pack. "Ready?"

Stephanie hugged Noah. "Yes, I so appreciate you staying here this long." She let him help her put on the pack.

Ann told her, "We all wanted to be with Eli."

"Fill your canteens with clean snow then put it between your wool clothes and coat. We'll add to it as we go."

When they started up the hill through the pine forest, it was ten in the morning, and the sun glared off the snow. Noah stopped. "We need to put on the goggles. I'll get yours out of your packs then you get mine."

Ann put on her goggles. "The world is green! We're going to walk in a green forest, under a green sky, on top of green snow."

Stephanie took hers. "But we'll be able to see."

Noah looked at his wife. Not only her eyes but also her skin was the color of the forest. "And move at a fast pace."

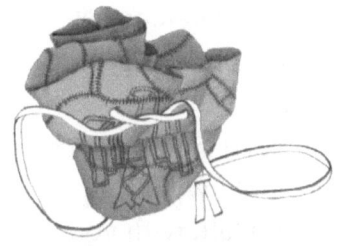

TWENTY THREE

When they stopped for dinner, Nancy brought the bread. Russell and Arnold brought ham, cheese, and mustard. William, one of Russell's men, sidled up to Nancy. "Hello, I'm Will. I thought you might like an orange."

"I'd love one." Nancy accepted the orange and then asked, "May I have six?"

"Sure." Will left to buy more oranges.

James told Nancy, "Don't encourage him."

"I'm not encouraging him. I just want to get some for all of us."

"Nancy, listen to me. I know how men think. He's going to believe you're giving him permission to go after what he wants."

"I think you're wrong. Melvin never acted that way. You didn't behave that way with Stephanie, and Noah didn't with Ann."

"Don't think we didn't want to because we did and besides that, we had a different set of circumstances."

Will came back. "Here you go." He hung around and talked about himself. James glared at him and hoped he would get the message to leave his sister alone. When they were about to move out, Will said, "I don't have to drive the wagon anymore today. I could ride with you."

Nancy brushed him off. "Thank you for offering your company, but I want to speak with my brother."

"All right, I'll talk with you later."

Once the caravan was underway, James told Nancy, "Tell Will you are not interested."

She replied, "He gave me oranges. I don't want to be mean, and I don't want to hurt his feelings."

When they stopped for the night, Nancy and Roscoe fixed the evening meal for everybody. Once again, Will sat beside Nancy and talked. Nancy said, "Umm Humm," repeatedly.

"This is real nice, Nancy." Will scarfed down supper.

Nancy replied, "Much obliged," but she was sick of Will following her around. "I'm going to bed. Good night." She went to her tent, wrapped up in her blankets, and then heard somebody come in. Roscoe usually went to bed early. "Roscoe, you turning in too?"

"It's me. I got your message to meet you in the tent." Will slipped inside.

Nancy scrunched into the corner. "I did not give you a message to come here. Get out this minute!"

"You don't have to pretend. I don't have any problem with you wanting to be together."

"If you don't leave now, I'm going to scream, and then you'll be in trouble."

James didn't see Will. He went to the wagon and

got a pistol. As he hastened to the tent, he heard his sister tell somebody to leave. He ducked into the tent and had the gun pointed in the right direction immediately. "Will, if you don't want to die, get out of this tent now, and leave my sister alone. Don't talk to her or even look at her ever again. Do you understand?"

"And take these back!" Nancy pitched the oranges across the tent.

Will wasn't sure if James would shoot him, but he figured there was no reason to find out. He got away as fast as he could.

Nancy begged, "James, stay in here. I'm afraid he'll come back."

James picked up the oranges and gave them to Nancy. He wrapped up in his blanket at the tent door with his pistol in easy reach.

Nancy contritely said, "I guess you're going to tell me that you warned me."

"You already understand that the oranges wouldn't have been worth what may have happened. Good night, sister."

TWENTY FOUR

In the forest, the rest of the family walked until the sun shone through the trees not far above the horizon. Noah knew it would take some time to set up. "Let's stop here."

Stephanie pointed out what she thought was a problem. "We don't have any wood or a place to make a fire."

"We can put the food packs in a pot with water. In the morning, it will be ready to eat. Tonight, we eat elk and apricots."

They dug to ground level then laid an india rubber canvas on the ground inside the hole and up the walls of snow. On top of that tarp, they joined the tin poles and made a long triangular frame. With the rope through the grommets, they drew the bottom tarp around the structure to the upper pole then laid the other tarp over the top and pulled it down over the outside. The tent was shut at the back but rigged to open or close at the other end. They climbed out through the small opening they had left at the front and examined the structure. The tent rose a foot too high, so they scooped snow on top and hid it.

Inside the tube in the snow, with their packs stacked at the far end, Noah sat on the buffalo hide. "How much water do you have?"

"I drank most of mine." Ann pulled her flat canteen out of her coat.

Stephanie did the same. "I don't have much either." They used every bit of Noah's liquid water to pour into the pot with three packs of the dried rice, chicken, and vegetable mix. Noah packed snow into the empty canteens and the other two pots to melt overnight. The three of them wrapped up together with the buffalo hide under them and the blankets around them. They barely fit, but they were warm, invisible, and protected.

Noah prayed with Ann every night, so he did the same this night. "Holy Heavenly Father, I ask that You give us eyes to see, ears to hear, minds to understand, and hearts willing to do whatever You ask. May everything we do, bring You glory and honor. I thank You for getting us safely to this place. While we sleep, watch over all our loved ones as well as us. Bring us all safely back together. I pray in the name of Jesus. Amen."

Both girls said, "Amen."

Stephanie thought, *maybe Noah does worship the real God.* Still, ever since Noah had performed an Indian ritual, she had her doubts.

The dim light of morning woke Noah. He opened his eyes and saw his beautiful wife lying in his arms, as well as Stephanie, snuggled up to Ann's back. His arm lay across both of them. Ann's lower hand lay inside his between them. He felt content. With him, he had the person most important to him in this world and a sister-in-law whom he loved, and he would be with the rest of the family in Little Rock in a few days. *Soon we'll be on our way to Harmony. I hope Tom will come with us. I think he will. Thank You, God, for letting me keep this family.*

Noah assumed the sun had just risen, so he let Ann and Stephanie continue to sleep while he thought about the fascinating green eyes that lay behind the eyelids he was admiring. Ten minutes later, the light still barely filtered into the tent. Noah thought the light was unusual. He woke the women, so they could leave early.

Stephanie removed the lid from the pot. "The food is completely rehydrated, and we did it without a fire."

Ann leaned back toward the packs. "I'll get our forks." They ate the survival rations directly from the pot and drank the water that their body heat had melted while they slept.

"Let me have the pot." Noah poured a small amount of water into the empty pot to rinse it and the forks. He drank the water out of the pot, performed the same procedure again, wiped dry the pots and their forks, and then repacked. Noah untied the front flap and pushed. It didn't budge. He pulled it in and discovered a wall of white. "We're buried."

Ann asked, "How did that happen? It hasn't snowed for weeks."

"I thought it seemed too dim in here." Noah offered the probable alternatives, "It must have snowed, or the wind blew it." *It is possible that somebody buried us, but I doubt that happened.*

234

Stephanie pushed against the top of the india rubber triangle they had slept in. "There's quite a bit of resistance. Can you get us out?"

Noah felt no fear. "Light is filtering in. We aren't deep. Let's untie the inside tarp."

After they took apart the bottom of the frame, the girls packed the poles, connectors, and canvas into Noah's pack. Noah untied and packed the rope. "You two stay as far back as you can get." The girls crouched beside the packs. Noah looked at them. "Ready?" They nodded. With one quick jerk, he pulled the tarp down, back, and up again. The snow above fell into the hollow beneath and opened the way out.

"It must have snowed after we went to sleep." Noah pushed the snow out of the way then saw two beautiful faces peek out from behind the flap of canvas. "Hand me the packs." Ann pushed the packs out. As falling snow came into the space previously occupied by their shelter, they took apart and loaded the rest of the tent.

Noah stood up. The wind whipped tiny snow knives into his cheeks. He squatted down out of the onslaught. "It's bad out there, but we'd be buried in no time if we stay here. Do you have on all your clothes and socks?"

Ann replied, "I have on my cotton, wool, and buckskin clothes, and my blanket inserts, and also my mukluks."

"I do too," Stephanie answered.

"Put on both your coats. Pull all the shirt collars

up over your necks and make sure you have the wool liners in your gloves. Keep your ear flops down. Put on your goggles and then pull your hood up. Tie your scarves around your hood, neck, and face, so only your goggles are exposed."

As the three of them covered up, Noah issued more instructions, "We can't open up once we get out there. Cram as much snow as you can fit into your canteens then tuck them under your outer coat."

Noah put the packs on the surface then knelt with one leg up. The women used his leg and stepped out. They pulled Noah up, strapped on their snowshoes, and hoisted their packs. For the second time, they left much later than they had planned.

Noah found something good about the weather. "The snow and wind covered all our previous tracks, and our new ones will be erased as we go." Since the dense pine forest reined in the wind, they traveled unaware of the strength of the approaching storm.

TWENTY FIVE

On the road by the river, the people in the wagon train woke. James made his way through the falling snow to the fire. He buckled on the gun belt, slid the gun into the holster, and made sure that Will saw him putting on his sister-protecting attire.

Arnold asked James, "You expecting Indians or something?"

"Something, yeah." James left to help Roscoe and Nancy melt snow for their animals. The wind barreling off the river did not let them put out hay. In addition, the animals needed heavier food to pull the wagons in the cold, so breakfast consisted of oats.

Will stayed far away from Nancy on the other side of the camp. Even so, she practically walked in James' shoes with him as they covered their animals with mule blankets. As the wagon train moved out, James climbed into the driver's box beside his sister.

The bitterly cold wind flung miniature ice daggers into their flesh and through the thick fur of the animals. Nancy scurried into the wagon and put on all her clothes before she went back to the driver's seat. While Roscoe bundled up, James related the idea he and Noah had when they thought they would be plowing through the forest in three feet of snow. "Noah and I had planned to cut up blankets and wrap the legs of the animals. I think we should do that. I see blood on their legs."

"And the snow has cut my face as well." Roscoe came out of the wagon. "Go tell Russell."

James ran to the front of the wagon train. "We're stopping to protect our animals better."

"All right, we'll have our midday meal now." Out of the howling wind, Russell and his men ate inside their wagons.

Instead of eating, James and Roscoe picked up the goats and put them into the hay wagon. Nancy stood beside them. *I don't think Ann, Stephanie, and Noah can survive in the open, especially if this storm gets worse.* Nancy assumed James felt frantic. "God will keep her safe. He'll keep them all safe."

The concern did threaten to overwhelm him. Eli reached out, "Stephanie, Ann, and Noah are somewhere in this storm, and they don't have a wagon or a tent. God, You know what they need. Keep them safe and bring us back together. Also, keep all of us who are here safe and our animals as well." He looked into Nancy's eyes. "I don't know what I'd do if they don't make it. Noah better do what he promised. He better get them safely to Little Rock."

The Bacons cut up blankets to make hoods to cover the heads and necks of their animals and also wrapped their legs and feet. Nancy climbed out of the wagon with two rolls of red ribbon. "This is all I can find."

Arnold looked at Roscoe, his nephew, and his niece wrapping their animals with red ribbons. He and the rest of his men laughed. "What are you trying to do, decorate your mules? They're designed to live outside, you know."

"Not in a storm like this." Nancy pushed Eyanosa's ears inside its hood.

James spoke up, "Look at your mules. Their legs are bleeding. You need to protect them."

"They'll be fine. Mules are tough. You're coddling your animals and you're wasting time and blankets you could sell."

Roscoe, James, and Nancy ignored him and continued to lash on the heavy wool coverings. Arnold, Russell, and their men left without them. Over the hoods of all the animals out in the weather, Roscoe put on bridles with the blinders attached. When they were ready, only the actual eyeballs were exposed but shielded at both sides.

TWENTY SIX

In the forest, the pines that had protected Noah, Ann, and Stephanie had given way to the bare shagbark hickories and white oaks that did not impede the wind. The storm swept away their shallow tracks almost as fast as their feet left them. Ann barely saw anything through the thick blowing snow that bounced off her goggles. She looked down at her feet as she walked then glanced up to remain oriented on Noah. He was gone.

Ann screamed into the howling wind, "Noah! I can't see you!" She looked back. She could barely make out Stephanie. "We have to hold hands."

As loud as they could, Ann and Stephanie hollered, "Noah!"

Ann stopped. "We don't know if we're going the right way. Noah's tracks are gone." Ann positioned her snowshoes between Stephanie's feet. They wrapped their arms around each other. "Noah, find us!"

Stephanie asked, "What are we going to do?"

Ann heard the fear in her sister's voice. She felt the same fear. *Father in Heaven, we'll die out here alone. Send Noah back to us.* Ann remained brave for Stephanie. "We stand still. Noah has to be looking for us. If we're all moving around, we'll never come together. Keep calling."

Noah looked back. He didn't see Ann or Stephanie. "Ann!" He listened for a reply. All he heard was the wind screaming past his ears. He retraced his steps until his tracks were gone then walked in a straight line away from his last step. "Ann! Stephanie!" *How could I have let this happen? I promised Eli, Chris, and Emma that I would protect them. I can't lose them again.* He hollered and hollered, "Ann! Stephanie!" No matter which way he looked, all Noah saw was a whirlwind of green snow. He reached out to the One who knew where Ann and Stephanie were in the ferocious storm. *God, there is no way I can find them in this blizzard. Help me.*

Stephanie held on to Ann, "The wind is going to knock us over."

"Put one foot back, lean into me, and keep calling for Noah." The girls braced against each other and screamed at the top of their lungs.

The shifting wind whispered Noah's name. He followed the ghostly voice along a twisting path through the blizzard. Soon, Noah had no idea which way he faced or had already been. *God, don't destroy Ann or Stephanie to take out vengeance against me. I know I've been arrogant. I acknowledge that I can't do anything without You. Please let me find them and a safe place.*

Through a thinning in the raging snow, Noah saw a vague darker shape like a short wide pine tree. Confusion came when his name was called to him from a different direction. Suddenly, a blast of wind evaporated the ghostly figure.

The girls slammed to the ground. Their

snowshoes tangled with Stephanie's leg. Tears started to well up in her eyes. "We're going to die."

Ann commanded her sister, "Don't cry. Tears will freeze your face. Get on your feet!" Ann stood and pulled Stephanie back to her feet. "You are not allowed to cry! Be brave! Holler!"

Noah tried to press toward the vanished ghost. The storm blew hard against him. He couldn't force himself even a single step forward. *God, take the wind away and let me move.* Before the image blasted away, Noah again saw what looked like people holding each other. The thought, *crawl*, grew in Noah's mind. He strapped one snowshoe to a hand and the other to his opposite knee. He inched forward on all fours.

Stephanie saw something creeping up on them. "It's a wolf!"

Maybe I can get my pistol fast enough. Ann dropped her pack off her back. She pulled out the gun, drew back the hammer, and turned. Buffeted by the blizzard, she fired. The animal made a strange maneuver with its feet. "Oh, no, I think I missed!" Ann tried to see what the wolf was doing. *That can't be a wolf. It has a huge hump on its back.* "You found us!"

Noah stood up. Ann let the tempest blow her into his arms. She asked, "Are you shot?"

Stephanie joined them a second later. "Thank God you found us!"

"And that Ann missed. I should have kept better watch. I'm so sorry."

Ann pressed Noah closer. "We didn't keep our eyes on you either."

Stephanie yelled, "How did you find us?"

"It was God. Get the rope." Noah turned so they could untie the rope. *There's no way I'm going to lose them again.* He tied all three of them to the same rope.

"Do you know which way to go?" Stephanie asked.

"I have no idea." Noah slipped his feet back into his snowshoes. "Keep out the gun."

Ann handed Noah the gun and put on her pack. "We have to get out of this blizzard and not get buried. We'd never get out from under the layer of snow this storm is laying down."

God had accomplished half of what Noah had asked of him. "God will show us a place."

Snow scalpels pounded against them as Noah looked for a safe haven. As they disappeared into the blizzard, Noah held his hands out to feel if something was in front of him. He also tried to feel with his feet, but the snowshoes prevented him from determining anything about the terrain.

Unable to see the person before them, the rope pulled Stephanie and then Ann, who had insisted that Stephanie be in front of her. Ann walked faster than Stephanie did. She accidentally stepped on the back of Stephanie's snowshoe. Stephanie stopped and screamed, "Ann, be careful!" Ann didn't see or hear her sister. She stepped forward and onto Stephanie's other snowshoe as well.

Noah picked up his back leg and shifted his weight to his front leg. The snow beneath him gave way. He dropped into the air. With Ann on her sister's snowshoes, the jerk of the rope didn't pull Stephanie over the cliff behind Noah. Instead, Stephanie went face first into the snow right where she stood. Her snowshoes popped up and threw Ann to the ground.

Noah's weight pulled Stephanie down into the snow and held her secure; too secure. She couldn't get up. She tried to push down to raise her face. Her arms didn't reach anything solid and became immobile in the snow. She couldn't breathe.

Ann stood up and followed the rope to Stephanie. She tried to pull her up. *This rope is so tight, Noah must be hanging from the other end. Stephanie has to stay in the snow until I get Noah back, or we'll all go over the edge.* She squatted and dug furiously beside Stephanie's head. "I'm digging you an air hole!" As fast as she could, Ann removed the snow and then turned Stephanie's face to the air.

As Stephanie gasped, Ann carefully made her way to the edge. She couldn't see Noah. She hoped he could hear her. "How can I get you back up here?!"

Noah looked up. He could barely make out a shape above him. "I don't know how secure you are, and the wind is blowing me everywhere."

"Stephanie is wedged in the snow. It can't withstand much tugging. Can you toss the rope to me? Maybe there's a tree I can reach."

Noah pulled and pulled until he had the whole length of the rope out of his pack. He looped it up as he dangled at the other end of the same rope. Ann lay in the snow and reached down. Noah gently swung the rope up. Ann hollered, "Too far to the left."

Again, Noah rolled up the rope and attempted to get his lifeline to Ann. It touched Ann's hand, but she couldn't grip it with her clunky glove. "Do it the same way again. Tell me when you're almost ready. I'll have to take off my glove."

Once again, he gathered a coil but tossed a little harder. Ann saw the rope coming. It went past. She thrust her hand through the hole at the center. The loop hung on her arm. "Got it! I'm going to check on Stephanie and look for a tree."

Ann carefully made her way back to Stephanie. "Can you hold out a little longer? I have the rope. I'm going to tie it to a tree."

"I don't have a choice. Go on!"

Ann was almost at the end of the rope when she saw a lone pine. She pushed herself into the branches and fastened the heavy hemp cord then followed the line back to Noah. "The rope is secured to a tree. I pulled it as tight as I could, but I think you're still going to drop some when I get Stephanie up. You shouldn't drop far."

"First, tie yourself and Stephanie to the part of the rope connected to the tree." Noah anxiously waited for the drop while Ann got them ready. There wasn't slack, so Ann freed herself and then tried to untie her sister from the line to Noah. With Noah suspended from it, the knot was too tight. Ann drew her knife and slid it under the rope. "I'm sorry. This is probably going to rub you raw." Ann sawed the knife back and forth under the line until there was barely a thread. It snapped and flew into the blizzard. Ann helped Stephanie up.

Noah not only dropped, but also swung to the side. The rope jerked into his armpits. Stephanie and Ann tried to pull the rope toward the tree. Instead, they slid across the top of the snow as they tugged the rope. Ann carefully navigated back to the edge. "We can't pull you unless we go to the tree. We won't know what's happening here."

"I can't be far down. I'll try to climb the rope." Noah shoved his gloves into his pockets, reached above, and gripped the rope. As he pulled, the wind blew him toward the cliff. He clung tightly until the gust died. He climbed another arm's pull up the rope before he drew his legs up, caught the bottom loop of the rope with one foot, pulled the rope over the top of his other foot, and clamped his feet together. He stood on the rope held in place by his feet.

Ann called into the whiteness, "Are you coming?!"

"I'm trying!" Since there was so much wind, and he now had enough rope below him, he wrapped the rope around his leg and then under his foot. With his other foot, he looped the rope back over, and again stepped on the rope with his free foot. He clamped his feet together hard as the blizzard drove him out into an angle.

So the wind wouldn't blow them over the edge, Ann laid with Stephanie in the snow. "Hold on!"

When he again hung straight, Noah let his feet loose to start another pull up the rope. Immediately, the gale carried him out. He got his leg secured back into the rope just before he slammed into the rocks.

Ann knew Noah needed help. "Stephanie, when you feel the pull, try to walk toward me." She turned and walked along the rope. At the tree, Ann braced and tried to draw Noah up. Stephanie attempted to help haul in her brother-in-law.

The rope from which Noah hung grew shorter. He wrapped the rope around his hands, put his feet against the rocks, and walked up the cliff as Stephanie and Ann reeled him in.

Once back on the snow-covered ground, Noah followed the rope to Stephanie and then they continued on to Ann.

"We have to get out of this storm." Ann leaned into the pine to detach the rope. "It's too dangerous to travel."

"I have an idea. Leave it tied. We need a tarp. You can't let it get away, and it's going to be very hard to hold." Noah held open some branches. "Get it in here." The large sheet flapped furiously as the girls pushed it into the tree. "Take off your snowshoes and step inside. Prop our packs, so we can sit on them and put the snowshoes behind."

Noah forced the rope through the branches as Ann and Stephanie got inside the shell and maneuvered everything into position. Noah hollered, "Help me hold the top!"

Ann struggled to keep hold of the slippery rubber canvas while Noah secured the top of their shelter to the pine. He explained what to do next, "Position our buffalo hide and blankets so they can be under us, behind our backs, and above our heads."

The girls retrieved the items. "Sit." Noah pulled the blankets and the hide up behind Ann and Stephanie. "Wrap these around you. Keep a space open for me. Don't make it so tight that we can't move."

Noah brought the rope down and wrapped it around the women sitting on the backpacks. He created a large pocket in the middle then once again, threaded it around at the bottom. He slipped inside and pulled everything closed, but left a small opening for fresh air. He tied off the rope. "This is the best I can do."

Ann snuggled against Noah. "I love our cocoon. We're warm, and we can't be blown away. Unless the snow gets over six feet deep inside this tree, we shouldn't be buried. If it does, we can climb the tree to get out."

Stephanie hauled out their food for the night and the morning. She put the dried survival food into a pot with water from her canteen then put on the lid.

They could barely hear each other, so they sat silently, drank the last of the water, and ate another meal of dried elk and apricots. Just as he had done the night before, Noah reached out and packed their canteens and the other pots with snow. Then, they leaned against each other and slept, lashed inside a pine tree.

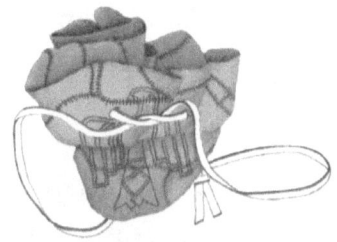

TWENTY SEVEN

On the road by the river, Russell's mules started to falter. The relentless onslaught of the tiny ice daggers had cut away their fur and eaten into their flesh. Much too late, Russell realized his mistake and attempted to protect his animals from the raging storm. He stopped at an outcropping that blocked some of the wind. "Use the wagons to make a windbreak then make covers for the mules." Back from the rock protrusion, they parked the wagons end to end in a line, parallel to the cliff, but with a space large enough for tents.

When Roscoe and his family arrived, they positioned their wagons in front of each gap between Russell's wagons. Roscoe screamed instructions through the storm, "Get all the animals on the protected side of the wagons and then we'll set up! Double stake their tent!"

Russell walked to Roscoe. "Will you set up your tent as a second shield for my mules?"

"I will."

Without a clue as to why the Bacons had set up a huge tent, Russell and his group once again thought that the Bacons' behavior was curious. This time,

Russell figured the Bacons knew what they were doing. As soon as the floorless tent was up, Roscoe, James, and Nancy shoveled the snow inside into ten-gallon tubs. Once they had it clear, the two men removed the goats from the wagon.

Arnold and Russell saw Nancy lead the goats into the tent. "Surely the Bacons aren't going to sleep with their animals?" Russell's group walked into the large canvas-covered structure. They saw the animal organizer suspended from the top and immediately realized the potential sales value. "Where did you get this?" Russell asked.

Nancy maneuvered the goats into their positions, and then Roscoe tied the dividers. James carried hay past Russell and said, "Nancy made it." He divided the hay into the goat feedbags before he went to get more. Nancy tied the inner corral closed. She left Russell and his group standing in the animal shelter and went to help bring in more hay. After they had filled all the feed bags, Roscoe and James brought in Ace and King.

Since the animal blankets would release too much moisture inside the tent, and since their body heat would warm the tent well enough, Nancy took off the blankets, leg, and head covers and carried them to Russell. Above the noise of the wind, she told him, "You can use these on your animals tonight."

Russell hollered, "Thank you. I've never before been in a storm that cuts away fur and flesh!"

After they had protected the animals, each group pitched their people tent against the side of the animal shelter and created a three-sided barrier on the inner side of the wagons. Russell brought his mules inside. It was not as good as being completely inside a tent, but it made a big difference for Russell's mules. Even wrapped in the blankets, leggings, and hoods, they bunched together with their rumps into the wind.

The animals were as well protected as they could get them, so Roscoe dispensed cold food to everybody. "Keep your plate with you until the morning." After he had served the last person, Roscoe joined Nancy and James in their tent. They sat on the extra tarp they had added to help insulate them from the snow under the tent, and ate while wrapped up in blankets.

Even inside the tent, the wind drew every iota of heat out of their bodies. Nancy complained, "I'm too cold."

Roscoe agreed, "I'll never get warm this way."

James knew what they had to do, but Nancy would not have her sisters to lie between. "Nancy, we have to get together like we did when we were going to Pine Bluff. I don't know how you feel about that."

"There's no other way to be warm."

James went to their wagon. He got another tarp and more blankets. "We'll wrap all six blankets and a tarp around us and sleep in a bunch."

In the other tent, Russell commanded his men, "Never tell another soul that we huddled up."

When the people exited the tents in the morning, they found that the driving wind had scoured the road clear of snow. They built the morning fire on the road. After the fire blazed, Roscoe started breakfast and lots of hot coffee. Arnold and Russell's men put ten-gallon tubs close to the fire and filled them with river water. Up the narrow space between the two ends of the dividers, James and Nancy squeezed to the center of the animal tent. They rationed oats and hay into all the feedbags as they stood in the goat pen. Russell's men brought hay and oats to their mules and fed them in a communal pile.

Nancy went out of the tent and instructed the men who were close enough to hear her. "Don't give Russell's mules any water until I tell you."

The men looked at Russell. Russell reckoned that Nancy had a good reason, but he felt he should know what she was about to do to his animals. He shook his head up and down to signal his agreement with her orders then asked, "What are you planning?"

"I'm going to pour boiling water over willow bark and let it steep. The hot water draws something out of the bark that takes away the pain. I also plan to cook cedar to make a poultice that helps wounds heal without becoming infected, and it also helps with pain. Will you let me treat your mules?"

"Are you sure none of that will poison them?"

"I've used it on myself."

Russell gave the go ahead. "Help them if you can."

Nancy prepared the willow tea and poured it into the warm water in the large tubs. Russell called his men over. Nancy told them the dosage, "Take the water to them. Half a bucket each."

After everybody had breakfast, the cedar poultice was ready to apply. Nancy instructed Russell and his men, "Watch how to apply this dressing and then do the same with the rest of your mules." She went to the animal that had taken the worst of the snow blasting. "What's this one's name?"

"It's Mule 17." Russell pointed to the number 17 seared into her flesh.

Nancy removed the coverings. Its right side, from head to hoof, was raw meat. Everybody knew the animal had to be suffering terribly. Russell tried to get the mule to walk. It barely hobbled a few steps. He pulled his gun. Nancy protested, "We can move our hay into your wagon and then bring Mule 17 into the empty one. I'll ride with her and make her lie down."

"If it won't ride that way, I'm putting it down." Russell slid his gun back into its holster.

"Thank you for letting me try. Now, watch how I do this." Nancy smeared the cedar poultice on the same wrapping she had removed, wrapped it back around the mule's leg, and tied it in place with the red ribbon. As she did so, she told Mule 17, "Don't listen to them. You're still beautiful. I'm going to call you Beauty, not Mule 17." Nancy instructed the men, "We want to make this go as far as we can, so examine the others and find the worst places. Use the same wrapping to secure the medicine over their injuries."

Russell removed the blanket of the first mule he planned to treat and told himself, *I should have known that Roscoe would do the right thing for his animals, and I should have too.*

Nancy continued to work on Beauty while she recited the names and uses of the plants that had been in Roscoe's storerooms. When she got to fumewort, she remembered that both Roscoe and Noah had said it was a sedative. That reminded her of Valerian. When she was done applying the cedar to Beauty, Nancy hung a pot of water over the fire and then dug in the wagon for the ingredients she needed to put the animal to sleep.

Meanwhile, James brought their animals out of the tent and let them drink as much warmed river water as they wanted. Russell's mules had only drunk the dose of painkiller. They needed more water, so his men did the same as James. It took over an hour to apply the poultice and get all the animals watered.

As people became free, they broke camp. Nancy spoke to Russell, "Your animals need the cedar treatment all day. Since the storm has passed and our animals aren't injured, we don't need to worry about ours. We'll leave the wrappings on your mules." Next, Nancy went to speak with Roscoe, "We only need eight animals to pull our wagons. We have thirteen more uninjured animals. I was wondering if we could use them with the three least injured of Russell's animals to pull his wagons and let the others walk. That is, except for Beauty. She needs to ride in the wagon because she can't walk, but she can get better, and we don't need to shoot her. They're your animals. Will you allow us to use them to pull Russell's wagons?"

"Little Jack and Little Jenny are too small to use.

Eyanosa is not mine to give permission, but you can use all the rest. They can rest in Little Rock when we get there."

Nancy hugged him. "Much obliged." She hurried off and found Russell talking with Will. When she saw Will, she turned and started away.

Russell called out to her, "Nancy, come here."

Nancy went over with her head hung low. She looked at the ground because she didn't want to look at Will.

"I'm sorry, Nancy." Will walked away.

"What's he sorry about?" Russell asked.

Nancy replied, "Nothing important. I came to tell you what we would like to do." She told Russell her plan to use their animals to pull his wagons and let all but three of his mules walk without a harness or a burden.

"Will and I were just discussing what to do about pulling the wagons with the mules in this condition. If I can use yours, I'd appreciate it very much. Did your uncle say we can?"

"Yes, I've already spoken with him."

"Wonderful, we'll hook up your mules and donkeys and then move on."

After they had moved the hay from Roscoe's wagon into Russell's, Nancy brought the bucket of water with fumewort, valerian, and willow bark to Beauty. It drank the medicine and then several more buckets of plain water. As they harnessed the teams, they decided that none of Russell's mules should work, and therefore used only Ace and King to pull the wagon carrying Beauty and only Redeemed and Big Jenny to pull the hay wagon. When everything except Beauty was ready to travel, James backed the empty wagon to the hillside. Beauty hobbled up the hill to the back of the wagon.

"That's a long step down." Russell looked at the four-foot drop into the wagon bed.

Will suggested, "Let's use crates to make stairs."

"Good idea." Nancy helped carry crates from their wagons.

Fifteen minutes after the mule drank the sedative, Russell led his mule down the steps into the wagon. The men then removed the crates. There was just enough space for Russell to get her to lie down. By the time everybody got to his position, Beauty lay completely pain-free, asleep in the wagon. They traveled at the slow pace of animals suffering from pain, barely held at bay by willow and cedar.

Russell pushed on into the night to get the animals into a stable in Little Rock. He knew, in their current condition, his mules would not survive another night in the extreme cold.

TWENTY EIGHT

Noah untied the rope and opened their shelter. He peeked out at the forest's stark beauty. Through the bare winter branches of the hickories and oaks, he saw a blue sky without a single cloud. A blanket of snow covered the earth. As Noah admired the scene, he noticed a large set of antlers rising out of pink snow. He recognized the bow shape. "I think there's an elk buried in the snow."

They stepped out of the blankets, put on their snowshoes, and hiked over to look. The elk sat with only its head and antlers above the snow. The creature looked at them with eyes that pleaded for release. Snow blasted by the storm, and in much worse shape than Beauty, its red blood had congealed into filigree tendrils and then frozen in the snow around its body.

Ann believed there was only one merciful action they could take. "We need to shoot it."

Stephanie also felt they should save it from a slow, painful death. "We're far enough away from anything. Nobody will hear."

Noah got the pistol that Ann had used to almost shoot him. He walked back to the elk. "Spirit of the elk, accept our gift of mercy to this elk." Noah shot it between its eyes. Its head dropped into the snow and added a large tendril of red to the pink design around it.

Ann looked at the elk. "Poor thing."

"There must be others around in the same condition." Stephanie scanned the surrounding land.

Noah knew they had to go directly to Little Rock. "We're only called upon to help the ones God puts before us."

Ann philosophized, "We would be lying in our own blood if we hadn't been in the tarp."

"Look at this." Noah held up the tarp that had been wrapped around them and then folded down behind them four layers thick. All that remained of the outer layer was tattered cloth. All the impregnated rubber had been eroded away.

Stephanie looked at the ruined tarp. "God sent a horrible storm."

"But He stopped it in time." Noah folded up what was left of the tarp and packed it, along with the blankets and the hide. They put on their goggles and set off through their private green world.

At the end of an uneventful day, they stood inside the Oakland Cemetery shed in Little Rock. They didn't know if the rest of the family had arrived before them or not. Either way, all they could do was wait. The temperature dropped drastically when the sun set, so they laid out the tarp with the shredded side down, pulled out the blankets and the buffalo hide, and wrapped up.

TWENTY NINE

Noah, Ann, and Stephanie were asleep in the shed when the sound of a wagon train woke them. They peeked out. Eli drove the rear wagon, so nobody would see him when he turned toward the shed. With his fingers, he made the symbol of a heart in front of his own heart. He held up his hand with the palm out and then held up one finger.

Eli prayed that his family was in the shed, had seen him, and had understood his message.

Stephanie turned from the cracks. "He says he loves us and to wait a minute."

Noah stepped back, "More likely an hour."

Ann had panic in her eyes. "I didn't see Sally."

Noah assured her, "Eli would have made a different signal if something was wrong. Let's get back into the blankets and wait."

Nancy told the sleeping mule she sat beside, "I hope they don't go to the same inn we stayed at the last time." When they stopped, Nancy loosened the pucker strings and cautiously peeked out. They were in a livery large enough to easily handle forty-five animals. She hoped the mules would get the medical attention they needed. Mule 17 was still asleep, but Nancy stayed in the wagon to calm her if she woke.

Nancy heard Russell as he approached. "Martin, I don't know how to get it out or if it's even alive." The back of the wagon cover opened.

The livery owner suggested, "Maybe we can remove the backboards, put some planks there, and let her walk down."

Nancy told the man, "I don't know if Beauty can walk at all."

"Why is it sleeping?" the man asked.

"I gave her a sedative, but she can wake up."

"I want to be able to sedate animals. What did you give it?"

"I used Fumewort and Valerian to put Beauty to sleep and willow to stop the pain. I'll tell you how to make it if you would like."

With complete confidence that he could get Mule 17 up, Russell stated, "Let's get her out."

The livery boy got all the other animals into their stalls while Russell's men watched them try to get Mule 17 out of the wagon. Russell and Martin pried the backboards off the wagon and then brought over strong boards to make a ramp. Russell tried to get Mule 17 up on her feet. The livery boy attempted to see what they were doing. He walked behind the wagon on every trip for hay or water.

Russell was not successful. Arnold jumped in and tried to help. They pulled on Mule 17, and they pushed against her, but the mule was too weak to get off the wagon bed. The pulling ripped open her injured side. Blood soaked through the horse blanket.

Nancy ordered, "Stop! You're hurting her!"

Russell decided. "Shoot it and pull it out."

Nancy pleaded, "Let her lay here until she gets stronger."

Martin hated to kill an animal. "Edwin can bring food and water to her in the wagon."

Russell agreed, "I'll give it a temporary reprieve. Nancy, I told you if it couldn't function that I would have to shoot it. If it cannot get up when we leave in the morning, I am going to shoot it. It has this one night."

Martin directed his worker, "Edwin, bring food and water over here." He turned to Nancy. "I'm Martin Harrow. Tell me what you gave this mule and what you have inside the bandages."

It disappointed Nancy that Martin didn't know how to provide basic medical care. She retrieved some of the plants from their wagon and then explained how to prepare them. Nancy handed the bags of willow bark, cedar, fumewort, and valerian to Martin. "Please give all the injured mules another treatment of cedar and willow tonight. Add the fumewort and valerian only for Beauty." Nancy left him to care for the animals while everybody went to the inn to secure rooms for the night.

The innkeeper led the group to the first available rooms. "These rooms have doors that open to the street. They're the biggest rooms."

Russell rejected them. "They aren't safe like rooms that open only to the inside hall."

One by one, each of the others declined the rooms. The innkeeper informed them, "Somebody has to take these rooms, or you'll have to share."

James spoke up, "No room sharing. We'll take these." Unknown to the others, the rooms served his needs just fine. As soon as he agreed, James tried to hurry into the room. "Give us the keys now. When you've got everybody else settled in, bring hot baths to our three rooms, and we want three big steak dinners tonight."

"I'll give the keys out after everybody knows which room they have."

James followed along unhappily. The innkeeper assigned the last room, doled out the keys, and then went off to tell his wife which of them had ordered a bath and to fix steak meals for all the late arrivals.

As soon as they were inside one of the rooms that opened to the street, James said, "Nancy, stay with Roscoe. Roscoe, do not leave Nancy alone for a single second. I'm going to get my wife. Tell anybody who wants to know where I am, that I'm resting and want to be left alone." James opened the street door. He looked around carefully, slipped out into the night, and hastened to the cemetery. Because of the storm the day before, he prayed with extreme concern, "God, let them be there." Eli now knew the way to the shed very well and quickly traversed the city to get Stephanie, Noah, and Ann. When he stood outside the shed, he knocked three times with a long pause between each knock. Noah opened the door, making sure his fingers were around the edge of the door and visible outside. Eli stepped inside. Noah peeked outside to see if anybody had followed. He didn't see anyone. Eli had his arms around Stephanie in the blink of an eye. "Thank God, you're safe. That storm was terrible! I've been so worried." Eli kissed Stephanie, and she returned the favor.

Noah hugged Eli. "I promised I would get your wife back to you."

Ann wrapped her arms around Eli last. "There were a few times I thought we weren't going to make it. That was the worst storm I've ever seen, and we were right in the middle of it."

"Pack this up. We've got rooms that we can enter from the street."

Noah and the girls were more than happy to get out of the shed that was not able to keep out the cold. Together, they sneaked up the streets to the rooms where Eli performed the appropriate knock but got no reply. He unlocked the door and cautiously looked inside. The only thing in the room was a full and steaming bathtub.

Ann entered the room. "That looks so inviting!" Eli knocked three times on the wall with a long pause between each, walked across the room and did the same on the other wall then stood at the door. When Eli heard the three knocks with a long pause between each, he opened the door with his fingers on the outside of the door. Sally and Roscoe crept into Eli's room. They hugged and quietly greeted each other.

Eli explained the plan, "We'll take our baths and go out to dinner since we should already be out there. Then, while we're eating, you three take a bath if you want one. We'll bring food when we come back."

They agreed, so Noah went with Roscoe, Ann

went with Sally, and Stephanie stayed in Eli's room. The three that had traveled with Russell's group washed and then joined the men already eating in the dining hall. Some of the men had chosen to spend money on baths, while others very obviously had not. Nancy sat next to those who smelled the best. Communal bowls and platters of food sat on the table for everybody to share. Roscoe, James, and Nancy ate with the guests that the innkeeper knew were staying at his inn. Ann, Stephanie, and Noah enjoyed soaking in hot water. Noah slipped over to Sally's room after his bath to wait with Ann in the warm, wind-proof room. When Sally stepped into the room, she had half a steak, a baked potato, and two rolls. She also gave both Ann and Noah one of the oranges that had almost led to a disaster with Will.

Sally passed on Roscoe's message. "Roscoe wants to sleep in the wagon, so nothing gets stolen. He'll bring the key to his room over here when he leaves." No sooner had she spoken than they heard the proper knock. She gave the signal that it was safe inside and then let Roscoe into the room.

"I want to protect our supplies. You two use the other room." Roscoe also brought forth the food he had taken with him from the dining room: a whole steak and a potato. He put the food in the washbasin with the food Sally had already placed there. "I even brought these." Roscoe gave Noah a knife, spoon, and fork and then pulled a glass full of buttered peas out of his pocket and put it on the table.

"How did you get the peas?" Sally asked.

Roscoe revealed his procedure for pea pilfering, "You put the glass in your lap. Every time people aren't looking, you take a spoonful of peas from your plate, you put your other hand around the top of the glass, so you can tell where it is, and dump the peas into the glass. Since we could keep helping ourselves to more, I kept putting more on my plate. I also got this." He pulled a glass of bread pudding out of his other pocket, "Same procedure."

Noah said, "I'm impressed and grateful."

Sally apologized, "Sorry, I didn't do as well."

Ann told her sister, "There's plenty. Don't worry."

Roscoe made sure everybody knew the plan for the morning. "Enjoy the night inside. I'll see you for breakfast in the morning. I'll knock on the door and come through my room to go to the dining hall."

"Thank you." Ann hugged Roscoe before he went to protect everything they had, especially what he had in the wagon.

Ann wanted information. "Tell us about your trip, Sally." Ann and Noah ate and listened.

Sally narrated the story and concluded, "When we got here they couldn't get Beauty to stand. He only gave me until morning. She's so injured. I'm afraid he's going to shoot her in the morning."

Ann complimented her sister, "I'm proud of you, Sally! It's a good thing you were there to help them. Maybe that's why God put the fear of caves into your heart."

Noah asked, "Do you want to sneak over there tonight and look at Beauty together?"

Sally wanted to save Beauty. "Would you?"

Noah asked, "Do you want to come, Ann?"

"No. You take the key. Be very careful that you aren't seen. I'm going to get in a warm bed and sleep."

While they ate bread pudding, Sally told them about Will. Noah paced in the room. "I want to knock his head off." Noah chastised Sally, "And you should have listened to Eli. He was completely right. You need to be careful about what you do. Men will take things the way they want them to be. You were lucky that Eli got there when he did. It might not have worked out that way. Don't let there be a next time."

"I won't. I learned my lesson. It's just that you and Eli aren't like that. Melvin, Roscoe, Smitty, and Zachariah aren't like that either, so I thought other men would be like you. I thought that I could trust them."

"Thank you for thinking I'm different. I try to do the right things, but when it comes to wanting love, I have the same thoughts. What I said in Judge Hall's courtroom was true. I did want to be with Ann before we were married, and it was very hard to wait, and remember that Zachariah didn't."

Sally still believed men could be honorable. "You wouldn't have forced Ann, and he didn't force Minnie."

Ann apologized to her sister, "I should have noticed that you've become a very attractive young woman. Men are going to want you. I should have talked to you before. I'm sorry that I didn't."

"It's not your fault, nothing happened, and I won't do anything to make any man think I want him around me ever again. You can be sure of that. The ones you do want around don't want to be with you. The ones you do not want around want to be. I guess I should tell you that Eli also had to get Arnold to leave George at Roscoe's place so he would leave me alone."

Ann sat on the bed beside her sister and hugged her. "I'm glad Eli was there, that he protected you, and that you're all right, but I'm exhausted. I'm ready to sleep."

Noah kissed Ann. "Keep the door locked and don't open it without the proper knock. I'm leaving the key with you. I don't want to lead anybody here if I get caught."

Ann commanded Sally, "Be careful. Sally, wait for Eli to get you in the morning, and you keep your door locked too. I love you both."

As she left with Noah, Sally said, "I will. Love you to the moon and back."

Ann went to Roscoe's room, got into the soft, warm bed, and immediately fell asleep.

Sally became Nancy again as she and Noah carefully crept through the shadows to the livery. Beauty thrashed on the wagon bed while Edwin stood and watched.

Nancy commanded Edwin in anger, "What are you doing? Help her!"

"I don't know what to do," Edwin cowered.

Nancy was extremely upset. She had told the

man to treat the animals, she had explained how, and she had given him the ingredients. "Didn't Martin give her the medicine?"

"I don't know what he did, but he left right after you."

Nancy ordered the boy with a tone that sent him running, "Go get my bags from him right now! I have a doctor here to treat them!"

"Yes, ma'am!"

Noah stood speechless. His sister-in-law had always spoken her mind, but this was different. She spoke with authority. She knew what to do, and she was not afraid to see that it happened. Noah was impressed. As the boy scurried away, Noah said, "That was great, Sally."

With the same tone, she said, "I'm Nancy here." She immediately realized that she had spoken too sharply. "I'm sorry. Please refer to me as Nancy Bacon, and Eli is James Bacon. We're Roscoe's niece and nephew. It makes me so mad that Martin didn't give them what they need, especially Beauty." Nancy softly cooed as she climbed into the wagon. She took the mule's head in her hands, laid its head in her lap, and stroked her between the ears where the skin was still intact, and it wouldn't hurt. The mule stopped thrashing, but it was obviously in pain.

"I think she knows you're going to help her. I'll get the things we'll need."

"Our other wagon is the one over there." She pointed to the wagon.

Noah walked toward the wagon. Roscoe had

overheard everything. He spoke to Noah as he approached, "Come on in. Those are not her mules. She should leave them alone."

"You want to try to talk her out of helping them?" Noah climbed into the wagon and listed the items he thought they should use.

Roscoe knew Noah was right about not being able to change Nancy's mind. "I'll get them. The boy has a fire going to stay warm. Here's water and pots. I'm staying out of this, not because I want the animals to suffer, but because they're not our property."

Martin hurried to the livery with the bags. "I was coming back to do what you said. I went home to eat. My wife wants me home on time."

Nancy ordered him, "Take them to the doctor by the fire!"

"Yes, ma'am!" Martin hurried to Noah.

"The lady told me to give these to you." Martin handed over the bags.

Noah wanted to give the man a chance to redeem himself. "Thank you. Are you able to help? I need somebody to give a painkiller to all the animals and to take off the wrappings carefully."

"Of course." Martin wanted to learn, and he was glad he would get a chance to help a doctor.

"Let me show you how to make the painkiller. Do you have clean water in here?"

Martin was proud of the artesian spring that vented water directly into his stable, "Lots." He listened as the doctor explained the procedure for preparing the willow tea. He also added Valerian.

Not enough to put them to sleep, just enough to relax them. When they had the first batch made, they divided it into several buckets and then added water to the mixture to fill them halfway.

The doctor told Martin, "Only this much, so they drink it all." Martin walked to the closest mule and put a bucket down for it to drink then did the same with the others.

"Pour warm water over the blanket until it's completely soaked. Leave it and move on. Go back later, and see if the coverings will come loose easily. If not, pour on more water." Noah then carried a bucket of water with a high dose of willow, fumewort, and valerian to Nancy.

"Let's knock her out, so we can work on her." Noah gave Nancy the water. Beauty could not even rise off her side to drink. "I'll get a canteen." They poured the water into the canteen and then helped the mule drink. "Do you want to stay with her until she's asleep?" Noah asked.

"Yes, she needs me."

Noah went to help Martin remove the wrapping from the other mules. Twenty minutes later, they had six mules out of their wrapping, and Beauty slept peacefully.

Nancy called out, "Doctor, she's asleep."

"I'll be right there, Nancy." Noah finished removing the bandage he was working on then took a bucket of plain warm water to the wagon.

They had a great deal of work to do before the town woke, so the doctor asked Martin, "Will you stay? We still need you."

270

"Of course, I'll stay. Will you tell me what you're doing for Beauty?" Martin followed the doctor.

"I promise I will later. Keep working on getting the cloth off the rest of the mules."

Noah got into the wagon. "We need to remove these coverings carefully." As they worked to soak loose the blanket and leg wrappings, Noah asked in a whisper, "Who am I?"

"How about Luke? He was a doctor in the Bible."

"I like it. What about my last name?"

"Smith is a common name."

"Dr. Luke Smith. I like it." When they finally got all the bandages off Beauty's right side and legs, Dr. Smith informed Nancy of the situation, "This is bad. So much of her skin is gone. She must have been in horrible pain. It might have been better to shoot her. I don't know if we can keep this much area free of infection while she heals."

Nancy begged for mercy, "Please try. I'll keep her asleep for as long as we can. I'll only wake her to eat. I'll do whatever it takes. She doesn't deserve to die. She was doing what she was told."

Dr. Smith could see that he needed to try. "We'll get some sinew soaking in cedar water, and then I'll sew the muscles and skin as well as I can."

"Thank you, Doctor."

Dr. Luke Smith told Nancy, "We'll work on the others while the sinew is soaking."

Nancy helped Martin remove the blood-soaked, scabbed-on wrappings from the other mules. They left the skin exposed, so Dr. Smith could examine the animals by lantern light. After the doctor had examined all of his patients, he gave Martin and Nancy their instructions.

"Both of you come over here." Luke again explained to Martin how much of each plant to use as he made another batch of the willow, fumewort, and valerian to make the tranquilizer and put the mules to sleep. "They'll sleep standing up, and there's no reason to torture them by stitching them while they're awake. We'll start after the animal is asleep. Give the sedative twenty minutes before you sew up the skin blasted open by the snowstorm. To protect it from the light, we need to make a salve or something and cover the eye of this one with an abraded eye."

They gave the first four mules the sleeping potion then Dr. Smith gave both Nancy and Martin detailed instructions on how to make an antiseptic wash and an antiseptic paste and how to apply the medications.

When the next most injured mule stood asleep on its feet, Dr. Smith took sinew, scissors, and a large needle and demonstrated how to sew the flesh. He cut the skin to make smooth edges, washed the area with the antiseptic water, and then joined the skin by pulling the pieces together with the sinew. After he had one wound stitched up, Luke applied the sticky antiseptic paste. "Any questions?"

Both Martin and Nancy replied, "No."

"Nancy, finish this one. Martin, go work on one of the other tranquilized mules."

Martin and Nancy started on their patients. Dr. Luke Smith went back into the wagon. He got a small potato, some tea, and a handkerchief. "Martin, do you have some long, dark, clean cloth?"

Martin told him, "Feed sacks, but they have oat dust on them."

Dr. Smith started a pot of tea, grated the potato, and then cut a feed bag into strips long enough to tie around the mule's head and eye. He washed the cloth strips as well as he could, put the handful of shredded potato into one of the strips, and strapped it around the mule's injured eye. Once he had the astringent, anti-inflammatory potato treatment on Mule 4, Dr. Smith took some of the antiseptic wash and went to work on Mule 17.

Nancy was still working on her animal when Martin finished his first patient. "I'll make another batch of the sleeping medicine and cleansing water." Martin went to the spring to get water.

Luke called out, "It's been fifteen minutes. Nancy, take the potato compress off the mule's eye, throw out the potato, and wash out the cloth. Pour the tea through the handkerchief into that pot of cold water then tie closed the handkerchief with the tea leaves inside. Pour the diluted tea over her eye to wash it and then secure the handkerchief of tea over her eye. After you care for her eye, make me more antiseptic wash."

Martin volunteered, "I'd be glad to do all that." He started the next batch of wash and did as Dr. Smith instructed for the mule's injured eye. After he had treated Mule 4's eye, Martin stitched closed the injuries of the next mule.

Another quarter hour later, Nancy finished the animal Luke had started. "I'm done. Is there anything you want me to do before I start on the next mule?"

"Take the tea off Mule 4. We'll leave her eye uncovered while it's still night."

Nancy did as instructed then took the antiseptic off the fire to cool and started another batch in a third pot. After she divided the sedative between the next four mules, she started another batch of sedative cooking. Nancy then commenced working on the last of the four mules that were already asleep.

When Martin had Mule 3 all stitched up, he took the cooled antiseptic to Dr. Smith. He stepped back and almost dropped the bucket when he saw poor Beauty without the blanket. So much skin was missing that it looked flayed. Even though he did not expect an answer, Martin asked, "How did they let this happen?"

"It's hard to believe that anybody would treat an animal like this, especially their own work animal."

"Will you be able to save it?" Martin handed the bucket to the doctor.

"Probably not, but Nancy wants me to try. Even with the willow, it's going to be in a lot of pain when it's awake. We'll keep it asleep as much as possible."

Martin couldn't stand to look at the animal any longer. "I'm going back to work on the others. Let me know if you need anything else."

The doctor worked on Beauty while Nancy and Martin worked on the other fifteen mules.

THIRTY

Almost all the animals were stitched up when Russell and Arnold walked into the livery. Bloody wrappings and blankets lay scattered across the livery floor. Pots, with they didn't know what inside, sat around. A cauldron hung on a spit over the fire, cooking a concoction that smelled awful. The skin of the mules that stood in the open central area looked like quilts with patches sewn on here and there, as well as lines of stitches holding pieces together.

"What's going on here?" Russell asked.

Nancy and Martin turned toward the voice. Nancy informed him, "We're saving your mules is what's going on."

With irritation, Russell loudly stated, "I didn't authorize this, and I'm not paying for it."

Roscoe heard Russell and thought he should tell the rest of the family what was happening. He picked up the key to Nancy's room that she had put in the wagon and slipped out the back door.

Martin explained what he thought had been his instructions. "You stood right beside Miss Bacon when she told me to treat these mules. You didn't alter those orders."

Russell came back, "This isn't what I thought she meant."

Nancy countered, "When we took the wrappings off, it was much worse than I thought. Cedar poultice

275

isn't going to be enough, and the doctor told us what to do."

"You hired a doctor?" Russell felt astounded that the girl had taken such liberties.

"I hired him to work on Beauty. He showed us how to treat these mules, but Martin and I took care of them ourselves."

"Where is this doctor, and who is he?" Arnold asked.

Martin informed him, "Dr. Luke Smith is in the wagon with Beauty."

Russell and Arnold walked away. Nancy whispered to Martin, "Finish before they make us stop." They continued to stitch their last patients.

Russell looked at the man who had spent the night sewing together Mule 17. "Dr. Smith?"

Dr. Luke Smith replied, "Yes, how may I help you?"

Russell informed him, "I did not authorize this treatment, and I'm not paying for it."

The doctor apprised the men of the arrangements, "I only treated this one animal at the request of Nancy Bacon. She's already paid me."

"Did you examine any of the other mules?"

"I looked them over."

"What's your opinion of them?" Russell asked.

The doctor felt peeved that the owner of the mules didn't want them to be cared for. "There's a fee for my opinion. Miss Bacon paid for my opinion, you can ask her."

Arnold asked, "How much?"

"Twenty-five cents per animal."

Russell gave him three dollars and seventy-fifty cents. "I don't need you to tell me about Mule 17. It's as good as dead."

Dr. Smith walked with Russell and Arnold to each animal. The doctor gave his medical opinion and chastised them slightly. "Proper care of your property could have prevented this! None of them are fit for work at this time. Except for Mule 17, they should all recover if an infection doesn't set in. In a few weeks, these three will probably be healed enough to work, but not in a harness pulling a wagon. They only need their skin to heal. These nine should be put out to pasture for at least two months. They have muscle damage as well as damage to the skin. These two will need months to recover from all the tissue damage. This one will have some vision loss. It may even lose all vision in its right eye."

Russell looked at Arnold. "We might as well shoot them all."

Dr. Smith was shocked. "Absolutely not! If you want to put them down, I'll buy them."

Arnold let the doctor know he was not going to let him take advantage of the situation. "You're saying they're bad because you want them."

Dr. Smith pointed out the financial advantage of not shooting them. "Sell them to somebody else and get what you can. Getting a few dollars is better than you paying to bury a dead mule."

Russell spoke to Arnold, "Get me sixteen healthy mules by the end of the day without depleting my inventory, or you can pay for the inventory, and I'll consider us even. Do what you want with these mules."

Nancy immediately asked, "What are you going to do with Beauty?"

"You paid the doctor to work on a dead mule. It's yours. You pay to have its body disposed of when it dies." Russell was sure he got the better end of that deal.

"Write me a paper of ownership."

"I don't have any paper," Russell replied.

"I do. Mr. Buzmann, I would like to buy however many you'll sell me for sixteen dollars, and I want a bill of sale for them." Nancy went to the wagon for paper and ink.

"I'll sell you the one that's going to be blind and these two." Arnold pointed to two of the mules that the doctor had said would take months to heal.

Nancy handed Arnold the paper, but Russell took it. "They're all mine. I'll write the bill of sale."

Arnold handed another sheet to Russell. "Write down the terms you gave me and sign it."

When Russell handed the papers to Nancy and Arnold, Nancy became the owner of Mules 4, 7, 8, and 17.

Due to the weather, Russell was behind schedule. He couldn't wait weeks or even days to move on. He hoped Arnold would put his excellent trading skills to work and manage to get him the mules by the end of the day.

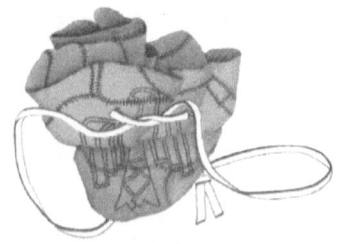

THIRTY ONE

The boy who had notified Martin that he had to go back to the livery walked into the mule hospital. "What happened in here?"

Martin told Edwin, "We're providing medical treatment."

Edwin's family horse was sick. It would devastate them if it didn't recover. "Mister, can you treat a horse? My horse is real sick. We could trade you some chickens."

Arnold suddenly had an idea. "Dr. Smith, if you treat the horse and don't want chickens, I'll buy them from you."

"Bring your horse."

On his way to get his sick animal, Edwin ran past Robert's house. Robert ran beside Edwin, "Where you going?"

"The animal doctor at the livery is going to look at our horse."

"Really?" Robert veered off to tell his girl, Bertha, about the animal doctor. He knocked. Her father opened the door. Robert came right out with his request. "If I get a doctor to heal your pig, will you let me marry your daughter?"

"I don't know if she wants to marry you."

Robert knew she did. Bertha was afraid to talk to her father, and so was Robert. Now, Robert had a solution. "If Bertha does, will you give us your blessing?"

Bertha's father firmly stated his conditions, "Daisy has to be completely healed first."

Bertha ran to the door. "I do want to marry Robert! Let's get the pig, Robert."

Bertha's father went to see his friend, Farmer Lull. "There's a real animal doctor at the livery!"

As Dr. Smith and Nancy helped Beauty drink another dose of sleeping water from the canteen, they heard a pig squeal. Nancy commented, "That sounds like a pig, not a horse."

This was what Arnold had hoped would happen. He walked to the young couple with a pig. "May we help you?"

Bertha replied, "We heard there is a doctor here who can help Daisy."

"How would you pay the doctor?"

"I have a wheel of cheese," Robert offered the only thing he had to trade for the doctor's service. Robert thought that it was too small a price to acquire Bertha as his wife, but that was everything he owned.

"Wait here." Arnold nonchalantly strolled to the wagon. "Dr. Smith, will you see a pig for this young man and woman? They'll give you a whole wheel of cheese."

The young couple heard the doctor reply, "I'm tired. I don't think so."

Robert strode over to the wagon. "Please. Bertha's father will let us get married if I get his pig healed."

How can I be the reason these two never get married? "Bring it over."

"Much obliged." Robert ran off as Bertha led the pig to Dr. Smith.

Dr. Smith climbed out of the wagon and looked over the pig. He remembered what he had been told by the medicine man in his village and diagnosed the problem. He gave Bertha herbal medication and instructions.

Robert returned with the cheese as Edwin arrived with his horse and six live chickens tied together at their feet and hung over the horse's back. Dr. Smith had not finished examining the horse before more people with sick animals stood outside the livery.

Arnold told him, "You can make some money, and these folks need an animal doctor."

"Nancy, is Beauty asleep yet? I'm going to need you again."

"What's this about?" Nancy got out of the wagon.

"Martin, do you have a table? Nancy, get more paper. Write down the owner's name, the type of animal, the animal's name, the symptoms, and how they'll pay then collect the payment."

Martin came back with a table. Nancy wrote down the information. The client named the payment. Arnold asked, "Do you want that or will you sell it?"

"Doctor, do you want to decide what you want?" Nancy asked.

Dr. Smith authorized Nancy to handle it all, "You figure it out."

Martin asked the doctor, "May I watch and take notes?"

Dr. Smith waved him over and allowed him to learn. "Come on."

It wasn't long before Mrs. Luke Smith entered the livery. Blood and other unidentified matter covered Dr. Smith. She backed up when he tried to kiss her. "Luke, we were supposed to be enjoying our holiday. You never came to the room last night, and here you are working again."

"I know, my love. I'm sorry. These people and animals need me. I'll be there as soon as I can. I promise."

"I've been sitting at the Hillcrest Inn with nothing to do." She looked at Nancy. "Who is this woman, and why is she here?"

Dr. Smith thought it was funny that his wife was pretending to be jealous and unhappy about an overly busy husband who wasn't spending enough time with his wife. "She hired me to look at her mules. Her name is Nancy. If you would like to help me here, I'm sure she would be happy to leave."

"I don't think there's any need for me to stay in this dirty place. Just remember to whom you are married. I'm going shopping." Now that she knew they were both all right, Mrs. Luke Smith walked out of the livery.

As Mrs. Smith was leaving, Nancy sashayed over to the doctor. "Luke, I'm happy to stay here and help!"

Mrs. Smith walked back to her husband. "You can give me your money bag, and don't be looking at anything other than animals, or you won't get it back." She took the money bag from his pocket and gave the young woman a nasty 'stay away from my husband' look.

Martin watched the woman walk away. *Dr. Smith had better be careful.* Later, he privately told Dr. Smith, "Two women fighting over you won't be as fun as you might think it will be."

Dr. Smith replied, "I only love my wife."

Martin liked the man, but he saw that there was a connection between him and the girl. He hoped he would not be stupid and ruin his life with a beautiful girl like Nancy.

Nancy sat with her head bowed. "State the type of animal, the animal's name, symptoms, the form of payment, and your name."

"She's a cow. Her name is Peppermint." The pen snapped. "She's lame. I'll pay you money. I'm Melvin Hatcher." Nancy looked up. Melvin saw the woman's face. "Sally?" He hadn't recognized her as he had stood in line. Everybody called the woman with short, dark, curly hair, shapely figure, and breasts, Nancy.

"My name is Nancy, sir." Her heart pounded so hard she was sure Melvin had to hear it. She could feel the heat of a flush on her cheeks.

Melvin saw the look of joy quickly change into fear and then to indifference. He looked at her flushed cheeks that matched her ruby lips. The girl he had known in December was gone. *I thought she would be a good-looking woman. She's incredible.* Melvin said, "Too bad. I haven't stopped thinking about Sally."

"You haven't?" Nancy asked.

"I haven't because I realized I love her."

"She was so young. How could that be?"

"There's more to a woman than her age. Besides, who can explain what a heart does?"

Nancy didn't know how to proceed. "It's a shame you haven't found her."

"I'd never hurt her or her family."

"You wouldn't?"

"No, and that's why I think you shouldn't see any more patients today." Melvin knew who was behind him.

"We shouldn't?"

Dr. Smith opened the stall door so that the man and his goose could leave. Martin finished his notes and started a new page. Dr. Smith turned toward Nancy. "Next." There stood Melvin, looking straight into his eyes.

Loudly Melvin repeated, "As I was saying, Nancy. I would never do anything to hurt Sally or her family."

The doctor ordered Melvin, "Bring that cow in here now!" He turned to Martin. "I'm so hungry. Would you get me something for dinner? I'll pay you when you get back, and I'll tell you about the cow later."

"What would you like?" Martin asked.

"Stew, milk, and bread."

Melvin took Peppermint to the doctor. Nancy got

up from the table. "That's all for the day." She hurried out of the livery and deserted the last person in line.

Wanting to bring everything possible to his trading table, Arnold walked to the table and wrote the information on the paper. He told the woman, "Wait for your turn."

Dr. Smith had seen many animals. Nancy had sold to Arnold most of the items that people had traded for the doctor's services. She had only kept the wheel of cheese, a jar of honey, and a sack of her favorite item: sassafras roots. Nancy didn't know the worth of anything, so she agreed to whatever amount Arnold offered and had allowed him to buy everything, one item at a time, for thirty-eight dollars.

Over the course of the day, Arnold had bartered his injured mules, and the items he had purchased from Nancy, with the people bringing their animals for treatment. Other items, he had traded with the store owner who had come to the livery after Arnold's first visit to the store. At the end of the day, Arnold had seventy-one dollars, ten chickens, one smoked ham, one wheel of cheese, a fifty-pound sack of bran, and six injured mules.

As Melvin led Peppermint into the examination stall, Dr. Smith notified him, "If you break her heart, I'll scalp you."

Melvin was surprised that Noah and his whole family were in Little Rock and that they were doing something that was drawing a lot of attention, but mostly, that Noah cared more about what happened to Sally than himself. "Don't you care about the fact that I know who you are?"

"Of course, I care."

"Don't worry. I didn't have any doubt anyway, but now you've convinced me that you're an honorable man. I swear, I won't tell a soul that you're here or that you're together. What can I do to help you?"

Dr. Smith avoided the topic. "What's wrong with Peppermint?"

Melvin hadn't told him her name. Noah wasn't pretending he wasn't who he was. "She's got a bad leg. She can barely walk."

"Which leg?"

"This one," Melvin touched the leg.

Dr. Smith carefully examined the leg and foot. "Anybody kick her?"

"Who would kick her?"

"Did any person or any animal kick her?"

"I don't know, but there have been a lot of mules in her corral."

"Her leg bone is cracked."

"I told Captain Cornish those mules would be a problem. Can you fix it?"

"I'll put on a splint. You take it off every day, wash her leg with soap and water, put on fresh cedar poultice with a clean wrapping, and then put the splint back on. Give her the willow tea to help with the pain. You know how to make them. Keep the splint on for three months, and keep her away from other animals or people who might want to kick her. If you can get to Harmony, Smitty makes an excellent liniment.

"And what you can do for me, Melvin, is not break Sally's heart or take advantage of her. Do you understand what I mean?"

"I understand, Noah. I wouldn't hurt Sally for anything, and I'm glad that you're with your family. I helped make that happen, you know. I know you love your family, and they love you."

"And don't tell anybody that we're here or anything about us, including Henry, John, Justus, and Jeremiah."

"Jeremiah isn't here. He was sent to train with the Corps of Engineers, but I won't tell anybody."

"I'm happy for him. That's the right job for him." While Peppermint drank willow water, Dr. Smith washed her leg. "Did Henry get back safely?"

"He spent a week in the stockade for spending the weekend with my cousin."

Noah applied poultice on a clean piece of blanket. "So, everything is fine?" He tied it on with red ribbon.

"Nobody realized where he really went, and everything is fine."

"I'm very glad. We were worried about him." On top of the duck cloth, Noah placed splints, which he tied on with a rawhide strip. "Do you need cedar and willow or can you get your own?"

"I'll get my own. How much do I owe you?"

"Talk to Arnold about providing the payment in mules if the army has any to sell." Dr. Smith figured they would, after hearing Melvin's comment about the mules injuring their cow.

Melvin led Peppermint out of the stall. The doctor called out, "Bring the next one."

"Arnold, I was told to talk to you about mules."

Arnold was happily surprised and hoped this man would have the animals he needed. "I need sixteen healthy mules by the end of today."

Melvin thought this was fortuitous. "I believe that we may be able to solve both our problems." As a woman led her young son in to see the doctor, Nancy stood behind the livery, peeked around the corner, and watched Melvin leave with Arnold and Peppermint.

"I know you're seeing animals, but I've taken my son to every doctor, and nobody has been able to help him."

Dr. Smith asked for details, "What's happening?"

"He has horrible pain in his stomach. Nobody can figure out what's causing it."

Dr. Smith asked the boy, "What's your name?"

"I'm Ansel. I've hurt for so long. I don't want to go on. I'm ready to go see God."

The doctor felt the boy's stomach, looked into his throat, looked up his nose, and then looked at his eyes. "What do you give him to eat?"

"Just regular food we all eat. We're not sick, so it can't be the food."

Dr. Smith had learned a lot about the effects of food since he had met Roscoe. The boy's eyes were puffy and had dark circles under them, his nose was full of mucus, and he could see it dripping down the back of Ansel's throat. The glands in his neck felt swollen. Dr. Smith thought it had to do with food. "Tell me what your typical food is anyway." He wrote everything down as Ansel's mother named them.

"Beef, chicken, ham, pork, bacon, green beans, corn, potatoes, bread, cheese, milk, apples, peaches, peas."

Dr. Smith told the woman, "This is what I want you to do: the first seven days, I want Ansel to drink only water. If the pains stop, add one item. He keeps drinking the water and eats only the one other food for the next seven days. If the pain stays away, add one more food for seven days until you find what brings the pain back. If he has pain drinking only water, it's not food, and you'll need to take him east to find a doctor."

Dr. Smith knelt beside the boy. "Don't give up, Ansel. I know the place where God lives is perfect because I've been there."

Ansel stopped him. "How did you go to the place where God lives?"

"I froze in a river. For a very short time, I was dead, but my wife saved me. I went to the land of God while I was dead."

"It's real, and there's nothing to be afraid of?" Ansel asked.

"I think it's real, and that there's no reason to be scared, but your mother needs you to be here, so don't give up. Promise me you'll keep trying for your mama."

The boy told Dr. Smith, "I'll try. I promise."

"Thank you so much." Tears flowed from the woman's eyes. She didn't want her son to give up and had been afraid he would. Now, he would hold on while they tried to figure out if food was causing his pain. Just for giving Ansel enough hope to keep going, she owed Dr. Smith more than she could ever repay him. "How much do I owe you?"

"I don't know if this will solve the problem. You don't owe me anything."

She put twenty dollars in his hand. "Take this anyway."

"This is too much," Dr. Smith told her.

"No, it's not enough."

She refused to take the money back, so Dr. Smith opened the door and let the two of them out. Nancy stood by the table with a paper in her hand, looking like she didn't have a drop of blood in her body. Dr. Smith walked over.

As he left the barn, the boy called out, "I'm going to hold on for Mama!"

Dr. Smith stood beside Nancy. "What's wrong? Is it Melvin?"

Nancy handed him the paper. Written on the last line were the words: Human, Ansel, stomach pain, cash, Mrs. Daniel Hall.

They stared at the paper for the longest time. Finally, Dr. Smith said, "I guess she won't know who I am, and they aren't to blame for anything Judge Hall did."

As Martin returned with dinner, Nancy replied, "We should leave Little Rock immediately."

"I brought enough for all of us." Martin put the food on the table.

Nancy handed Dr. Smith his money. "We can

settle up with Martin while we eat." Dr. Smith counted the money. He put it in his pocket then poured some of the milk into a pot and set it beside the fire.

"I've been talking with my wife, and we'd be honored if you would stay with us tonight. I'd like to learn how to find the plants you used."

"We might leave today, but thank you for the offer."

Everything Martin learned would be useless if he didn't have the items he needed to treat the animals. "Dr. Smith. I need to know how to acquire these plants."

It would take a long time to explain how to identify all the plants he had used. However, if he didn't, he would deprive a whole town of the medical assistance they didn't already possess. Martin might be able to provide a version of what they needed.

Martin took a guess and offered a deal, "Tell me what you did for the cow, the woman with the boy, and Beauty, plus explain how to find the items you used today, and neither you nor the Bacons owe me anything."

Dr. Smith replied, "Get your paper."

Martin retrieved his stack of papers and went back to the table. Dr. Smith explained the problem with the cow and the treatment. He explained about the boy's pain and what he had suggested. Last, Dr. Smith informed Martin that for Beauty, all he had done was wash her with the antiseptic, stitch up what he could, and keep her asleep. Martin carefully wrote the information into his notes and then put all the papers into the leather binder he had brought with him to the livery with their dinner.

"Let me ask my wife if she would like to stay with you and your wife. Show me where you live after we finish eating." Dr. Smith decided to think about staying. Information in exchange for boarding all their animals was a hard deal to turn down.

Arnold arrived back at the livery with sixteen good mules and a sealed letter. "Nancy, Melvin asked me to give this message to you. I'm going back to the armory to take the rest of what I owe them. Do you want to read the letter and send one back?"

Nancy took the letter and walked to the wagon to read it.

Dr. Smith said, "I see you got the mules. Did you meet all your partner's requirements?"

"I paid Melvin the seventy-one dollars I earned today and added sixty more dollars. In addition, I have to give him the things I was going to keep, but I didn't use anything of Russell's. The way I see it, I bought the twelve injured mules for the sixty dollars."

"I'd wondered if you'd be able to do it." Luke had counted the money that Nancy had given him. *Arnold shouldn't have that much when I only have thirty-eight dollars.* Dr. Smith told Arnold, "You owe me for the treatment of the cow. I told Melvin to see you about mules for the payment."

"I can't give you one of these good mules, but I can give you an injured mule. I only wanted four of the wounded animals anyway. These were mine in the beginning, but I had to give them to Russell to stock the trading post. I'm taking them back."

"I want the last two. One is the payment for medical treatment of the cow, and the other is for finding you a source of mules."

"I can sell that mule."

"These mules aren't worth much, but I'll also continue to take care of your animals until you leave on Monday."

"Do you think these animals will heal and they'll be as good as ever? Is it worth paying for your time by giving up another mule?" Arnold tried to negotiate the best deal possible for himself.

"Let me look at them again." Dr. Smith looked them all over. "They're big mules, and they'll be good work animals when they're healed, but they need to have the cedar treatment continued, or their wounds will probably get infected. With proper care, they should heal up fine."

"Those two are yours. I'm taking these four." Arnold took the four biggest and least injured mules, whether they had originally been his or not. They were all his now anyway, and he could pick the ones he wanted.

"Write me a bill of sale. Did you see how we've been treating them?"

"I put on the stuff that Nancy made on the way here. I think she cooked cedar to make it."

"Do you know if you can find cedar around the place you bought?" Dr. Smith asked as if he didn't already know.

"There's probably some up in the forest."

"Pick the very ends of the branches and the blue cones. Cook them in boiling water for an hour, let it cool down, mash it up then put it on a cloth and secure it to the injured areas. It will keep the injuries free of infection. They'll heal faster and hurt less. Will you do that daily?"

"Would twice a week be enough?" Arnold didn't want to go through all that every day.

"Most likely not, but it's possible."

"Thank you for the advice." Arnold thought he would get George to do it. So Russell could pay for their keep, Arnold put the new healthy mules into stalls separate from his.

Dr. Smith separated his two animals from Arnold's. He put them with Nancy's mules. *Arnold got the better of us today, but at least this makes it more even.* After he got his mules into the stall, he carried the warm milk to the table. "Nancy, I need to use some of our honey to treat Mule 4."

Nancy brought the jar. She told Arnold, "I'm not sending back a letter. Thank you for bringing this one."

Arnold handed Luke the bill of sale for Mule 11 and Mule 20. He loaded the chickens, cheese, ham, and the sack of bran onto one of the new mules and left. Dr. Smith poured a quarter of a cup of warm milk into his glass then added the same amount of honey. While he finished his stew, the doctor stirred the honey and milk until it was completely mixed and smooth.

"Is that another treatment?" Martin asked.

"Get your papers and write this down on the page for eye treatments. Equal parts honey and warm—not hot—milk, stirred until smooth and thoroughly mixed. Two or three drops in the eye several times a day or used as a compress." Luke ate his last bite of bread then carried the milk and honey mixture along with a spoon to the hot water. He rinsed his spoon in hot water and used it to drip a few drops of the mixture into Mule 4's eye before he put the cloth on again.

Martin was ready to go home. "You ready to see where I live?"

"Let me look at Beauty before I go." Dr. Smith climbed into the wagon and found, even though she was asleep, that Beauty wasn't sleeping soundly. The wounds were clean, but he rinsed them again with the antiseptic wash. He left her uncovered, so nothing would stick to any wounds during the healing process.

When the doctor got out of the wagon, Nancy said, "I'll come back tonight and treat them all. Thank you for helping with the mules. How much more do I owe you, doctor?"

"You helped me with the whole process today. That's enough."

Nancy whispered, "Why don't you stay with Martin tonight?"

"Is that what you want?" Dr. Smith asked.

"I need to talk with Melvin."

"Don't let him take advantage of you." Noah was

worried about what might happen. He knew that Nancy had feelings for Melvin. He hoped he had made it clear to Melvin to be a gentleman.

Nancy assured him, "I won't. I promise."

Luke and Martin walked to Martin's home. Martin had seen Luke and Nancy whispering. Luke was considering giving him information about the plants to pay for Nancy's animals. He was sure there was something between them.

"I lost my first wife when I got involved with Dollie. I love Dollie, but I didn't want to lose Mary. I loved her more than anything. I was stupid." Martin spoke as if making idle conversation while they walked. He hoped Luke would hear what he was saying and back away from Nancy.

Nancy walked to the inn with the cheese, honey, and sassafras. She gave the proper signal that all was safe outside and waited for the correct inside signal. Ann and Stephanie both sat in her room, and there was a hot bath waiting for her.

Ann informed her sister, "I thought my competition for the heart of the doctor would like to clean up."

"Don't worry. I heard him assure Martin that he only loves you." She waved her sisters away from the door and then went into the inn. A few minutes later, she returned with a loaf of bread, a plate, knife, cup, and a large pot of hot water.

"Fix us some sassafras tea, bread, honey, and cheese." She stripped off the filthy clothes and submerged herself.

"Roscoe told us the mules were in bad shape, and you had to do a lot to help them. He also told us your names, but I want to hear what's happened while we've been hiding in this room." Stephanie washed her sister's hair with the bar of rose-scented soap left in the room from the previous night.

"It's been so long since we've had sassafras tea." Ann poured the delicious hot tea into the cup. They enjoyed the food and tea while Sally told them about the animals Noah had cared for and what they had done for the injured. She explained how bad Beauty was and that Russell had given her the mule. Then, so she could save them, she had bought three more of the most injured animals, including Mule 4 with a damaged eye.

"Noah earned thirty-eight dollars. I sold everything we got to Arnold for cash, except what I brought here. He traded it around and ended up with just over seventy dollars, plus ten live chickens, a smoked ham, a wheel of cheese, and a sack of bran." Sally didn't know about the twenty dollars Mrs. Hall had given Noah.

Stephanie said, "That doesn't seem right."

Ann agreed, "Arnold shouldn't have ended up with more than Noah."

Last, Sally told them about the last two patients Noah had seen that morning: Melvin and Judge Hall's son. "Maybe we should leave right away, but I want to talk with Melvin. I'm going to meet him later tonight. Besides, we have to wait for Roscoe to complete his sale on Monday."

"I think Noah's right. Mrs. Hall wouldn't know who he is. I don't think Melvin's going to tell, but look around carefully and be sure it's not a trap before you meet him." Ann knew Sally had fallen in love with Melvin. Sally would have to decide what she was going to do. If Sally wanted a life with Melvin, Ann wasn't going to stop her. As much as she loved Sally and didn't want to lose her, she understood how a woman felt about the man she loves.

Sally stepped out of the tub, got into bed, and had a cup of sassafras tea. "It's been so long since I've slept. Wake me up in time to meet Melvin."

"I will. We'll go to the other room and let you sleep. Tonight, when you're talking with Melvin, remember that we love you no matter what you decide." Stephanie hugged her younger sister because she also understood about loving a man.

Ann hugged Sally. "Sleep well."

In the room she shared with Eli, Stephanie voiced her opinion, "She hasn't known Melvin very long. I hope she doesn't go with him. She can find somebody else."

Ann sat on the bed beside Stephanie. "Sally needs to be well-rested when she meets with Melvin. I want her to be thinking right."

"Maybe he'll come with us. I want her to be loved."

"Having an AWOL soldier with us is a bad plan."

"You're right, but Sally's intelligent. She'll make the right decision."

James had been in the dining hall with Roscoe, Russell, and his men all morning. He would rather have been in his room with Stephanie. They all knew Nancy was in the livery with Dr. Smith and Arnold. Therefore, he should have nothing else to do except sit with the other men. Ann had hardly been in Stephanie's room long enough to speak those few sentences when she heard the proper knock, but it was at Roscoe's door. She cracked the door with her fingers in the correct position to signal that everything was safe inside. Noah saw the other door open and the fingers wrapped around the outer edge of the door. He moved over to that room and stepped inside.

"Come here, my jealous wife. Let me hug you thoroughly. I want you to know I love only you."

"No way!" Ann told him, "I just bought this dress, so I can be the doctor's wife, and I don't want it covered in blood and muck."

"Standing there in that dress, you're the most beautiful thing I've ever seen." A second later, he ruined the compliment. "Actually, I have seen one thing more beautiful, but I still don't want to dirty your fine dress. Would you like to stay as a guest at Martin's home tonight? He offered for us to stay with him and his wife because he wants me to tell him how to find the plants we used today. We wouldn't have to hide here, and we could say that Stephanie is your sister and she's traveling with us."

Stephanie quickly declined, "I'd rather hide here and be with Eli."

Ann felt irritated. She didn't have the right to ask Noah what he found more beautiful, and she certainly shouldn't think that she was the most beautiful thing in the world. She tried to shrug it off, and she didn't want to have to hide in the room until Monday when Arnold could go to the bank. "I bought us two sets of the proper attire for Dr. Luke Smith and his wife, and bags to carry them. Let's go stay with the Harrows."

"Don't forget to remind Sally how much we love her." Ann hugged Stephanie.

THIRTY TWO

After Noah had bathed and put on his new clothes, as Dr. and Mrs. Luke Smith, they went to Martin's house. "What's my name?" Ann asked on the way.

"Who do you want to be?" Dr. Smith noticed his wife looked very tense.

"How about Isabelle?" *That sounds like the name of a beautiful woman.* Ann wondered what he found to be more beautiful than she was. She thought maybe she would lose him to somebody he thought was more beautiful, and she also might lose her sister if Sally decided she wanted to be with Melvin. On top of that, they were openly walking the streets of Little Rock together. All of this was out of her control, and she worried about what might happen. She felt as defeated as she had when the snake had bitten Noah the previous fall.

Luke saw that his wife was lost in thought and her brow was furrowed. He tried to make her feel better. "That's a lovely name. I like it."

Maybe he likes the name Isabelle better than my real name. She silently told herself; *stop it. You're making one little comment into something big.*

Luke and Isabelle Smith knocked on Martin and Dollie Harrow's door. Martin opened the door. "I'm glad you decided to stay with us."

Martin's wife greeted her guests as they came into her house, "Dr. Smith, Mrs. Smith, welcome to our home. I'm Dollie."

"Call me Luke. This is my wife, Isabelle."

After a short round of polite conversation between the four of them, Luke and Martin moved to a table across the room and discussed how to identify the needed plants as Luke sketched them. Isabelle and Dollie sat in rocking chairs and talked about being the wife of a busy man.

Isabelle liked being the wife of a man so well respected, but what she liked most was that Luke was getting the respect and admiration he deserved. He was a doctor who cared about animals and people and would risk himself to help them. Ann watched Noah explain where to find the plants and how they looked so that Martin could continue to help the community. Luke glanced at Isabelle and saw her looking at him with obvious love and admiration. She didn't have the irritated look she had worn since they had left the inn. It made him stop and send her a silent kiss floating through the air. Martin saw them look at each other. He knew there was not any other person who was going to get in the middle of that love affair and stopped worrying about Nancy.

THIRTY THREE

James told Roscoe and Russell's men, "I'm going to my room to read my Bible and rest." He walked to the innkeeper behind the bar. "I'd like to take my supper to my room. I'll wait here until you have it ready."

"It's roasted chicken tonight. How much and what else do you want?"

"A whole roasted chicken, a big serving of green beans and mashed potatoes, a loaf of bread, a jar of jam, lots of fresh butter, two large slices of cheese, a large pot of tea, and a sugar jar."

Russell called out, "You have a tapeworm, James?"

James figured he would tell the truth, and nobody would believe him. "I'm hiding a beautiful, blonde-haired, blue-eyed woman in my room, and I need to feed her."

Roscoe swallowed hard. *What's he doing?*

Russell replied, "Yeah, I've got one in my room too." They all laughed then described the woman they wished was in their room.

James joked with them, "And if I find one like that, I'm going to scoop her up and marry her."

One of the other men told him, "Good luck with that."

Roscoe said, "Your father might not like you bringing home a wife out of the blue, so you better keep your eyes closed."

As James picked up the tray of food, he said, "Nope, if I see her, I'm keeping her."

As he jabbed his elbow into Roscoe's side and winked, Russell told James, "Tonight, enjoy the woman you've got hidden in your room."

James replied, "I will."

In their room, Stephanie told Eli the news while they shared the chicken dinner. Eli replied, "Arnold didn't operate with the utmost integrity when we were doing the inventory at Roscoe's. He tried to alter the numbers. I pointed out mistakes several times before I took over the recordkeeping."

"Keep a close eye on him for us, darling. He can't deceive you."

"I will." Eli didn't like how Arnold had manipulated the trading with the goods his brother-in-law had earned, and he planned to keep Arnold from finding another opportunity to do the same again.

Stephanie told her husband about what concerned her most. "Melvin brought Peppermint in with a fractured leg bone. He saw Sally. He told her that he loves her and he wants to talk with her tonight. She's meeting him later. Let's pray for them."

"God, you are our Father. You want us to understand the love You have for us, so You put us in families and created love between a man and a woman. Love is a powerful feeling and a mighty force. We know this because of how much Stephanie and I love each other. Now, Sally and Melvin, under the influence and power of love, have to make a decision that will have a significant impact on both of them and all the rest of us. It's an enormous burden, and we ask that You will fill them with Your love and wisdom. Bring about what You know is the best outcome and help us all to accept that outcome, no matter what it is. We ask in the name of Jesus. Amen."

"Amen. Eli, I love what you said. I love you powerfully." Stephanie's heart filled to overflowing with appreciation for Eli's thoughts, and she wanted him to understand how much she loved him. She showed him passionately.

THIRTY FOUR

Outside in the night, Nancy watched Melvin until she was sure he was alone and then slipped through the darkness to join him.

"Sally, I was afraid you weren't coming."

"Why did you want to meet me like this?"

"Because I don't want the wrong people to find you. I want you to know how I feel about you, and I want you alone to decide what you want to do." Melvin reached out to hold Sally's hand.

"I'm listening."

"When we left Cadron Creek, I felt so miserable. I didn't want to leave you. I thought it was just the stress and stupidity of the whole situation, but I never stopped thinking about you or missing you. I realized I loved you and that you're the person I want for the rest of my life. We think the same. You're sweet, beautiful, and interesting, and I enjoy being with you so much. We can go back to Virginia and run the tavern together. We would spend every day doing what we love with the person we love. I'll take good care of you and love you always. I want to marry you now, but we'd have to stay here until my time in the military is over." Melvin hoped Sally felt the same. He held her hands and waited for her answer.

"I love you too, and I've thought about you all winter, but I can't leave my family. You could come with us."

"I would be AWOL. The Army would look for me, and they'd find your family. I do not want that to happen. Don't you want to be with me?"

Sally wanted Melvin to be part of her life very much, but family was everything to her. She was in the family she wanted, and she wasn't going to tear it apart. "I do want to be with you, but I'd end up resenting you for taking me away from my family. Find us when you leave the Army."

"I won't be able to find you a year from now. I love you. I don't want to lose you. Please, stay with me."

"I love you, Melvin, but I can't leave my family."

Melvin pulled Sally over into his arms. His heart reached for hers through her lips. Her heart and lips responded. She wanted to spend her life loving him. "Stay with me," Melvin whispered.

"I wish it was that simple. Roscoe told me we didn't have a choice last December. You belong to the Army, and I belong to my family. I guess we still do." She stayed in his arms and kissed him again. "Life won't let you be my husband, but it can't make me forget you or stop loving you."

"And I'll always love you, and I won't forget you either." He kissed her one last time then turned and walked away.

Sally wanted to run after him and say that she had changed her mind, but she knew it couldn't work. She turned and forced herself to walk the other way. She went to the livery. The animals needed her, and she couldn't walk away from them either. She had to take care of them. She put lots of hay in the wagon with Beauty to make her bed soft, plus the mule hadn't eaten in two days, and she needed food to heal. Sally brought oats into the wagon and woke Beauty up. She immediately gave the mule more of the sedative water, so it would be awake only long enough to eat the oats and hay. Beauty sat up on her own. That was more than she had done since she had been in the wagon. Sally looked at the side the mule had been laying on. The snow and wind had battered her on the side facing the river, but her other side was all right.

"Thank you, God. Help Beauty heal and grow healthy again and help me not to hurt either." Tears rolled down her face as she grieved over not having Melvin. She stroked Beauty between the ears where it wouldn't hurt and softly told her mule that she was going to take care of her.

Melvin watched from the shadows. He saw Sally's tears and knew she wanted him. He wrestled with himself. Just like the previous fall, he saw that Sally had a beautiful soul, and he wished he could go with them. If they could escape, maybe he could too. However, Captain Cornish wasn't interested in tracking this family, even though Judge Hall had told him to look for them. He was sure the Captain would search for an AWOL soldier, and if he found Noah and Ann together in the process, he would arrest them and bring them back for a second trial.

Melvin had told both Sally and Noah that he wouldn't do anything to harm any of them. He studied the girl he loved as she ministered to Beauty.

She washed the mule's injuries and then put shredded potatoes on another mule's eye. She cared for all the other injured mules before she took hay and water to Roscoe's twenty-four animals and Eyanosa. He could see the softness of Sally's touch and the strength of her care. He was not going to be able to share that wonderful life, and it broke his heart. *Noah should have told Sally not to break my heart.*

When Sally left the stable, Melvin knew it was the last time he would see her. He wished her love and happiness and then slipped unobserved back toward the barracks.

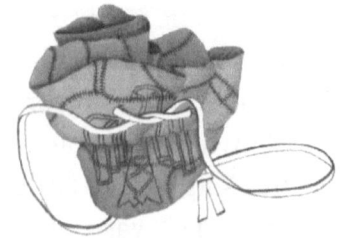

THIRTY FIVE

That night in the Harrow's spare room, Isabelle whispered, "Luke, will you help me get out of this dress?"

"I'd love to help you out of your clothes." Luke thought Isabelle was beautiful in the dress. That made him think about how much he loved her, which brought his mind again to wanting to make love with her, and then he thought about what was under that dress. He unbuttoned the back of her dress then lay on the bed and watched as she took off her petticoats. She walked to the bed in the nude. Luke told the woman he loved and desired, "Now, I'm looking at the most beautiful thing I've ever seen."

He saw his wife soften. The tightness in her shoulders left. He remembered what he had said earlier when he had first seen Isabelle in the dress. He had gone through the same thought sequence faster than he'd known what he was thinking and had thought about the beautiful naked body of his wife. He had said that he had seen something more beautiful than Isabelle wearing the dress. Luke wanted her to understand how he felt about her and never to worry that his heart was somewhere else.

"Every desire I have is for your beautiful body and the lovely woman inside. Share your love with me. I need you."

As Luke and Isabelle ate breakfast with Martin and Dollie, somebody knocked. Mr. Harrow discovered Edwin at the door.

"You better come to the livery, Mr. Harrow, and you too, Dr. Smith." They swallowed the last of the coffee in their cups then put on their coats and went to see what Edwin thought they needed to see. Before they got to the livery, they saw the line of people and animals. "I think we better go back home and change clothes. Martin, are you ready to start your practice?"

"I'm ready."

"Isabelle, holder of my heart, would you get Nancy and Roscoe? Tell them to come to the livery prepared to look at and treat animals, if they're willing. Then go change your clothes and come back to sign everybody in."

"Yes, my love." Isabelle went to the inn, walked in the front door, and over to Nancy. "If you're willing to help look at and treat sick animals, Dr. Smith requests your help. Also, Roscoe's help if he's here." Isabelle wanted to hug her sister. She had worried all night. She hadn't known if Nancy would be there, and she was jubilant when she found her at the inn.

"I'm Roscoe. I'll help." Roscoe guessed after the lessons the three of them had given to each other in the storeroom of plants that they would all be able to help.

Nancy wanted to know what Ann was calling herself. "I'll help, Mrs. Smith. What may I call you?"

"Isabelle."

"That's a lovely name."

"Thank you. Get ready and go to the livery."

Arnold called out, "Before you go!"

"Yes, sir?"

"Can I do like I did yesterday?"

"What was that?"

"I gave Dr. Smith money for the items people brought to trade."

Ann's eyes narrowed. *So, he's the scalawag, Arnold.* She hoped Nancy would get James to keep an eye on him. "I don't see any reason why you shouldn't. Come along too."

Russell stood up. "Arnold, I'll walk to the livery with you then continue on my way." Russell issued his orders, "Men, finish up and then come to the livery, ready to move out."

Arnold and Russell walked over without the rest of the people. Russell said goodbye, "You did a good job getting those mules, and I appreciate it. I'm going to miss having you as my partner and friend."

Arnold replied, "We've had some good years for sure. I'm going to miss the business and you. It's hard to find a true friend."

"Don't stop considering me as your friend. I'll see you every time I come to resupply your trading post. Marry your girl, have lots of children, and be happy."

"Thanks, Russell. I will." Arnold helped Russell get his new mules out of the stalls.

Nancy knocked on a door three times with a long pause between. "James, we need you. Dr. Smith, Roscoe, and I are going to take care of animals at the livery again today, and Arnold is going to buy what people bring for services."

James said, "I'll be over soon."

Nancy, Roscoe, and Russell's men arrived at the livery and found the people impatiently waiting, hoping the animal doctor would be there again. Nancy went to the wagon. She found an orange and a note. "I'm sorry." It was signed, "Will."

Nancy got a stack of blank paper, went to the table, and sat down. She told the first person in line, "State the kind of your animal, its name, what's wrong, how you will pay, and your name."

Will led two mules past Nancy on his way to the wagons. Nancy called out, "Will, stop!" Will stood still. "You're forgiven. I'm sorry that I gave you the wrong impression."

Will replied, "Thank you," and then continued on his way. He had been around Nancy for the last several days and had realized that she wasn't a person to use and then throw away. He had decided, in the future, to make sure he knew the woman and knew for sure if she was willing. He wondered why Nancy and James had never said anything to Russell. They were different. Anybody else would have hollered bloody murder about it, and his life would have been ruined. He was glad they had not told anybody. He was gladder that James had stopped him.

Nancy told the man with the sick donkey, "Go to the third stall and wait." She wrote 'Roscoe' on the ledger page line. She had written down the information for several people when Luke, Isabelle, Martin, and Dollie arrived. Martin went with Luke into the first stall to work together for a while. Nancy handed the pen to Isabelle then went to treat the injured mules. Edwin had already given food and water to all of Russell's new animals, so he helped Nancy. She had scared him to death the first night, but yesterday, Edwin had seen that her motivation was to help and that she would never have hurt him. Luke let Martin look over the animal and decide what he thought was the problem and how he thought he should treat it. Martin already had a good idea about what was wrong with animals from owning and running a livery. It wasn't long before Luke said, "Martin, I'll go to stall two. You don't need my help."

When James and Stephanie arrived, Russell asked, "Who is this beautiful woman you have with you, James?"

"I found one! This is my new friend, Marie." James turned to Isabelle and requested permission to join them. "Nancy told me you might need help. Since Marie likes animals, I thought maybe I could win her heart if I brought her with me to help."

Nancy suggested to Isabelle, "I think James should help Arnold with our payments. Brother, do what you think is best with my payments and Uncle Roscoe's." Nancy then said, "Follow me," to the owner of the chickens.

Isabelle was concerned. They were drawing all kinds of attention. *This is not going to be good if the wrong people are in that line.* She silently prayed. *God, keep the wrong people away. Hide us even though we are stupidly drawing attention.*

She wished it wasn't Sunday, so Roscoe and Arnold could complete their transaction, and they could leave. "Marie, maybe you would check out the line, but don't alarm anybody. James, you have complete authority over Dr. Smith's payments as well."

Marie knew what Isabelle wanted and left to observe the line. She didn't see anybody who might recognize any of them.

Dollie and Isabelle logged everybody. They waded through hours as Luke, Nancy, Roscoe, and Martin looked over animals and then sent them out to a healthier life.

Much to Arnold's dismay, James traded the items given for payment to Nancy, Roscoe, and Luke. He had sold very little to Arnold. What he did sell, James had insisted on fair payment. Arnold thought James had an uncanny ability to know the value of everything. Dollie had instructed Edwin to take the items her husband earned and to secure them in the tack room.

Marie relaxed when it was close to the end of the day. There wasn't a large population living in Little Rock. She thought, *surely they must already have seen every single animal in the area.* Nobody had joined the line in the last hour. The line had grown short and barely wrapped the corner. Marie was about to leave her lookout when somebody she recognized joined the line. *It was only last fall that we stayed at his inn. Even with her short haircut, he'll surely recognize Ann.* It wouldn't be long before the man rounded the corner. Marie jumped down from her perch and hurried to the livery.

When a boy left with his dog, Marie slipped into the stall. Luke put the lizard the boy had traded to save his dog from certain death onto the stall ledge and let it run away. The dog was going to be fine, as soon as the smell of the skunk faded away. It had brought its problem with him. The overpowering smell filled the stall.

"Isabelle, I'm moving to the other side of Nancy." Dr. Smith and Marie fled the fumes. Dollie reviewed who had received what to determine if the division was fair. As she concentrated, she failed to hear Dr. Smith announce his change in location.

Marie delivered the news. "Remember the man who was running the inn where we stayed the first time we were in Little Rock, the one who told us to be glad we had an exciting life?"

"John Peabody."

"He's in the line."

"How long before he gets here?"

"He's right around the corner."

Noah told his sister-in-law what he wanted. "Get Roscoe to sign him in and direct him to Martin. Make sure Roscoe knows which man he is. Get Isabelle out of here. Nancy and I can stay hidden in our stalls. You leave with Isabelle and James."

"I'll go tell Roscoe and get him to take over at the sign-in table. Isabelle can leave then I'll tell Nancy to keep out of view."

Luke told Marie, "Perfect," so she left to organize the family. Luke called out, "Send the next patient."

Isabelle wrote Luke on the line. "Fifth stall down." She directed the patient and owner to the new stall.

Dollie focused on how to get the next patient to Martin. This patient planned to pay cash. Roscoe opened the stall gate. His patient exited. *It's not going to work out.* Dollie saw Marie walk into the stall. She hoped, *maybe Marie will hold Roscoe up long enough.*

Roscoe walked out of the stall and over to the table. Marie went to Nancy's examination booth and waited at the gate.

"Isabelle, I'm an old man. I can't see any more animals. Let me sign up the people. You go with Marie. She needs your help." Roscoe offered what sounded like a reasonable explanation as to why they needed to shift positions. Isabelle knew what this meant and went into the livery.

Martin opened his stall. *It worked out.* Dollie quickly wrote Martin on the line and took the money, "First door."

Roscoe saw the man he had to get to Martin. The minutes ticked away. Isabelle tried to signal to Nancy to hurry up, but the woman was telling Nancy all about last summer when her rhubarb pie had won the blue ribbon.

"I'm sure it will be delectable. I'm impatient to

get done here, so I can try it." Nancy opened the door. Since she wanted them, Nancy called out, "I want my pies."

James put them aside.

Arnold thought, *too bad.* He had wanted to buy one for himself.

Marie motioned James over. "The innkeeper of Peabody Inn is in line. Roscoe is going to direct him to Martin. Nancy, keep out of view in the stall. Isabelle, James, and I have to go."

Nancy whispered, "I understand." James, Marie, and Isabelle went out the back door. Nancy called out, "Next."

Dollie wrote Nancy on the line. She directed the woman, trading one act of mercy from her husband, "Fourth stall down." *How ridiculous. Nobody wants an act of mercy.*

That second, Luke opened his door to allow his patient and its owner to leave. He called out, "Next." The woman and boy hurried over to see Dr. Smith. Roscoe saw that Luke had moved. He erased Nancy and wrote Luke on the line. Still unaware of the move, Dollie handled the next patient, "Second door." The man and his horse stepped out of the line and into the livery. He walked down the row of stalls. Nobody was in the second stall, but the fourth door was open. "They can't even count to four. This is probably going to be worthless." He walked past two and on to four. Everybody waiting outside in the line moved forward. The last man in line came around the corner.

Luke now knew who the woman and her son were. He didn't know if they knew who he was. "Mrs. Hall and Ansel, so nice to see you again."

Ansel spoke up, "Dr. Smith, I held on, and now I don't hurt."

"You don't? That makes me very happy, but it's barely been a whole day." Luke looked at Mrs. Hall for confirmation.

"We had to tell you. I've been praying. I begged God to send me to the person who could help my son. He sent me to you. God brought you here for my boy. I'm sure of it."

"Let me look at you, Ansel." Dr. Smith wanted to see for himself. Ansel's eyes were clear. His nose and throat were mucus free.

Martin finished with his patient and called for the next. Dollie didn't want chickens. She stood up. "Martin, take a break." Then, she saw that the second stall was open. *That last one was fast.* She wrote, 'Luke', on the line and told the man, "Go to the second stall." The man went into the empty stall. "Never mind, Martin." The last person was another rare cash customer. Dollie hoped to get him to her husband.

They logged everybody in the line. Roscoe realized if Dollie sent the next person to her husband, he wouldn't be able to send Mr. Peabody to Martin.

In the fifth stall, Luke asked Mrs. Hall. "What does Ansel eat every day?"

"I don't know. I guess milk. I usually give him a big glass to coat his stomach first thing in the morning and before each meal."

"Wait the rest of the seven days then drink milk only for a few days. If the pain comes back, stop the milk. Go back to water only for seven days and don't drink more milk. Try something else, but only one thing."

It was the first day Ansel could remember that he wasn't in pain, and he didn't want to hurt anymore. He told them, "I think it's the milk. I'm not going to drink it. I'll eat something else."

Dr. Smith told him, "You can do it that way if you want. Add other foods one at a time and don't drink milk."

The man in stall two waited for somebody. Nancy still looked over the wrong animal in booth four. The woman looked at Martin, waiting for his next patient. "Are you going to send me in?"

"Go to stall one." Roscoe wrote Martin on the line and made sure he didn't look at Dollie.

Mrs. Hall and Ansel left. Luke called out, "Next."

Dollie instructed the next man in line, "Second door."

The man stood outside the stall. "Somebody's already in there." Luke went over to look. Everybody in the line came forward to see what was happening. He quickly stepped into the second stall.

Nancy realized that something was wrong. "We're done. Do as I told you. Come back here to get more when you run out." She hurried them out. "Next!" She got the misdirected man into her stall.

Dollie crossed out Luke and wrote Nancy. Roscoe had to notify Luke and Nancy that they had to see the next two before Martin finished with his current patient. Roscoe spoke up loudly, "Everything's all right, just a little mix-up. It's no problem. There's only three of you left. You will all be seen."

Luke called out, "Go ahead and send the next to stall five." He tried to rush.

Nancy tried to hurry, but this one was difficult.

Martin didn't know his wife wanted him to see the last one and sent his patient out. "I'm ready for the next."

Dollie wrote Martin and sent the man before Mr. Peabody to her husband. Mr. Peabody now stood where he had a clear view into the livery. Therefore, Luke now needed to drag out the examination he had been hurrying. He couldn't let the man leave, or he'd be looking into the wrong eyes. Maybe he could slip to stall five when Mr. Peabody wasn't looking. Nancy had nothing else she could stall with either, so she opened the stall door. Noah saw the door open. He was free to be in Little Rock, and so was she, but it would give them away to be there together.

Dr. Smith called out, "Nancy, go to number five. I'm ready for the next in here." Roscoe went to Nancy and walked beside her to shield her. He wasn't letting her get into this. He walked her right out the back door. Dollie wrote Luke and told the man, "Go to stall two and give the man your money."

Roscoe stepped back into livery. "I believe it's my turn. Please come to stall three." Mr. Peabody didn't care which person he saw. He followed Roscoe.

"It's not this chicken with a problem. It's me."

Roscoe drew Mr. Peabody's attention away from the door behind him. "Tell me what's wrong."

Luke quietly slipped past and ducked into stall five with his last patient.

Roscoe listened to John Peabody explain the problem. He was surprised that a man who ran an inn and served food every day would have let this happen to himself. Roscoe knew what the problem was. He had seen it before. It was clear that the man was suffering from scurvy.

"Mr. Peabody. What do you eat?"

"Beef, potatoes, pinto beans, bacon, eggs, bread, a little cheese, ale."

"Do you eat fruits or vegetables?"

"No. I don't like them."

"You have to eat oranges, lots of oranges, green beans, corn, carrots, okra, beets, pickles, and all kinds of things. Your body needs different things. Eat that chicken. Each animal and plant has different things inside. You can't eat only a small variety and get everything your body needs."

"I don't even know how to cook other things."

"Experiment and try different things. If you enjoy beef, make a stew and add vegetables. If you like bread, dry some spinach then crush it up and cook it into the bread. Try anything. Your body can recover if you start feeding it what it needs. You have scurvy. You have to eat oranges, lemons, or limes."

"That makes sense. I'll try it. Much obliged." Mr. Peabody wrung the chicken's neck. "I'll eat this chicken tonight." He handed over his money and then walked out.

Martin finished his last exam, prescribed the treatment, and sent them on their way. Dr. Smith contemplated over his last patient a long time. He wanted to be sure that John Peabody was long gone. It was late in the day. They were all tired and glad the work was finished. Three times, potential disaster had loomed before them. Dr. Smith informed everybody, "I'm not doing this tomorrow, no matter what."

THIRTY SIX

Dollie wanted to look through her pay. "Edwin, do your end-of-the-day work." She walked to the tack room to pack everything into a wagon.

All day, Arnold and James had let people trade with items they had in the back of the wagon. James thought he had given everybody who traded with him a good deal. Arnold thought James had given people too good of a deal. They both felt they had increased the value of the goods. The results of their trading sat in the wagon. Most of the items belonged to Luke, Nancy, and Roscoe, but Arnold had done well. Arnold further separated his goods from the rest and then walked across the livery. "Do you want to look at what you have here? I don't know how you want to divide everything. You could sell it all to me."

Roscoe, Luke, and Nancy went to the wagon and looked at the items. Roscoe asked James and Arnold, "Do you think you can sell any of this at the store?"

"Not today. I've traded with Clark for years. He won't trade on Sundays."

Nancy wanted to share the one item that she had specifically wanted. "Dollie, may everybody come to your house long enough to wash their hands and have a slice of rhubarb pie?"

"All right, but come now. After the pie, I want to rest. It's been a long day."

Nancy joined Edwin and shoveled manure. "You come too, but leave your shoes outside."

Isabelle asked, "Dollie, may we sort everything out at your place?"

"If it doesn't take too long."

"We can go now."

Except for Arnold, who decided he was a trader—not a stablehand—the others worked the evening rounds in the stable. A piece of pie was not enough pay for Arnold to muck out a stable. "It was a pleasure working with all of you." He took his goods and went back to the inn.

Dollie and Isabelle took their wagons of booty and started for the Harrow's home. By the time they had carried everything except the chickens into the house, the others had finished at the stable and had arrived to eat pie. They cut the two pies into pieces. Martin, Dollie, Luke, Isabelle, James, Marie, Nancy, Roscoe, and Edwin shared the pie. While they enjoyed the rhubarb, they looked over the ledger.

Isabelle commented, "Can you believe some of the things people brought to trade?"

Marie informed everybody, "My favorite is this pie."

Nancy expressed her preference, "I wish we had gotten more sassafras."

Isabelle asked, "Edwin, what do you think was the best item?"

"The chickens, of course. Eggs, cheese, and pie

are great, but once you eat them, they're gone. Chickens keep giving you more."

Dr. Smith said, "I'm glad you said that. According to this ledger, I own twenty chickens, and I don't have a way to take care of them. I want you to take them for me."

"Are you sure?" Edwin's family had traded all six of their chickens for the care of their horse. He thought he was never going to eat another egg. Now, he would have even more eggs than before, and they would have some to trade or sell.

The chickens lay in the wagon with their feet tied. They needed to get into a warm place, or they would freeze during the night. Dr. Smith asked, "Can you get them home tonight?"

"I'll carry some home now then come back and get the rest." Edwin wanted his family to hear the rooster crow in the morning then go outside and see all the chickens. He had heard his mother praying that God would not kick them down anymore. Now, they might be able to go forward. His parents worked hard. Edwin thought they deserved something good.

Luke told him, "Good. I'll leave them in the wagon for you."

Edwin licked his plate. "That was good. I've never ate rhubarb pie before. Thank you for including me, Miss Nancy. I'm going to go on home with some of those chickens now." Edwin left with four chickens.

"With all the trading we did, I don't know how to determine who owns what, but I divided what little money was paid for the items in the wagon between the three of you." James gave them each an equal share.

Nancy suggested, "We could take turns, and each pick something we like. What nobody wants, we try to sell tomorrow at the store and then divide the money."

Dollie said, "Some of that I might like to buy from you or maybe trade. You take the things you want to keep, and then I will see if there is anything I want. I'll take the things I want out of Martin's, and you can see if you want any of the rest."

Martin had looked over his share while he had eaten his slice of pie. "I want this." He picked up a Bowie knife.

"May I look at it?" Dr. Smith examined the blade. *It looks as good as mine.* He handed it back. "It's a beautiful knife."

Martin told his wife, "Do what you want with the rest, honey."

Nancy selected an item then Roscoe, Luke, Marie, James, and Isabelle. They made three rounds between them all then decided the rest should go to Nancy, Luke, and Roscoe. Nancy took an embroidered shirt. Luke didn't see anything else he wanted. "Isabelle, is there anything you want?"

One item had caught Isabelle's attention when she had driven the wagon to the Harrow's home. Isabelle had even looked through the ledger before the others got there. She had not discovered what it was. She decided it had to have been something

James had traded at the wagon. Even though she didn't know what it was, it looked interesting. *I'll take this thingamajigger as a curiosity.* She picked up the metal object with what appeared to be multiple tools inside that were able to rotate out individually. "Thank you, my husband."

They traded items until there was nothing else they wanted from each other. Then Dollie bought the other things she wanted and divided the money between Luke, Nancy, and Roscoe.

Luke said, "Tomorrow, we'll try to sell the rest."

Dollie rejected the suggestion. "I'll deal with mine later," and then tried to get the crowd to leave. "Are we done?"

"I am." Nancy picked up the pie dishes out of Dollie's washbasin. "These go with the pies."

James excused himself with Marie, "We better leave. I'm sure Marie has to get home."

Roscoe gracefully excused himself as well, "I'll walk with you."

Isabelle said, "We can go to the inn."

"No, not you two. Please stay again tonight." Dollie liked having high-quality people in her home. She planned to make sure her friends knew that Dr. and Mrs. Smith had stayed in her home. After they had removed the dirty reminders of the many sick animals they had treated that day, the four ate a meal made from items they had received for payment of their healing services.

Luke asked Martin, "Are you going to help people with their animals?"

"I'm sure I won't be able to figure out everything, but I'll try." He wanted to help the animals and their owners because he hated to see creatures suffer, and he knew people depended on their animals. Therefore, he now had a different opinion of Russell and Arnold after what they had allowed to happen to their mules.

While they were eating, they heard somebody outside. Martin and Luke went to the door to see if it was Edwin, back for more chickens. They found him at the wagon with a grown man.

When Edwin saw Dr. Smith and Martin, he said, "Pa, that's Dr. Smith." Edwin and his father walked toward Luke and Martin with the rest of the chickens hanging by ropes over their shoulders. Luke and Martin met them partway between the house and the wagon.

Edwin's father said, "Hello, Martin."

"Hello, S.R." Martin added, "Meet Dr. Luke Smith. Luke, this is Edwin's father, S.R."

"Pleased to meet you. You have a fine son."

Edwin basked in the compliment.

"Thank you, sir. He is a good boy, and we're much obliged for these chickens."

Luke told the man, "You're doing me a favor by taking them. I don't have a way to take care of them, and I don't want them to freeze."

"I'm glad to be able to help." Since he was not accepting charity but was doing the man a favor, S.R. was happy. Mostly, he felt good about owning twenty chickens, and a horse he hoped was recovering.

"How is your horse?" Luke asked.

Edwin replied, "She isn't better yet, but we did have moldy hay."

"We don't have much, and it's the only horse food we have left. We're doing as you told Edwin. We've been soaking it before feeding her, and we moved it all out of the barn to a shed. I was hoping spring would come early. After that storm, I don't think it will."

Luke intimately knew how bad the storm had been. "That was a wild storm!"

"If there's ever anything I can do for you, let me know." S.R. and Edwin turned and left with the rest of the chickens.

As Martin went with Luke back to their wives in the house, he said, "This winter has been hard on everybody."

THIRTY SEVEN

James hoped to get business done early. "I'm going to the store. Nancy, will you help me put everything back into the wagon?"

Arnold offered to help. "Nancy, would you like me to sell those for you? I can get a better deal from Clark. He knows me."

"That would be nice, but take James with you." Nancy had seen how Arnold traded. Not dishonestly, but always working things more to his favor than what Nancy thought was fair. She figured that he offered because he planned somehow to get more for himself. However, his relationship with the store owner might be an advantage. They got everything into the wagon. Arnold and James went to see what they could sell at the store.

Arnold called out, "Good morning, Clark."

The owner of the store returned the greeting. "Good morning. I hear you had another big day of business. You want me to take a look at what you've got?"

"I would."

Clark walked out to the wagon. "Who is this you have with you?"

"Roscoe Bacon's nephew, James Bacon."

Clark wanted to know what he was getting into. "So, who does all this belong to?"

James asked, "Does it matter? These items are worth what they're worth, no matter who they belong to."

Clark explained, "Yes, but I have a margin of profit that I can adjust. I don't want high prices for the people of this town because I want to be able to sell my goods. I want to pay a fair price to the person I buy from, and I have to earn a profit for myself. If a person is my friend, I might take less profit for myself."

Arnold started to answer. James cut him off, "These belong to my sister, Nancy Bacon, and to Roscoe Bacon, and to Dr. Smith. Arnold is here because he helped. He did an excellent job trading what was given for veterinary services. The people here in town got things they wanted and gave up things they were willing to let go. Arnold managed to make it into a good value, and he wants to complete his process of getting the most for his efforts. Also, he is our friend, and he wants to help us."

Clark turned to Arnold, "Is that how you see it, Arnold?"

Arnold would not have gone about selling this way, but the hand was dealt. "I guess so."

"Then I'll give you the same as I would give to Arnold. I'll buy it all for fifty dollars."

Neither Clark nor Arnold had any idea that James and his father had run a store in Harmony, or that James knew the value of the items in the wagon. "You're sure you know what's here, and you didn't overlook anything?"

Clark glanced in the wagon again. "I'm sure."

Arnold also knew how much those items were worth. Suddenly, he saw himself. That was what he would have done, but he had seen Dr. Smith, Roscoe, Nancy, Isabelle, and James work hard. He thought they deserved to get what the items were worth. He didn't want them to have done all that work for Clark to make an unreasonable profit. "Clark, I think you should look again."

Clark looked at the items in the wagon more closely. "I guess I didn't see everything. I'll take it for sixty."

James got back on the wagon and tapped King. "Clark, I'm going to keep everything. Thank you for clarifying the situation."

Clark changed his mind. "Wait! I can give you sixty-five!"

James drove away. He would pack everything into their wagon and take it with them. They would get more value by using the items themselves.

"James is not ignorant, Clark, and neither am I." Arnold walked off toward the bank.

THIRTY EIGHT

Instead of going with James and Arnold, Nancy went to the livery to check on the animals. Edwin had already fed most of the animals and had given them water before Nancy joined him.

Edwin called out, "Good morning!" He was happy to be doing his job. He was helping his family by earning money, and he was learning about animals and their care. He didn't know how to read or write, but he listened, watched, and remembered. He had learned a lot over the last two days and was already cooking cedar and willow for the injured animals.

"And good morning to you, Edwin," Nancy returned the greeting so pleasantly that Edwin smiled. She went to check on Beauty.

Roscoe climbed out of their wagon. "How are the animals this morning?"

"I think they're doing much better, but I want you to look at one of them." Edwin pointed at puss squeezing out from under the stitches of the mule of his concern. "I think it's an infection."

Roscoe asked, "Edwin, you know of any place where there's rotting food?"

Edwin thought that was a strange request. "Sure. Why?"

"We need maggots."

Edwin led Roscoe to the back of Peabody Inn. "Why do we want maggots?"

"Maggots will eat that infection, but they won't eat healthy flesh."

Edwin remarked, "I wouldn't want them eating on me."

"Then you're lucky that you don't have an infection because I would put them on you, sure enough." Roscoe picked up a maggot and tossed it onto Edwin's arm.

Edwin jumped back. "No, you won't!" He ran away and left Roscoe to collect the creatures alone.

Nancy thought Beauty was doing well. The mule sat up to eat oats and hay, so Nancy didn't give her the sedative. Instead, she gave her willow water. *It will be best for Beauty to sit up for as long as she can. I'll give her the sedative right before we leave.* Nancy noticed some infected places, so she washed the mule's side, neck, and face with the antiseptic water. She rubbed Beauty between the ears and then left her to eat while she went to look at her other mules. The one that Edwin wanted Roscoe to check had infected stitches. The other two animals seemed to be healing well, except for the damaged eye that still looked cloudy. They couldn't fit two mules in the wagon, so Nancy pondered about what she could do if the mule couldn't see well enough to travel.

Edwin ran into the livery. "Nancy, Roscoe's going to feed the mules to the maggots!"

Nancy thought about that. Maggots did eat rotting garbage. "Maybe that would work."

Roscoe walked into the livery with a handkerchief in his hand. Nancy called him over, "Beauty needs some of those maggots."

Edwin watched Roscoe put a maggot on top of the infected flesh. It made him feel nauseous, but he was fascinated as the creature started eating. He watched one burrow under the fur.

Roscoe climbed into the wagon. "I'm glad Beauty can sit up."

Edwin went to the wagon and looked in as Roscoe and Nancy put the rest of the maggots on areas seeping white goo. Martin arrived at his livery in time to see the maggots being applied. He got out his folder and added another entry about treating infections. After all the maggots had been correctly placed to eat their meal of rotting mule flesh, they treated all of Dr. Smith's and Nancy's mules with cedar and gave them willow water.

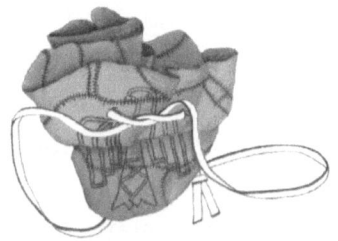

THIRTY NINE

Dollie strolled into the butcher shop. She hoped to trade some of the items that Martin had earned for their favorite meats and then do the same at the bakery.

The other woman in the butcher shop asked, "Aren't you the wife of the livery owner?"

"Yes. I'm Dollie Harrow." She remembered that the woman had been at the livery the day before.

"My husband, Judge Hall, wants to meet Dr. Smith."

Having Judge Hall and his wife to dinner was better than Dollie had ever dreamed of in the way of social status. "Would you and your husband care to have dinner at my house this afternoon? Dr. and Mrs. Smith will be there."

"We'd love to. What time?"

"Noon."

"Thank you for the invitation. We will go to your house at noon." The woman completed her purchase and went to tell her husband that she had arranged for him to meet the man who had healed their son.

Dollie wanted to put on a dinner to remember. "I need enough of your best cut of meat for six. Come

337

look at what I have, and we'll talk about what you want for the meat."

When she got home, Luke and Isabelle Smith were ready to go. They had waited to thank Dollie and say goodbye. "I have guests coming who want to meet the doctor. Please stay. You can leave directly after dinner."

Luke looked at Isabelle. The town had told her husband that he was less of a person because he was part Indian. The town owed him the respect he deserved, and now, some of them were going to do that. Isabelle didn't want to take that away from him or herself. They could continue on their trip after dinner and enjoy the morning with the Harrows. "I think we can stay, but just through dinner."

"I'll go ask the Bacons if they'll wait a while longer, so we can travel together." Luke and Martin went to the livery while Dollie prepared the meal. Isabelle stayed at the Harrow's house and sipped tea. She felt like they were somebody, and she liked it.

Arnold arrived at the livery with the money he needed to buy Bacon's trading post. "You ready to complete this sale?"

Roscoe headed toward the door. "Do you have the money?"

Arnold assured him, "I'm all set." The two men went to see William, the Clerk of the Court. William was not on duty. The associate clerk, Harold LeBarron, completed the transfer of ownership. He recorded the deed in the name of its new owner, Arnold Buzmann. In less than an hour, with both sadness and anticipation, Roscoe was free of his bonds to Arkansas and Arnold was the owner of a place to settle down and have a family. While Arnold was out of the livery, James packed their wagon and then went to get Marie. When Luke and Martin arrived at the livery, Nancy and Edwin were the only people there.

"Nancy, do you think it will be all right with your family to wait until after dinner to leave? Martin and Dollie have some people they want us to meet." Noah liked being Dr. Luke Smith, and he wanted to enjoy the prestige a little longer. Nancy thought it would be better to leave as soon as possible, but Luke wanted to stay and meet these people, and it wasn't up to her to tell him no. "If that's what you want. We'll leave when you're ready to go."

Luke asked, "How are our mules? Should I look at them?"

"Roscoe, Edwin, and I have already taken care of them. Go enjoy yourself."

Martin shook his head. *It's clear that Luke and Nancy are together. I warned him once, but it was rather indirectly. I'll advise him one more time. It's probably already too late, and it's such a shame. Isabelle is such a lovely and charming woman. I don't know why he even wants to have anybody else, but Nancy did bring Luke here, and I benefited. I'll help them all.* "Nancy, Russell took all the hay and oats. I think some of that was yours, so fill up with hay and oats."

"Beauty's in the wagon. We don't have space."

"Pack as many oats as you can get in the wagon

with her. Fill in all the empty space in your other wagon with hay. Edwin, help Nancy load up. We have to be home for dinner at noon, and I need to be clean." Martin and Luke left Nancy and Edwin to load animal food.

Roscoe and Arnold walked into the livery. Arnold gave Edwin the money he owed Martin for feeding and stabling his four mules. Roscoe spoke with Nancy, "Come to the inn as soon as you can. We'll get something to eat then move on."

"Dr. and Mrs. Smith want to have dinner with the Harrows. They want to meet somebody."

Roscoe thought that was a bad idea. "We should be going."

Nancy shrugged her shoulders and continued to load hay. Roscoe left with Arnold. He had known him for many years and considered him a friend. They walked to Hillcrest Inn. "Arnold, take good care of Bacon's Trading Post or whatever you're going to call it."

"I will. You made the trading post into a good business. I'm lucky to buy it."

"I remember that bad year. I didn't have money to buy anything, but you and Russell stocked me. You trusted me to pay you when you came again in the fall. That year could have been the end of Bacon's if you hadn't done that, and it wouldn't have been here now for you to buy."

"It's funny how things work out, isn't it?"

"Nancy and James would say God is rewarding you for doing something right."

"I think it just happened that way is all." They continued to reminisce about old times as they walked to the inn.

Edwin got Arnold's four animals ready to go. He was about to put a blanket on the first mule when he noticed an infection. He checked the others. Arnold had not once put a cedar compress on his mules or given them any willow water. Edwin was concerned. He threw the blanket over the stall door and ran to the butcher shop. Much to his relief, the garbage was crawling with squirming, little white worms. He shoved them into his pocket and ran back to the livery. He put the maggots on the infected animals, hoping they would conceal themselves and continue to heal the injuries. Edwin decided to feed the mules more oats, put fresh cedar poultice on their injuries, and give them willow water. After he saw to their needs, he put on their blankets, their packs, and four bales of hay each. That was all he could do for them.

Nancy watched Edwin care for Arnold's mules. She knew Edwin didn't have to help them and would get nothing for doing so. She expressed her appreciation, "Thank you for everything you did for Arnold's mules. God sees what you do for His creatures. Keep being the person you are, and God will reward you. You never know what He'll do for you. It may only be when you get to Heaven that you'll get your reward, but He sees what you're doing."

Edwin replied, "Thank you for treating me like a real person."

"You are a real person. You're as valuable as any other person is. Don't ever forget that."

At the inn, Roscoe knocked on James' door with the proper knock. James barely cracked it open. He stood behind the door but signaled that all was safe inside. "Don't come in. I'm not ready to go."

"Get ready. I'll settle for our rooms. However, we're not leaving right away. Luke and Isabelle are attending a dinner party at the Harrow's, so when Nancy gets here, we'll eat too."

Marie got out of bed. "We've been here too long already. It's stupid and selfish to hold us up to go to a party."

"We don't know what's happening over there. They probably have a reason why they think they should stay."

"Maybe." Marie went out the street door and then re-entered the inn through the front door. "Is James here?"

"I don't keep track of what my guests are doing. You can knock on his door. It's the second one down that hall." The innkeeper pointed her in the proper direction. As she headed to the room, James met her in the hall.

"Marie, I'm glad you came. We're leaving today, and I want to talk with you." They stood in the hall and spoke quietly before they joined Roscoe at a dining table. Arnold was there too. He had already paid the innkeeper and had returned his key when James and Marie joined them. Roscoe called out, "Add one more meal." He had known they would need four meals, but he wanted to make it look like they didn't know that Marie was going to be there. As they waited, Nancy walked in.

Roscoe twisted toward her. "Get ready and then come eat."

"May I take a quick bath? I'm a mess."

Marie waved her hand in front of her nose. She didn't want to ride with her sister reeking so badly. "You do smell."

Nancy spoke to the innkeeper, "Make me a bath, and sell me a bar of plain soap and an india rubber bag."

"They'll be at your room in a few minutes."

While Nancy waited, she laid her clean clothes on the bed and packed the last of the cheese, the jar of honey, and the bag of sassafras roots. After Nancy bathed, she got out of the water and then washed her dirty clothes in the tub. She put the wet clothes into the india rubber bag, got dressed, took everything, and joined her family. Roscoe gave the innkeeper the keys to the rooms and paid for everything, including four tasty, hearty meals.

Luke and Isabelle sat in the Harrow's living room and waited for Dollie's guests to arrive. Dollie heard a knock and went to the door. Luke and Isabelle stood to greet the people arriving.

Dollie ushered the woman into her house. "This is my husband, Martin."

"Come into the sitting room. Where's your husband?" Martin inquired.

"At the last minute, he wasn't able to come, but I

knew you had prepared, so I came without him. I hope that will be acceptable."

"Of course." Dollie was disappointed. However, even if Judge Hall had not come, his wife had, and she felt honored.

Their guest walked into the room. Luke put down the teacup he was holding, turned toward the doorway, and choked on the tea he was about to swallow. He held the napkin to his mouth and looked at Isabelle with panic in his eyes. When he was able to speak, he said, "Mrs. Hall, what a pleasure! I didn't know Dollie had invited you."

"It's so nice to see you," Mrs. Hall replied.

"Is your husband coming? I was told he wants to meet me." Luke needed to know if he should go out the back door with his wife.

"I'm afraid not."

Luke breathed out a sigh of relief. "Meet my wife, Isabelle."

"So pleased to meet you, Mrs. Hall," Isabelle cordially greeted the wife of the man she thought was the worst person on the planet.

"Would you like tea before we eat?" Dollie asked.

"Yes, please."

Isabelle knew if she and Luke jumped up and ran away, the Harrows and Mrs. Hall would know something was wrong, but maybe Judge Hall would still decide to come. Her stomach knotted as they drank tea.

Luke fidgeted. "How is Ansel today?" He hoped the boy was still pain-free.

"It's working so well, Dr. Smith."

"Please, call me Luke."

"He hasn't had anything except water for three days, and he isn't hurting at all. Daniel wanted so much to meet the man who helped our son."

"I'm sorry we won't get to meet him, but we'll be leaving today." Isabelle planned to make sure they got out of town as soon as possible. They finished their tea and moved to the table for an excellent meal. When they were ready for the last course, Dollie went to the kitchen to get the pastries.

Arnold, Roscoe, James, Nancy, and Marie walked to the livery. Arnold tied his mules to each other and led them out of the stable. "It's been a pleasure. Enjoy living with your brother, Roscoe."

Nancy said, "And you enjoy the trading post." She did not think it had been a pleasure. He wasn't a horrible person, but she didn't like what he and Russell had done to the mules, or that he more or less had swindled them the first day that Dr. Smith had treated the local animals. Nancy asked, "Edwin, would you help us get ready to go?"

Edwin was completely infatuated with the kind, intelligent, and very beautiful fifteen-year-old girl. He told Nancy, "I hate for you to leave. I'm going to miss you."

Nancy replied, "I'll miss you too. Don't forget what I told you."

They gave Beauty and the goats the sedative then hitched, King, Ace, Redeemed, and Big Jenny to the wagon carrying Beauty. Shaggy, QuickSilver, Blue, and Chief, they harnessed to the other wagon. They put the planks to the back of the wagon carrying Beauty, walked the goats in, and closed the rear boards that James and Roscoe had made removable. Roscoe tried to pay Edwin what they owed.

Edwin told him, "No, sir. Mr. Harrow said not to charge you anything."

Nancy stated what they all knew, "But you fed them your food this whole time, and we just stocked up with your hay and oats."

"No, ma'am. I won't take any money. I'm doing what Mr. Harrow said."

James told Edwin, "Well then, please go see if the doctor and his wife are ready to leave. They're going to travel with us." Edwin strolled to Martin's house.

Dollie heard a knock, hurried over, and opened the door.

"I'm so glad you were able to get here! I'll get the pastries. We'll join Dr. Smith."

"Let me carry them for you, Mrs. Harrow."

Dollie walked into the dining room. She stepped to the side. "Judge Hall, meet Dr. and Mrs. Smith."

Judge Hall, Dr. Luke Smith, and Isabelle Smith locked eyes. "That is not Dr. Smith!"

Dollie stated emphatically, "I assure you that he is."

"They are Noah Swift Hawk and Ann Williams." He set the pastries on the table and drew a pistol from his pocket.

"I told you, if I found you together, that you would get maximum lashing and a year hard labor. I'm going to whip you both myself. Especially you, Ann Williams."

Mrs. Hall stepped in front of her husband. "You will do no such thing. I don't care who they are. He is the man who treated Ansel. You will not harm him or his wife."

Judge Hall told his wife, "They're breaking the law!"

She didn't believe him. "What law could they possibly be breaking?"

Dollie, Martin, Noah, and Ann sat paralyzed. Dollie and Martin didn't understand what was happening. Noah and Ann thought Judge Hall was surely going to shoot them if they moved.

Judge Hall explained, "He's an Indian man, and she's a white woman."

"You've got to be out of your mind! That man gave your son a pain-free life. It doesn't matter if he's an Indian or a—she paused—gorilla!"

The white man, Beamis, who had made a family with a person of color, had escaped because he hadn't found them, but he had these two. Judge Hall wasn't letting them go. "It's the law."

"Dollie, do you have the ledger in which you wrote who we were and what we were paying?"

"It's right here." Dollie stepped across the room and picked up the ledger.

Mrs. Hall flipped through the pages. "Read this line, Daniel. What does it say?"

"Human, Ansel, stomach pain, one act of mercy from my husband, Mrs. Daniel Hall."

"I had money that day. When Dollie asked how I was going to pay, a feeling swept over me that I should say that you would pay for Ansel's care with an act of mercy. You will honor that payment."

Judge Hall looked at the ledger. He looked at his wife. She would never forgive him. Noah was the man who had told her how to remove Ansel's pain. He looked at Noah then Ann.

"I'll let him go, but not her." Ann had told him she was going to be with that Indian and be right before God and that he would still be wrong. He wanted to whip her.

Judge Hall's wife stepped up to him and held the pistol to her heart. "Then shoot me now because that's exactly what you'll be doing. You'll be putting a hole through my heart if you hurt either one of them."

Edwin sauntered up the Harrow's walkway. Through the window, he saw Judge Hall with a gun pointed at the heart of Mrs. Hall. Mr. and Mrs. Harrow looked as white as the snow that still lay on the ground. Edwin realized there was a worse storm going on inside the house than the one that had raged across their town a few days before. He sneaked up to the window and listened.

"Leave, before I change my mind," Judge Hall spit the words from his mouth. He would grant them one act of mercy. Judge Hall would allow them to leave the house. However, as soon as he could get to the arsenal, he was sending soldiers to track them down and bring them back. He planned to enjoy ripping the flesh off their bodies.

Noah Swift Hawk and Ann Williams shot out of their chairs, grabbed their bags, and flew out the kitchen door.

FORTY

Edwin slipped away from the window and ran after them. He already knew all about the Judge. His family had helped Mr. Beamis escape with his wife and their children, and they had helped others before them.

"Dr. Smith!"

Luke recognized Edwin's voice. He turned to look as they sprinted away. "We have to go! We can't talk with you."

"I have a place for you to hide."

Isabelle tried to speak as she ran, "We have to get some people!"

"James said you were going to travel with them. I'll tell them you weren't able to wait and to go on without you."

Dr. Smith had to spill the beans. "We haven't been honest with you. We're all one family. We have to go together."

"You're a family with Nancy?" Edwin didn't want any of them to tangle with Judge Hall, but especially not Nancy.

Isabelle confessed, "Nancy is my sister."

"Can you hide all of us?" Luke asked.

"Yes. I'll get you to the first stop then I'll bring them."

Luke knew that Judge Hall wasn't letting them go. He knew what hatred looked like, and it was written all over the man's face. "We're going to trust you to get them and hide us."

"How will your family know that I'm on your side, so they'll come with me?"

Dr. Smith said, "Tell them, Chris and Emma's child says she loves them to the moon and back."

Isabelle agreed, "Perfect."

Edwin hurried them to his house. He opened the door. "Railroad procedure. Large depot."

S.R. grabbed his shotgun. "Follow me, Dr. Smith."

Edwin left Dr. and Mrs. Smith in the care of his father. He entered the livery. James asked, "What took you so long?"

"I'll explain on the way. You have to come with me now. Chris and Emma's child said she loves you to the moon and back."

Nancy and Marie exclaimed, "What?"

"Judge Hall found them. We have to go."

"Climb up here and tell us where to go." Roscoe flicked the reins across King's back as Edwin jumped on.

"It would be easier if you let me drive." Edwin held his hands out for the reins. Roscoe handed them over. "Follow me." Edwin drove out of the livery. James and Marie followed in the other wagon. They went south on the main road out of town. Edwin pointed, "You see that wash?"

Roscoe replied, "I see it."

"Remember it. We'll come back and turn in."

After they had traveled another mile toward Pine Bluff, they turned the wagons a hundred and eighty degrees. "Drive back on the same track." There were tracks in the snow from their arrival and Arnold's departure, so it probably didn't matter, but Edwin thought it was best if it looked like one new set of tracks went out of town, but none came in. He carefully erased the evidence of their reversal then jumped onto the wagon with James and Marie.

When they got back to the wash, Roscoe turned off into the water followed by the second wagon. The runoff from the melting snow removed any evidence of their passing. Edwin took them up the wash for a few miles before he led them out onto a hard, rocky bank. For another mile, the exposed bedrock was a perfect concealment of their route until they came to the only place able to hide two large wagons, six people, and thirty-one animals.

The cave opening was not high enough to get in without taking off the wagon bows. They stopped in front of the entrance. James encouraged Marie, "Go talk to Nancy," then he started taking down the wagon cover.

"Do you think you can go inside? If you can't, we'll send James and Roscoe in with the wagons and animals, and we'll stay out here."

"I'm going to try." Nancy breathed short, shallow breaths of fear, as she walked to the entrance. She stood beside her sister and looked into the opening.

Nancy didn't like it. "You go in and look. Tell me what you see."

"Of course," Marie narrated what she saw as she went. "The entrance isn't high or wide. It doesn't look like we can get a wagon through, but we must be able to, or they won't have brought us here. It's not a long tunnel, and there's plenty of light. I've come to a very large—she didn't want to say cave—hollow. There is more than enough room for the wagons and animals. Others have been here before us. I see a fire pit. There are some rails set up as a corral, and it looks like lots of firewood is stacked in here."

"Come get me. I want to make up for the problems I caused the last time a cave came into the picture."

Isabelle walked up behind her sister. "Do you want me to walk in with you?"

"You're here!" Nancy threw her arms around Isabelle. "Marie," she hugged Luke, "Isabelle and Luke are here!"

S.R. told Edwin, "Go back to the livery. Tell Mr. Harrow that you ran away and hid because you saw the Judge holding a gun to Mrs. Hall's heart and you were afraid."

Edwin hated to leave, but he wanted these people to get away. "God keep you safe." He hugged each of them. "Goodbye." He hurried away on foot.

S.R. repeated the same information that he had told other people in the past. "Two days from now, somebody will come and take you to the next stop. That person will ask you, "Have you made the items?" You say, "Look in the wooden box." Keep your fire in the fire pit around to the right. I'm sure you understand that you can never speak of this place, my family, or any part of this route."

Isabelle replied, "We understand, and I'm sure you won't tell anybody about us either."

"Do you know how long this trip will take or where we will end up?" Noah asked.

S.R. explained, "I only know this stop. I don't know who is on either side or where you will go. The people I bring here don't know where they are, so they can't tell anybody. That makes it safer because nobody knows anything except their one little part."

That was not the case this time. Luke had remained oriented to the sun with every turn and had calculated how far they had traveled between each turn. He knew, even after the long walk, that they were only half an hour out of town. He easily could have gotten back, but he didn't think there was any reason to give away that fact. Even though he knew where they were, it didn't help him to know where they were going. He handed S.R. a dollar. "This is to thank you for helping us. I want you to buy fresh hay for your horse."

S.R. knew his horse would run out of hay long before the spring grass was up, and he didn't feel the money was charity. He and Edwin were taking a great risk for them. "I should be able to buy fifty bales of hay with this." S.R. took the money and left them at the beginning of their journey of escape.

Acknowledgments

This gorgeous cover was created by
Hristo Argirov Kovatliev.

Follow Me Online

https://www.ChanceAndChoicesAdventures.com

Did you like this story?
Please write a review!

https://www.amazon.com/dp/B076HMPPWW

Chance and Choices Adventures
by Lisa Gay

Pray for Justice
Choose Your Consequences
No Remorse
Means of Escape
Torn Hearts
Xida People
Stone Cold
Goodbye Hideout
Along the Way
The Western Sea
Sally's Sketchbook

Books by The Traveler

Provence: a land of lavender and olives

www.ingramcontent.com/pod-product-compliance
Lightning Source LLC
Chambersburg PA
CBHW022004050726
47499CB00002BA/291